No Ordinary Matter

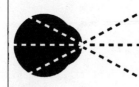

No Ordinary Matter

Jenny McPhee

Thorndike Press • Waterville, Maine

Copyright © 2004 by Jenny McPhee

Acknowledgments can be found on page 8.

Published in 2004 by arrangement with FREE PRESS, an imprint of Simon & Schuster, Inc.

Thorndike Press® Large Print Basic.

The tree indicium is a trademark of Thorndike Press.

The text of this Large Print edition is unabridged.
Other aspects of the book may vary from the original edition.

Set in 16 pt. Plantin by Carleen Stearns.

Printed in the United States on permanent paper.

Library of Congress Cataloging-in-Publication Data

McPhee, Jenny.
    No ordinary matter : a novel / Jenny McPhee.
      p. cm.
    ISBN 0-7862-6762-3 (lg. print : hc : alk. paper)
    1. Women — New York (State) — New York — Fiction.
2. New York (N.Y.) — Fiction.   3. Sisters — Fiction.
4. Large type books.   I. Title.
PS3563.C3887N6 2004b
   813'.54—dc22   2004051609

For Tommaso and Leandro

As the Founder/CEO of NAVH, the only national health agency solely devoted to those who, although not totally blind, have an eye disease which could lead to serious visual impairment, I am pleased to recognize Thorndike Press⋆ as one of the leading publishers in the large print field.

Founded in 1954 in San Francisco to prepare large print textbooks for partially seeing children, NAVH became the pioneer and standard setting agency in the preparation of large type.

Today, those publishers who meet our standards carry the prestigious "Seal of Approval" indicating high quality large print. We are delighted that Thorndike Press is one of the publishers whose titles meet these standards. We are also pleased to recognize the significant contribution Thorndike Press is making in this important and growing field.

Lorraine H. Marchi, L.H.D.
Founder/CEO
NAVH

⋆ Thorndike Press encompasses the following imprints: Thorndike, Wheeler, Walker and Large Print Press.

This was a very innocent planet, except for those great big brains.
— Kurt Vonnegut, *Galápagos*

Truth is stranger than fiction,
  but it is because
Fiction is obliged to stick to possibilities;
Truth isn't.
— Mark Twain

The Brain — is wider than the Sky —
For — put them side by side —
The one the other will contain
With ease — and You — beside.
— Emily Dickinson

Acknowledgments:

The author wishes to thank Professor David Freedberg, Director of the Italian Academy for Advanced Studies in America at Columbia University, for his sustained generosity and support. The writer would also like to thank Massimo Fedi, Alexis Hurley, Maris Kreizman, Anne Maguire, Maria Massie, David Forrer, Vesna Neskow, Luca Passaleva, Lisa Springer, Grace Suh, Rick Whitaker, Stephen Zimmer, and, most especially, her agent, Kim Witherspoon, and her editor, Amy Scheibe. No small thanks are due the author's father and mother, sisters and brothers.

One

I

Veronica sat in the back of the Hungarian Pastry Shop waiting for her older sister, Lillian. She surveyed the compact room, while contemplating a dash outside for a smoke. The café's clientele were mostly regulars who came laden with dog-eared, beverage-stained reading materials and stayed for hours sharing a table with fellow bohemian throwbacks while consuming innumerable cups of coffee. A laptop was as rare a sight in the Hungarian Pastry Shop as was a pencil in Silicon Valley. In keeping with the times, however, the patrons had been forced to give up smoking, at least while inside the café. When Veronica was a student, smoking Lucky Strikes or Gitanes with your coffee was de rigueur. Now smoking was permitted only at the tables on the sidewalk out front, which lay in the formidable shadow of the Cathedral of St. John the Divine.

As she waited for Lillian, Veronica sipped a cup of Viennese coffee and ate a hamantasch, a triangular pastry with poppy-seed, prune, and walnut filling. For nearly fourteen years, since Veronica was a freshman at Barnard and Lillian had just started in the M.D./Ph.D. program in neuroscience at Columbia, the two sisters had met more or less consistently the first Monday of every month at 9:00 a.m. in the dusky but warm and sweet-smelling hangout.

Veronica, a half-pack-a-day smoker, hated being told she couldn't smoke, because it reminded her that she shouldn't smoke, which made her defensive and angry, a state of being she found very uncomfortable. But perhaps it was better under the pastry-shop rules that she wasn't allowed to smoke on these Monday mornings with her sister, since she was then spared Lillian's medically detailed descriptions of the long and painful death that awaited her if she continued to smoke. Veronica, however, wasn't in the habit of thinking quite that far into the future and, besides, she just loved to smoke — she loved the taste, the smell, the way she

10

looked with a cigarette in her hand, and most of all she loved feeling, even if just for the duration of the cigarette, defiant. What exactly she was defying — death, her sister, the surgeon general — she wasn't at all sure.

Veronica wished desperately for a cigarette to go with her coffee as she strained her eyes in the dim light shed by the blue-bell-shaped wall lamp just above her table. She was reading over the script she had written for an episode of *Ordinary Matters*. Later that morning, the draft was due to be delivered to a head writer for his review, which would lead to inevitable rewrites before final approval by the associate producer, Jane Lust. Not once, in the five years Veronica had been a sub-writer for *Ordinary Matters*, had the head writer flat out accepted what she'd turned in. Veronica believed the head writers returned each and every script for rewrites, regardless of its merit, to ensure that none of the sub-writers got big ideas about moving up. They needn't have worried about Veronica. She had no desire whatsoever to become a head writer. Such a promotion would mean more money, benefits, and perks, but it also would mean joining the office corps, which would seriously curtail the pursuit of her greater ambition to write musicals. When Veronica was hired, Jane Lust had told her that if she had any sense she wouldn't take the job, that writers shouldn't write as a sideline, that she would end her days as a soap-opera writer. She said that statistically Veronica would have a greater chance of breaking into a writing career if she were an actor on the show, that the names of sub-writers who ever went on to write anything, much less get published or produced, could be easily scribbled on the inside cover of a pack of matches.

Veronica closed the script and pushed it away. Soap operas, she decided, were even more implausible than musicals. Her eyes were wandering over this month's art exhibit on the pastry shop's walls — watercolor landscapes of industrial New Jersey — when she felt a stir go through the café. Whenever Lillian entered a room, heads visibly turned. Both men and women did double takes, repeatedly sneaking glances to discern which famous movie star or supermodel they had spotted on her day off. And there she was, placing her order at the counter, six feet tall, blond, gorgeous. Years of living with her sister's beauty had not made Veronica's pangs of jealousy any less sharp, but what had evolved was this:

Veronica's desire *to be* Lillian was now only a desire to know *what it was like to be* Lillian. Taken on its own, Veronica's beauty was quietly arresting, but her average height, dark eyes, short dark hair, became mothlike beside Lillian's flame.

"So who is Dr. White's wife going to sleep with this week?" Lillian asked, gesturing at the script. Veronica knew Lillian was just winging it with this question — she never watched the show. Even when Veronica had arranged for her to become the show's consultant on neurological issues, Lillian still never watched. Since Lillian was a neurologist at St. Luke's Hospital and a researcher in Berlin Hoshi's lab at Columbia's Center for the Neurobiology of the Mind, Jane Lust was eager to hire her. Amnesia was a staple on *Ordinary Matters*, but now and again narcolepsy or Alzheimer's disease would turn up and Lillian would give the writers the appropriate medical jargon.

Professionally, Lillian was something of a renegade. Her Ph.D. was in neuropsychology and her medical specialization was neuro-rehabilitation after head injury. While some of her colleagues thought she was a genius, "a scientist before her time," most thought she wasn't serious enough about her work. She was employed by a hospital that had no neurology department to speak of, she was an associate in a notorious eccentric's lab, her publications were all over the place in terms of subject, and, worst of all, she hired herself out to lowbrow ventures such as soap operas and insurance companies. In Veronica's opinion, by far the most deplorable thing said about Lillian was that she owed the continuous publication of her work and her position in Berlin Hoshi's lab entirely to her exceptional beauty. Some of this Veronica had learned from Lillian and some of it she got from her own boyfriend, Nick, whose childhood friend had gone to medical school with Lillian. Veronica told Nick not to pass along his friend's gossip to her, but she secretly loved to hear about her sister from another source.

"This week's candidate," Veronica said, "is Dr. Roger Norman, the psychiatrist who is trying to cure her nymphomania." Eve White had already slept her way through the entire Paramount Medical Center staff — in fact, the scriptwriters had to keep writing in new doctors, orderlies, male nurses, and patients for her to seduce. "I doubt it will get by the head writer, though, since Dr. Norman is Eve's only hope. If *they* have sex, she either has to be killed off or cured. And those options are unlikely, since this nympho thing has been a ratings bonanza." Veronica ate the last bite of her hamantasch. "I think they'll want to milk it a few more months, but we're just about out of men for Eve."

"How can you eat that thing? Poppy seed and prune?" Lillian said. Even with her face smooshed up in a sour look, she was ravishing.

"Lillian, you've been watching me eat these pastries for years," Veronica said. "What's different about it today?" Her sister loathed the sugar-drenched pastries from Eastern Europe which, she had once said, suggested the added ingredient of the sweat from the brow of a fat, sharp-tongued housewife.

"Nothing. I'm pregnant. I home-tested positive this morning."

"Lillian," a waitress called out, then delivered a cup of black American coffee.

"That was quick," Veronica said, referring to the conception, not the coffee.

A few months earlier Lillian had announced to Veronica that she had decided to have a baby. She was thirty-five, she explained, and it was time. There was no man she was particularly interested in and

15

certainly no one she wanted to share the experience with. As for raising the child, men didn't seem to do that much anyway unless, as in the case of widowers and househusbands, they did it all. She would just have to rely on Margaret Mead's dictum: Fatherhood was a social invention.

"It's a new millennium and an election year. That should fill up your newness quotient for a while without your having to go and have a baby," Veronica had said at the time, and then swiftly repressed Lillian's plan. Veronica now realized that she had refused to believe her sister because she dreaded the possibility of being replaced. She knew she should be experiencing joy and elation at Lillian's good news, which she was, but she was also, unreasonably, irrationally, jealous.

"Is there a father?" Veronica asked. She looked around the room to make sure no one was listening. The only person nearby was wearing headphones. He seemed thoroughly engrossed in his heavily highlighted copy of *Ulysses*. Of course, she thought, there had to be some sort of father — even if he was just a sperm donor — but Veronica could imagine her sister devising some way even more incredible than divine intervention.

"Alex Drake, a patient at the hospital," Lillian said, sipping her coffee. "He came to the ER. He'd fallen into a mirror while doing a headstand in yoga and had lacerations on his shins and thighs. The nurse at reception heard 'head injury' instead of 'headstand' and I was called. When I got there, I was told I wasn't needed, but I caught a glimpse of him. His physical beauty indicated a solid gene pool, so I got hold of a blood sample and did some tests." She sipped her coffee. "I obtained his address, waited until I was ready, then followed him into a juice bar. I'll spare you the rest."

"How —" Veronica had to ask.

"Doctored condom." Lillian shrugged.

"Jesus, Lillian, the guy doesn't know?" Veronica asked.

"Of course not. He's an out-of-work actor with an apartment full of aromatic candles." She rolled her eyes. "If this zygote has any luck, the new-age genes will be regressive. I did ask him all about his family, trying to get a better sense of his gene pool. His mother and father are both doctors, which I found encouraging. I started probing deeper into the origins of his surname — was he descended from Sir Francis Drake? — when he told me he had been adopted and was currently in the process of trying to locate his birth parents." She laughed and rolled her eyes again. "What he doesn't know can't hurt him. Just think how many men *willfully* don't know who their children are."

"Still," Veronica said, "I'm not sure it's fair."

"If this world were fair, we would be sea anemones — self-fertilizing hermaphrodites. How's Nick?"

Lillian did not like Nick. In the four years he and Veronica had been together she had met him only a few times and yet her negative opinion of him was solid. She was the only person in the world Veronica knew who wasn't completely seduced by Nick's boyish charm, sophisticated intelligence, and quick wit. When Veronica had asked Lillian why she didn't like him, she had explained, "Neither he nor his paintings suspend my powers of disbelief." Since then, Veronica had rarely mentioned him and Lillian used him only to change the subject.

"His next opening is in April. You're invited of course." Veronica's eye landed on a brightly colored painting of the bridge over the Delaware River in Trenton. Written in large red lettering across the trusses was the slogan TRENTON MAKES THE WORLD TAKES. Growing up in a nearby town, Veronica had crossed that bridge many times and had always felt sorry for Trenton not being able to keep what it made. "Lillian, it's Valentine's Day. Do you know what that means?"

"A lot of people will pretend they love each other. Flower shops, chocolate shops, card shops, and restaurants will make a mean profit." She sighed, pushed her hair behind her ears. "And our father died exactly twenty-five years ago today."

In the course of Veronica's life, the impact of that fact ebbed more than it flowed, but somehow Lillian's simple statement just then made Veronica feel as if sorrow might drown her. Perhaps it was her sister's tone, so full of muted anger and disappointment and, Veronica was sure, the hint of accusation. She wished she would never think again about being the only other person in the car when the accident happened. She remembered the button on her father's shirt. It had been unbuttoned. Just before the crash she had reached over to fix it. Veronica, however — out of habit, disposition, perhaps even self-discipline — never stayed long on the brink of despair. She forged ahead, sure that the moment

19

would right itself soon enough.

"Yes, but Lillian, isn't it a remarkable co-incidence that you found out you were pregnant today?" she said.

"I don't believe in coincidence."

"Did you ever blame me?" Veronica blurted out. She and Lillian spoke about the past even less than they discussed Nick. Every so often they would talk about their mother, Agnes, when she called from New Zealand — but even those conversations were short.

"For what?"

"Dad's death?" The guy with the head-phones had fallen asleep, *Ulysses* his pillow.

"Probably," Lillian said, then drained her coffee. "But mostly I was jealous that you were in the car. I still want to know where he was taking you. I always had the sense from Agnes that she believed he was taking you to meet his other family. I just want to know why he chose you to go with him and not me, wherever he was headed."

Veronica's memory of the accident was very muddled, but she was pretty sure they had no specific destination. "We weren't going anywhere. He just felt like getting out of the house, going for a drive." For a while after his death, her mother would ask, "Where was he taking you, Veronica?

It's okay to tell me. It's over. You can tell me now." Veronica remembered her father singing to her in the car. She remembered reaching over to button his shirt. And she remembered believing she had been the cause of the accident, even though her mother assured her that her father had suffered an aneurysm, that there was absolutely nothing that anyone could have done.

Veronica wanted to ask Lillian what she meant about being jealous of her as the one who was in the car, especially since Veronica had spent her life since the accident wishing that this one fact were not true, wishing for it, much to her own horror, even more than wishing her father hadn't died. But Lillian looked at her watch and stood up to leave.

"So which would you prefer," Veronica asked, "a boy or a girl?"

"Oh, I don't care," Lillian said, putting on her jacket. "My zygote is doomed either way." And she left the Hungarian Pastry Shop to the requisite swivel of a head or two.

II

Veronica and her father were home alone on a Saturday. Her mother and Lillian had gone out to buy a chocolate cake for Valentine's Day dessert. Veronica, who was eight years old, had decided to stay home with her father at the last minute. Their father was rarely home — he traveled on business three to four days of every week and sometimes would stay away for a couple of weeks straight. When he was home, Veronica and Lillian, and to some extent Agnes, competed for his attention, but as far as Veronica was concerned, it wasn't really a competition since Lillian usually won. Veronica now wished she had gone with Lillian and her mother to the store. She felt very awkward sitting on the living-room floor drawing while her father lay on the couch with a headache, chain-smoking and staring at the ceiling. She glanced in his direction repeatedly but never looked straight at him, afraid that if she did, he might disappear, or worse, might have never been there in the first place. Instead she remembered him. He had short silky brown hair, dimples, a wide smile, and very blue eyes that had a way of looking right at you without seeing you.

After overcoming her shyness, she decided to use this time alone with her father to its fullest potential. She needed to get him to notice her, but she didn't want to say something stupid so she wondered what she might ask him that would make her appear smart — like Lillian. She could ask him to help her with her homework, but that would be boring for him. She could ask him about his job, but he and her mother were always fighting about it. Death could be a good subject. Veronica noticed that whenever a child mentioned the word, a hush would go around the room and the adults would stop their conversation, listen, and ask questions.

"Are you going to die?" she asked.

He stubbed out his cigarette and sat up. "Not any time soon."

It worked.

"When then?" she followed up.

"Not until I'm very, very old, Nica, with white hair and a crooked back."

He was using her baby name, treating her as if she were little.

"Will it be scary or interesting?" she persisted.

Her father looked at her with curiosity and surprise, as if he had discovered a secret treasure or had made a new and unexpected friend. The distant look in his eyes was gone.

"I have a feeling," he said, "it will be the most interesting thing I have ever done. C'mon." He stood up. "Let's go."

"Where?" Veronica asked.

"Somewhere, anywhere, let's just kill some time," he said, rising from the couch. He stopped, stared at her a moment, then added, "No, actually, there's someone I want you to meet. You should know the truth, Veronica. Let's go."

"What about Mom and Lillian?" Veronica asked, not so sure "the truth" would be fun.

"They will find us, sooner or later, wherever we are."

Veronica had to stretch her neck to see over the dashboard and out the front windshield of her father's turtle-green Dodge Charger. For as long as she could remember her father had driven that car, and like a turtle's shell it was in many ways his home. The backseat was strewn with books, shirts, files, socks, T-shirts, newspapers, a large leather toiletry bag, and two red coolers on the floor. Her father's arms were resting lazily on the steering wheel. She noticed he had forgotten to button the third button on his shirt. She began to tell him about it and then decided not to. The novelty of it made her feel close to him. He lit a cigarette.

After a while he said, "Nica, don't ever believe a word they tell you, okay?"

"A word *who* tells me, Daddy?"

"Anyone, anyone at all. Your mother, your sister, your teachers, your doctors. It doesn't mean they're all liars, it just means they're blind even if they can see. But you can look at a situation from all sorts of different angles. Always explore the angles, baby. Will you promise to do that for me, no matter what anyone tells you, no matter what happens?"

"Of course," she said, looking away from him.

"That's my good girl. They will tell you things about me that aren't true, but you won't believe them, now, will you? No, you won't, because you are a good girl, a girl who knows how to explore all the angles."

Veronica's palms began to sweat. His tone of voice had become unfamiliar, falsely enthusiastic like a TV car salesman or a game show host, and she knew there was something wrong about what he was asking her to do. It was as if she had mistaken a stranger for her father and had agreed to get into his car. She wished Lillian were there. He put out his cigarette and they rode for a while in silence. Then, much to Veronica's relief, he began to sing his favorite Beatles song: *"When I get older, losing my hair . . ."*

Veronica loved it when her father sang. His voice was deep and smooth, and it was as if there were nothing else in the world but the two of them and the song. He almost never sang when Lillian was around because if he did she would leave the room. Once he had followed her around, serenading her while she yelled at him to stop. Agnes had told him to quit it, that he was embarrassing Lillian. Veronica found that hard to believe because nothing embarrassed Lillian. Eventually he had given in, saying, "You're a tough nut, Lillian. Every once in a while, you have to give in to the things you love." Since then, he sang almost exclusively to Veronica.

"Will you still be sending me a Valentine . . ."

Veronica reached over to button the undone button on his shirt, and that little white circle was the last thing she remembered seeing. Then nothing. She heard things. Distant sounds, clicks, tinklings, at once sharp and hollow like the noises she heard coming from the radiator in her bedroom late at night. She heard a siren, at first faint and disturbing, like a scratched record, then loud, vertiginous. A horrible metallic crunching made her open her eyes. An upside-down man holding a crowbar was prying open the car door. Behind him she saw flashing lights.

"Are you alright?" he asked.

She didn't say anything. She saw that the windshield was smashed through on the driver's side. She saw blood. She didn't see her father.

She thought: He's dead, then entered the black velvet of unconsciousness.

When she woke in the hospital, she smelled her mother's lilac perfume. She tried to roll over and bury herself in her pillow, but the effort made her feel as if she were being stabbed in the chest with a knife. She felt someone squeeze her hand very lightly. She opened her eyes. The skin on her mother's face was creased and blotchy and her shoulder-length auburn hair unbrushed. Her lips were chapped and without their usual dark shade of lipstick. Her brown eyes were bright and blurred, the way they became when she drank wine. A muscle in her cheek twitched.

"Oh, Nica," her mother whispered.

Lillian was standing at the end of the bed with that angry look she got when Veronica borrowed something without asking.

"He's not dead yet," Lillian said. "He's in a coma. Agnes says it doesn't look good."

"Lillian," Agnes said sharply. "Do you always have to be so insensitive? She just woke up. Let her be."

"You broke your collarbone and a few ribs," Lillian went on, "and you hit your head hard enough to get a concussion. They want to run some tests, but they think you'll be fine in a couple of weeks."

"That's enough, Lillian," Agnes said. "Leave your sister alone now."

Veronica tried again to turn away, but she felt a sharp jab in her shoulder and stopped. Instead, she stared up at the ceiling. Was it really possible that she had caused the accident?

Over the next couple of days, nurses came and went, taking her temperature, giving her pills, helping her to the toilet. Doctors pushed and pinched every limb and organ. She was taken by wheelchair to be X-rayed. Lillian came to the hospital after school and stayed with Veronica. Agnes, a nurse at the hospital, stopped by often during the day and came at the end of her shift to have dinner with the girls before taking Lillian home for the night. During these visits Agnes never failed to find an opportunity to ask her the same questions.

"Veronica, where were you going with your father? Where was he taking you? What did he say to you?"

Veronica would see the white button. She would look into her mother's tear-stained face and tell her everything she could remember.

"We weren't going anywhere, just for a drive, to kill time. He didn't tell me anything. He just sang to me."

Two days after the crash, she woke up to Lillian and Agnes standing at the foot of her bed.

"He's dead," Lillian announced. "The funeral is tomorrow, but Agnes says we're not allowed to go."

Veronica started crying. Through her tears she looked at Lillian, who was staring out the hospital window.

"I'm so sorry," Veronica sobbed.

"At least *you* were there," Lillian said.

Veronica pulled the covers over her head, causing a good deal of pain in her chest. She couldn't understand why her sister was so cruel — she had to know that the last place Veronica wished she had been that day was in the car with their father.

III

From the window of Veronica's office in her apartment she could see the Empire State Building, the Chrysler Building, a sliver of the Hudson River, and a billboard across the street that displayed a photograph of a padded coffin. Under the coffin a slogan read, CIGARETTES WILL KILL YOU. The phone rang and Veronica lit a Marlboro Light. The sound of the telephone was a huge relief. She had spent most of the morning staring at her computer, typing nothing. Hours had gone by in which she waffled over the title of her musical about Boss Tweed and Tammany Hall, the corrupt political machine that dominated every aspect of post–Civil War New York City life. It was a bad sign when she spent hours mulling over the title of a project she wasn't at all sure she would finish. Nevertheless, she now had a working title: *Quid Pro Quo.*

She picked up the phone.

"Hello?"

"Hello, darling."

Veronica took a long drag on her cigarette, exhaling a soft pillow of smoke into the room. On the other end of the line was Jane Lust, thirty-year veteran head writer for five soap operas. She'd been with *Ordinary Matters* as associate producer for the last six seasons. For a long while "real-life" dramas as seen on the talk shows were *in* and the totally unrealistic fantasy world of soap operas was *out*. *Ordinary Matters* was on the verge of cancellation when Jane took over. Knowing her career was finished if something radical didn't take place, she somehow convinced the network to give the soap its last gasp on prime time. She refused to tell Veronica exactly how she had done it. Whether it failed or succeeded, it would be big, Jane had argued. She had gambled well, and not since *Mary Hartman, Mary Hartman* had a soap hit it so big. Nowadays there was nothing more chic than *Ordinary Matters*, nothing more socially acceptable than the lowbrow plots. Its stars received endless invitations to Park Avenue salons. Dinner party conversations among the elite and the literati centered around dissecting the show's characters. Speculation on future plots could last deep into the night. Once upon a time,

31

among Nick's avant-garde artist friends, Veronica had felt the need to explain that she wrote for the soaps only for the money to support her true artistic endeavors. Now when she told Nick's set what she did they were in awe of her ability to reach such a wide audience using the ultimate-in-kitsch material — melodramatic, stilted, 1950s' etiquette-riddled language.

"Your work is superlative, Vera," said Jane. "It worries me."

Jane had decided to make Veronica her pet project, which was both flattering and disturbing. Jane had wanted to be a novelist in her youth and now decided that she would relive her life through Veronica. She had invited Veronica to her house for several tête-à-têtes, trying to convince her to quit writing for a soap opera while she was still young and capable of producing a subtle sentence. When Veronica would bring up the fact that she needed the money, Jane would say, "Starve." When Veronica would tell Jane that even with her job she was managing to work quite a bit on her musical, Jane would look at her skeptically and say, "Well, then, why isn't it finished?"

"So, how much rewriting is there?" Veronica asked. The head writer had evidently passed the script on to Jane, which either meant he thought it very good or very bad. As predicted, Veronica had a feeling that the nymphomaniac-sleeping-with-her-psychiatrist subplot hadn't flown.

"Just a dab here and there," Jane said diplomatically. "It won't take you more than a few hours."

At least she'd said "hours" and not "minutes," Veronica thought. If she'd said "minutes," that would have meant "days." As it was, hours was probably a straight-forward estimate.

"I appreciate your plot suggestion, but Eve White will *never* have sex with Dr. Roger Norman," Jane said decisively. "Some lines just aren't crossed, even in soap opera. A rapist and his victim can fall in love and get married, but a psychiatrist simply isn't allowed to have sex with his patient. It's strong taboo as opposed to weak taboo, which is the stuff we trade in. Strong taboo — things like infanticide, sex with children, and incest — is to us as a wooden stake is to a vampire. You'll have to leave those story lines to the tabloids or to literature."

This kind of talk was what made Jane a producer. But it didn't solve the problem of finding someone for Eve White to screw.

"By the way," Jane went on, "we've finally hired an actor to play the new doctor at Paramount Medical Center. Why don't you start writing him in as Laralee's latest quarry?"

Laralee Lamore was the name of the actress who played Eve White. She was in the middle of high-profile divorce proceedings with her onscreen and offscreen husband Nigel Thorpe, a.k.a. Dr. Trent White, chief of neurosurgery at Paramount Medical Center. Nigel was accusing his wife in court and to the press of multiple acts of adultery. Laralee was having a hard time defending herself because the character she played on *Ordinary Matters* was a nymphomaniac. Everyone just assumed she was a slut in real life, too. Both Nigel and Laralee's contracts were up for renewal.

"I'll see what I can do," Veronica said, staring out her window at the coffin billboard.

"We've named him Dr. Night Wesley and made him a neurosurgeon. He's to start appearing right away, even if initially just in walk-ons."

It struck Veronica as curious that almost all doctors on soap operas were neurosurgeons.

"Night? That was daring." They always

chose the blandest, most standard-issue names for the characters under the assumption that Middle America would find it easier to identify with a Tom than with a Tobias. As a result most of the actors on *Ordinary Matters* had boring, forgettable screen names while their real names were unusual, even exotic. There was Tripp Jones (Dr. Grant Monroe, an incorrigible playboy), who was gay but never seen publicly without a blonde on each arm. Bianca McGee (Faith York, Eve White's sister), married to a network executive, had been having an affair with Nigel Thorpe for more than a decade. Ashley Diamond (Crystal Clear, the head nurse and Dr. Grant Monroe's barbiturate-addicted ex-girlfriend) was leaving *Ordinary Matters* to pursue a career in reality TV. And Melody Weaver (Lily White, the date-rape by-product and teenage daughter of Trent and Eve) was having an affair with Bianca McGee's network-executive husband. Jane Lust regularly plagiarized plot lines from the actors' real lives.

"We went a little wild on the first name since the actor's real name, Alex Drake, sounds as if he had been born on the show."

Veronica smiled. The name did sound

familiar. They probably had used it on the show a few seasons back. "Night Wesley. I like it. It sounds sophisticated. Is he supposed to be sophisticated?"

"Honey, you can do with him whatever you like."

"Sure," Veronica said, laughing, "whatever I like, just as I always do." Veronica had almost no direct input on plot and character. She was given a very rigid outline and was supposed simply to connect the dots with stilted, morally conscious dialogue. Very gradually, over the several years Veronica had been filling in the lines for *Ordinary Matters*, Jane gave her a little leeway, but inevitably she was reined in.

"So what else is wrong with my script?" she asked, drawing hard on her cigarette and thinking there was indeed something very familiar about the name Alex Drake.

"Nothing else much," Jane said. "Shall we get tickets to see Patrick Stewart in Arthur Miller's *The Ride Down Mt. Morgan*?"

Periodically, Jane and Veronica went out and had fun. Probably thirty years separated them, though it was hard to tell exactly how old Jane was. All she would ever say about age was that, much to her surprise, each decade was better than the last. Veronica never would have predicted such a strong friendship, but there was something about Jane that allowed Veronica to relax. With her own crowd, which was really Nick's crowd, she felt so self-conscious that even going to the movies was exhausting. Was eating popcorn in or out? Was she supposed to like the movie or not? Comment on it afterward or not? Comment on it during the movie or not? There was a very strict set of rules of comportment with their friends that was, though exacting, constantly changing. Who exactly was making these rules was unclear, but the rules themselves were incontrovertible as long as they lasted. Jane wanted nothing more from Veronica than for her to be who she was, which meant a certain amount of pressure on the musical-writing front but for the most part Veronica appreciated that about Jane, too.

"I'd rather see a musical even if I do love Patrick Stewart. Hey, do you know if he can sing? Anyway, Jane, quit stalling. Let's have the full damage report on the script," Veronica said, stubbing out her cigarette. Hadn't Lillian mentioned Sir Francis Drake the other Monday at the Hungarian Pastry Shop?

"Again, nothing that a few minutes won't fix."

Ugh, Veronica thought, minutes.

"The Lily White subplot is much too small — you've got to draw it out for several more pages."

"Jane, mine is not to reason why," she complained, "but Lily's work with the elderly and underprivileged children is a total snooze. There's not much more I can wring out of that one. Can't we give her kleptomania or maybe a biker boyfriend? I mean, with that mother of hers the girl couldn't be so — how shall I put it — lily white."

"Just do it. The order comes from on high." Rumor had it that the twenty-year-old actress Melody Weaver, who played the sixteen-year-old Lily, was putting pressure on her fifty-five-year-old executive producer-lover for more air time. Yet she didn't want her character to do anything unseemly, in order not to offend her real-life parents, who were Mormons and regular watchers of the show.

"Okay then, back to the orphanage I go."

Alex Drake, Veronica suddenly realized, was the name of Lillian's sperm donor. "Jane, did you say the new actor's name is Alex Drake?"

"Yes, why? Do you know him?"

"No, no. My sister knows someone with

that name, but I'm sure it's not the same guy." She dismissed the possibility that the Alex Drake who was about to become Paramount's latest recruit to the corps of neurosurgeons was the father of her unborn niece or nephew.

"If you want to meet him, we'll be having our usual welcome-to-the-show party for him at Tavern on the Green. How is Lillian? Does she still fancy having a baby on her own?"

Ice skating at Chelsea Piers a month before, Veronica had told Jane about Lillian's idea, thinking it was a notion that would pass. Jane, who found Lillian's willful abrasiveness tiresome, had been duly impressed. "I'll always root for a sperm bandit," she had said. As Veronica and Jane were gliding around the rink, arms linked and in synchronized step, Jane had told her that if she had a chance to do things over she would have had a kid, with a husband or without one. (Jane had been divorced twice and was presently widowed, a state she described as "much easier than divorce.") "Of course, I'd do anything in retrospect," she'd said.

Veronica had always just assumed that sometime in her thirties she'd have children. Now she was thirty-two, and, to be honest, she wasn't at all certain Nick would be the father of her children. She was in love with him. He was successful, handsome, adored by all. But if a child was in the room, a child to whom even one adult was paying any notice, Nick would vie with the kid for attention. Even that rather immature trait Nick somehow managed to make charming and endearing, but Veronica really did want a father for her children, not a competitor. Besides, it was hard to imagine their having a child when, after five years, they had never seriously discussed moving in together — the excuse being that they each had impossible-to-give-up rent-controlled apartments.

"Does Lillian still fancy having a baby?" Jane asked.

"She's pregnant." Veronica tried to remember how Lillian had described the father of her baby: handsome in a positive-gene-pool kind of way, into yoga, candles, new-age stuff. He actually sounded rather pleasant. And what did he do for a living? Artist? No, Veronica would have remembered that because of Nick. Musician? No, she would have remembered that, too, since she was in search of one to write the score for her musical. Doctor? No, Lillian scorned other doctors. Writer, no. Electrician? Maybe.

"Nothing if not efficient, that sister of yours. Who's the father?"

"A sperm donor," Veronica said, remembering with a jolt Alex Drake's profession: *out-of-work actor.* Apparently, he had found a job.

IV

A long line of tourists was standing on a red carpet waiting for the elevator to the observation deck on the top of the Empire State Building. Veronica had last been there with her sister and parents when she was six years old. The only thing she remembered about the trip was Lillian showing her, before they left home, an old photograph from *Life* magazine she had found in the library. In it a woman lay on the smashed roof of a car. Lillian explained that the woman had jumped off the top of the Empire State Building, and though her body looked intact all 206 of her bones had probably been reduced to dust on impact.

This time Veronica and Lillian had an appointment with Bryan Byrd, private investigator, in his office on the seventy-ninth floor. It had been Veronica's idea to hire someone to look into their father's past and she was shocked that Lillian had said okay. Their knowledge of him had stopped abruptly when they were eight and eleven years old and that knowledge was shrouded in mystery. Their mother had rarely talked about him after his death and if pressed would become angry or develop a migraine or simply get in her car and drive off, leaving the girls to wonder if she would come back. After Agnes moved to New Zealand, the subject of their father had been closed. At the very least, Veronica argued, they should know where his body was buried, if there was a grave somewhere. And the detective could resolve once and for all if their father did have another family and was taking Veronica to meet them when the accident happened. Second families were, in fact, quite common. On *Ordinary Matters* the phenomenon had occurred already twice in the five seasons Veronica had been writing for them.

A security guard — a tall black man with a football player's build, who manned the reception desk for non-tourists — asked them where they were headed.

"The seventy-ninth floor?" he repeated, looking first at Veronica, then Lillian. "Going to see the Byrd? Well, it's his lucky day."

Veronica was thinking it was a positive sign that their potential detective was on such intimate terms with the security guard when she noticed a miniature television set on a shelf behind the desk. Eve White and the newly hired Dr. Night Wesley were on the screen, falling passionately, and convincingly, onto a bed, and Veronica realized the guard was watching a daytime rerun of *Ordinary Matters*. As they waited for the elevator, Veronica stepped between Lillian and her line of sight to the television. She was ignoring every moral bone in her body urging her to tell her sister about Alex Drake and his doppelganger. For Veronica it was an entirely new sensation and she found it thrilling.

The elevator doors closed and Veronica was relieved to be out of the lobby, even if it meant traveling in a metal box with several people she didn't know to nosebleed altitudes. If he turned out to be a different Alex Drake, then why worry Lillian? Veronica reasoned. Of course, Lillian never worried about anything, so Veronica had to admit that her logic was paper thin. The elevator ride was so smooth, Veronica had to check the number panel to assure herself that they were actually moving. The truth was, in a world where her sister had exclusively the upper hand throughout their history, Veronica was savoring, delighting in the frisson of power this potential knowledge gave her. It was like mainlining a massive dose of Nick's school friend's gossip.

The elevator stopped at several floors along the way, the doors opening and closing with a neutral electronic tone. Veronica wasn't particularly proud of the fact that she was indulging in this silly fantasy, but she didn't see the harm in it yet. In fact, once she knew that the two Alex Drakes were not actually the same person, it would even make a funny story to tell Lillian. Gold-leaf logic, Veronica knew. Anecdotes were to Lillian as chocolates to a diabetic — they just didn't go over all that well. From the fifty-seventh to the seventy-ninth floor Veronica and Lillian rode alone. Veronica made a point of thinking about what she and Nick were going to eat for dinner, just in case Lillian, as Veronica once had believed she could do, was listening in on her thoughts.

A black sign with white lettering listed

the businesses on the seventy-ninth floor:
Apples and Oranges Film Production Co.;
Bryan Byrd, Private Investigator; East West
Furniture Imports; Fabulous Fashion Designs; Galleria Benevento; Buena Vista
Photographer; Singh Singh Travel. A small
white arrow next to Bryan Byrd's name
pointed down the corridor to the right. Veronica and Lillian stood in the hallway in
front of the sign, not moving. The elevator
doors had long since closed behind them.

"We don't have to do this," Veronica finally said. "We can turn around and call
the elevator back and that can be the end
of it." Now that they had come this far,
leaving was the last thing Veronica wanted
to do, but she knew that if *she* offered her
sister the option of backing out Lillian
would never take it.

Lillian flashed her a look that said
"Don't think that I am not fully aware of
the fact that you are manipulating me,"
then followed the little white arrow. The
floors were covered with green-and-brown-
speckled linoleum, and the air smelled
faintly of cigars. Veronica would have liked
to have a cigarette but knew that little gift
to herself was a long way off.

"I'm not at all sure what we're up to
here," Lillian said. "It feels dangerous,

which leads me to believe we are doing the right thing. On the other hand, this could be an exercise in boredom." She stopped walking and pushed her long blond hair back over her shoulders. A loose strand was left behind, out of place and alone down the front of her sister's black jacket. Veronica was tempted to push it back along with its mates but knew better.

"What is it exactly that we want to know that we don't know already and why do we want to know it?" Lillian asked.

Veronica ignored her better judgment and adjusted her sister's hair.

"You're the doctor," she said gently.

"You're the writer," Lillian shot back. "You specialize in motivations. I don't look at why, I look at how." She took a step backward, away from Veronica, toward the elevator. The cigar odor became stronger and Veronica saw that they were standing in front of Fabulous Fashion Designs. She wondered if it was Bryan Byrd who smoked cigars and if the Fabulous people complained bitterly. The fluorescent lighting in the corridor made Lillian's skin glow.

"Hold on," Veronica said, trying to save the situation before it deteriorated. "Let's just think about what we're afraid of finding out about our father." She counted out the possibilities on her fingers. "He was having an affair; he had another family; he was a member of a religious cult. Are any of those really so bad?"

Lillian said, "He was in the KGB, CIA, American Militia, Ku Klux Klan. He was a serial killer. I would be quite interested to know if he was up to any of those things, but, Veronica, I'm afraid our dear dead father was simply a frustrated businessman from New Jersey whose time came a bit prematurely."

"One way or another, I think I would rather know." Veronica imagined a lit cigarette dangling from her fingers just waiting to be sucked upon. She put her hand lightly on Lillian's arm. Lillian hated to be touched, but years of experience had taught Veronica that the right brief touch at the right moment could be persuasive.

"Oh, fine," Lillian sighed, turning on her heel. "Let's go talk to the guy."

At a desk in the waiting room outside Bryan Byrd's office, a secretary was painting her toenails black.

"Lillian and Veronica Moore?" she asked. Her short hair was blue and a large silver tongue stud flashed as she spoke. She couldn't have been more than twenty

47

years old. "Have a seat, he's on the phone. Excuse the nail polish. We don't get many clients in the office." There was a slight whistle in her speech. She put the nail-brush back in the polish, rose from her desk, and walked barefoot into Bryan Byrd's office. She was wearing a pink polyester pantsuit. "I'll tell him you're here," she said. Veronica wondered if this secretary-boss relationship was in keeping with every last one on *Ordinary Matters*.

In Bryan Byrd's office there was not a trace of the smell of cigar smoke. By his desk sat a shiny light brass tuba, like a dutiful pet, its case lying open on the floor. And like a pet, the instrument, in an impressionistic way, resembled its master. He was a large man, though not fat, and he had a surprisingly handsome face — surprising because each of his features was odd. His hazel-green eyes slanted upward, his nose was large, his mouth wide and curvy. He was almost entirely bald. What little hair he did have was in a halo and as blond as Lillian's. He wore a marble-white linen suit (and this was February) that fell over him loosely like a toga, contributing to an overall impression of his being a man out of time. Roman, Raj, Jazz Age, Martian. He was talking on a cell phone while pacing in front of a set of windows with a spectacular northeast view — the Chrysler Building, the East River, the Triborough Bridge. On his desk was an amaryllis in full bloom, four red-and-white flowers at the top of two long stems, like medieval trumpets blaring the arrival of something or someone spectacular.

"Still no sign of her, Mrs. Goodwin; New York is a big city," Bryan Byrd said. "But don't worry, she'll turn up sooner or later." He winked at his secretary, who left the room, closing the door behind her. He motioned to Veronica and Lillian to sit down in the two black wooden armchairs in front of his desk, and he sat down also. His words to the woman on the phone had not been exactly reassuring. The office was neat but by no means spare. The oversize desk and filing cabinets were made of dark mahogany. A teak and rattan coffee table and chairs were over to one side in a sitting area. The two standing lamps with milk-white glass shades and a silver desk lamp were all on even though the room was flooded with daylight. The maple blades on the overhead fan spun lazily. The whole package, Veronica mused, might well have come from East West Furniture Imports down the hall.

After nodding into the phone for a while, Bryan Byrd finally said good-bye to Mrs. Goodwin and hung up. He clasped his perfectly manicured hands together in front of him on the desk.

"How can I be of service?"

"Our father died in a car crash in 1976," Veronica began. "I was in the car with him. Our mother always believed he was taking me somewhere, perhaps even to meet his other family." She paused, looked at the detective's face for an indication of shock, or humor, or confirmation. Instead, he seemed distracted. He was staring straight at her but even so he seemed to be observing Lillian with some sort of alternate vision. "Our grandparents died before we were born and both our parents were only children," she went on. "Our mother lives in New Zealand and won't talk to us about him. We don't know where his grave is and we're not even sure what he did for a living. We were always told he was a businessman. Lillian thinks he sold insurance."

"So where do I fit in?" Bryan Byrd asked.

"Start with the body," Lillian said. "Then you can move on to his employment, the other family. I think you will find

50

this to be a very simple assignment, Mr. Byrd."

Bryan put a hand on his tuba. "Whenever I get that line it means I'm in for it."

"Does that thing," Lillian said, indicating the tuba, "work better than wood?"

"Far better." He stood up, walked over to the window. The light in the room suddenly shifted from lemon to ginger. "I'm superstitious, paranoid, counterphobic, suffer from mood swings. I've got several neuropsychological complaints that hover on the brink of turning into full-blown pathologies, all of which might interest you professionally," he said, turning back toward Lillian and staring at her. But his was not the usual ogle. It was as if he were examining some rare specimen on display at a county fair.

"You've done your homework, Mr. Byrd, and I've done mine," Lillian responded. "You have a solid reputation for obtaining desired results for most but not all of your clients. You have been described as peculiar and whimsical. You are a dabbler in the neurosciences, and, as you say, you have a highly complex personality. I assume it is your counterphobia that accounts for your offices being on the seventy-ninth floor of the Empire State Building?"

51

Bryan hesitated; a shadow of fear seemed to cross his face and then he smiled. Veronica looked at her sister, then at Bryan, then out the window, as if she might find an explanation for what they were talking about out there.

"In July of 1945," Bryan explained, "on a morning thick with fog, a B-25 bomber crashed into the seventy-ninth floor of the Empire State Building, killing ten people."

"Oh," Veronica said, wanting to get the hell out of there. Who was this weirdo? He had been highly recommended by a friend of Jane Lust, but now she felt terribly guilty for having exposed her sister — pregnant, no less — to this obvious nutcase, although Lillian, always thorough, apparently had compiled a dossier on the guy and so presumably had had some idea of what she was getting into.

"Well, I'd be happy to see what I could find out about your father for you," Bryan said, returning to his desk. "But since everything ultimately leads back to the mother, don't you think we should begin by asking her?"

The sisters answered in unison. "Not a possibility."

During the summer before Veronica

started college their mother announced she was leaving New Jersey for New Zealand "to begin afresh." A few months after she arrived there, she bought a farm on the Canterbury Plains four hours from Christchurch, where she raised chickens, geese, lambs, llamas, goats, pigs, and peacocks. She never failed to call each of her daughters on their respective birthdays and on Christmas and occasionally and randomly in between. She had long since made it abundantly clear to her children that as far as she was concerned she had done her duty by them, but a sense of guilt seemed to permeate all her dealings with them. Talk of mutual visits was common, but concrete details were scrupulously avoided by all. The preferred subject of conversation was comparative weather.

"Well, that's a relief," the detective said.

"What do you mean?" Veronica asked.

"You two spoke in unison. It's a sign of good luck," he said.

The three of them spent the next half hour discussing all possible leads, details, thoughts, ideas, memories that might help the detective find out about Charles Moore and where he might have been heading with Veronica in the car twenty-five years earlier. Bryan Byrd never took a note. At a certain point he looked at his watch, stood up, and came around to the front of his desk and leaned against it. "I charge fifty dollars an hour and I need one hundred fifty down. You will pay all my expenses," he paused, "and I will be up front and tell you that in all likelihood you will spend upward of five hundred dollars and be none the wiser about your father." Directing himself to Lillian, he added, "You're a scientist. The human desire to know is unquenchable, for better or for worse. The best-case scenario, and the most likely, is that I don't find out anything about your father and you never know where he was going with Veronica. The second best case is that I find out something banal like he was indeed an insurance salesman and was taking Veronica" — he nodded toward her — "to the cinema. It will then be a while before you get over the disappointment of how mundane the information is, given the fact that your conscious or subconscious imaginations have been working on this mystery for some twenty-five years." Bryan Byrd stroked his tuba. "Worst-case scenario is that I do find out something horrible or scandalous about your father, which will only present you with infinitely more unknowns. No matter what happens, I get paid."

"I believe we are paying you for your professional expertise, Mr. Byrd, not for your advice," Lillian said, putting on her coat. Veronica was glad they were finally getting out of there.

"The advice is free," Bryan Byrd said. "I went to see the new Rose Planetarium at the natural history museum the other day." He opened his office door. His secretary, tongue stud glistening, was chattering on the phone. "A big part of the exhibit," he went on, "tries to put the earth and people in some sort of relative scale to the rest of the universe — the earth in relation to the sun, the sun in relation to the Milky Way galaxy, and so on until we realize we are entirely insignificant in the grander scheme of things. The exhibit also displays a life-size model of the brain. Standing in front of the mass of thick squiggles, a girl, who happened to be French, turned to her mother and asked, *'Maman, pourquoi on a besoin d'un cerveau?'* "

"I see what you mean," Lillian said. Again, Veronica had absolutely no idea what they were talking about, although she had enough French to know the little girl was asking why we needed a brain.

"If you do decide to engage my services," the private investigator added, "please leave the retainer fee with my secretary. I'll be in touch within a couple of weeks." He disappeared back into his office, closing the door behind him.

If there was one thing about her sister that Veronica found consistent, it was her ability to surprise. Veronica would have sworn that for Lillian the deal was off, the detective idea deemed a failure and relegated to life's ever-mounting heap of regret that, like Sisyphus, we grow wearily accustomed to over time. Veronica stood by silently as Lillian gave Bryan Byrd's secretary $150 cash. As they rode the elevator down, Veronica wanted to ask Lillian what she thought Bryan Byrd's point had been at the end there with his little girl and the brain story. Veronica speculated that he was probably trying to say something meaningful like "the mind is what makes it possible for anything at all to matter to anybody" or "we are incapable of explaining ourselves." But there must have been more to it than that to get Lillian to pay up front for a journey heading who knows where with a tuba-playing, self-confessed psychopath as tour guide. Lillian, however, didn't seem in a mood to talk.

V

Tavern on the Green was Jane Lust's home away from home. It was just four blocks from the studio and one block from her Central Park West apartment, so she held all her breakfast meetings, lunches, and dinner parties at the "dazzling" restaurant in Central Park. Like Jane, it was the epitome of kitsch. Veronica had been there before for a number of Jane's *Ordinary Matters* affairs but she mostly avoided them. The party for Alex Drake, however, she was not going to miss. How exactly she was going to find out if this Alex was Lillian's Alex, she wasn't sure. She could be subtle: "Do you like yoga?" Or cagey: "Aren't the emergency rooms in New York City's hospitals an outrage?" Or direct: "Have you had sex with a tall blonde within the past month?" She would just have to wing it.

Jane's "small" dinner party welcoming Alex to the *Ordinary Matters* "family" was a sit-down dinner for fifty people including executives, the cast, and select members of the staff and press. Veronica, dressed in a white wool sleeveless dress, purple fishnets, and high black boots, was directed by a maître d' to The Terrace Room. She had come early just in case the guest of honor was also early and in need of company. It might be her best opportunity for the evening.

Very few people had arrived and they were hovering around the open bar. The room was above-average wedding fare — a glassed-in pavilion with wedding cake-shaped Waterford crystal chandeliers, a hand-carved plaster ceiling, a movie-set view of Central Park and Manhattan's skyscrapers, and, of course, the renowned half-million tiny blue lights encircling the trees just beyond the windows of the Tavern. All very magical, Veronica mused, until you looked a little closer at the decor — the gold-painted bamboo chairs with stained upholstery, the knockoff Martha Stewart floral-motif tablecloths, the indoor/outdoor multicolored wall-to-wall carpet, the mandatory fan-folded faux-linen napkins that had wiped too many mouths. Wafting through the restaurant's halls and ballrooms were the mingling smells of mass-produced food, air fresheners, and cleaning products. And for all the glory of the sparkling chandeliers, the wattage was too high, the light near searing.

Sweeping her gaze around the room, Veronica immediately determined that Alex Drake was nowhere in sight. On the other hand, most of her fellow writers were already there, drinks in hand, hors d'oeuvres in mouth. Writers as a breed were notoriously cheap and hungry. At these events, she was always seated with them and had to endure their heated and unsubtle debates as to who among them was actually the better writer, the most prolific, the best at character, plot — all in a desperate attempt to deny the fact that every last one of them was an expendable hack. But the real reason she tended to stay away from these parties was because of Nick, who would come and gawk at the middlebrows all the while pretending that by intellectually and artistically slumming it, he was a better person. He also inevitably became a party's center of attention — an eventuality that did not particularly please the hostess (Jane) or the guest of honor.

Veronica had asked Jane Lust to seat her anywhere but with the writers. She knew she couldn't be seated with the actors — it was tacit policy that the writers did not mix with the actors because they quickly would begin making "helpful" suggestions to the writers about how their characters might be developed and how this or that plot twist would best serve them. And the writers, never able to take anything in stride, became, at best, offended, at worst, confused about the character, which would then become manifest in subsequent scripts. Veronica didn't want to be labeled standoffish by the other writers, so she got a drink and, while the room began to fill, chatted with them amiably for a few minutes.

Jane Lust made her entrance in an emerald-green suit, matching eye shadow and shoes, her strawberry-blond hair puffed in a cotton-candy swirl. And not far behind her was Alex, sandy-haired, blue-eyed, far more handsome in real life than on TV, healthy, athletic. He wore dark-chocolate wide-wale corduroy trousers and a black-wool turtleneck sweater. It had to be Alex, Veronica thought. It made no rational sense, but she immediately felt a deeper bond with him, as if she were recognizing an old friend instead of seeing someone for the first time. Of course, this profound "feeling" could easily be explained by the fact that she'd seen him already many times on television. She looked again. Still gorgeous. But she noticed he had something on his face, a raspberry-colored

60

smear just beneath his left eye at the pinnacle of his cheekbone. Perhaps a bruise from his yoga accident?

Veronica was heading over toward Jane and Alex when she was waylaid by a colleague named Jim, a short, skinny, intense guy with a mustache. They had once been in a playwriting group together, but it had fallen apart after a few months and he had switched to writing screenplays. He had written and sold one a year for the past five years, but they were never produced. "The day of the premiere, I'll quit my day job," he always said. He felt a certain camaraderie with Veronica because they both had "higher" ambitions. He was telling her how close he had come on the last one — money raised, Steve Buscemi to star and direct, actors signed, DreamWorks interested, when "Steve" got a huge festering boil on the tip of his nose and had to pull out indefinitely. Veronica watched as Jane and Alex worked the crowd, moving off in the opposite direction, while listening patiently to Jim's trials and tribulations. At a certain point, Jim stopped talking and followed her gaze. "Oh, him," Jim chuckled. "Laralee may have met her match. Did you hear about the bed?"

"The bed?" Veronica asked.

"Yeah, they were doing the scene where the new doctor and Eve fall into bed together for the first time. They were so into it, they literally broke the bed. It came crashing down off its frame and Laralee sprained a knee." He was shaking his head laughing. "I'm sure the story will make all of next week's soap magazines."

A waiter announced that the appetizer — lobster bisque with tarragon crème fraîche — had been served and they each went off to find their soup. As Veronica made her way across the room to her seat, she thought, accident-prone Don Juan, it's just got to be him.

Seated at Veronica's table were a cameraman, a lighting technician, a set continuity person, and a makeup artist named Candace. Veronica couldn't believe her luck. Candace would surely know all about the mark on Alex's face. Veronica bided her time through all the initial table chitchat, waiting for her chance. Pasquale, the cameraman, was saying that the last time he'd been to Tavern on the Green was for the premiere party of *Santa Claus: The Movie*. "They had this place looking like the goddamned North Pole," he said, "and they hired real dwarves to dress up as elves." This led Lucy, the set continuity person, to suggest that they try to list all the films they could remember with scenes shot in Tavern on the Green.

"That's easy," Veronica said, "zero."

"Oh c'mon," the others said in perfect chorus — and she remembered Bryan Byrd and his luck theory — "don't be such a spoilsport."

So while chewing on herb-crusted salmon or lacquered organic duck they racked their cinematic memories while Veronica despaired of turning the conversation to her purpose. By dessert — New York cheesecake or peanut butter bombe — they had identified and recounted the plots of *Crimes and Misdemeanors, Arthur, It Had to Be You, Ghostbusters, Wall Street, New York Stories*, and, appropriately enough, thought Veronica, *The Night We Never Met.*

It began to snow and Veronica felt as if she were in a pristine snow globe. Pristine did not exactly describe her present situation. Over coffee, Veronica realized that the opportune moment was never coming. She would just have to ask straight out.

"Candace, I noticed a bruise on Alex Drake's face. Where'd he get it?" she demanded, as if it were entirely her professional right to know.

"It's not a bruise, it's a birthmark,"

Candace said, obviously familiar with the question. "Easy as pie to cover with makeup. I once had an actress with a pigment problem — without makeup her face looked like a patchwork quilt. Took me an hour and a half every day, but she had peaches-and-cream skin when I was done with her. That little strawberry Alex has, piece of cake. He's not mine, though. Luigi does him."

That settled it, thought Veronica, standing up. Lillian would never have chosen anyone with a birthmark on his face. And if she had, she would have mentioned it to Veronica.

"If you'll excuse me," she said, "my carriage is about to turn into a pumpkin."

Outside, it was still snowing and a crowd of people was waiting for a taxi. Wouldn't Lillian have told her about the birthmark? In any case, her ruse was ridiculous. She would go home, call Lillian, tell her about the Alex Drake coincidence, ask her to watch *Ordinary Matters*, and settle the issue. In the meantime, she had to worry about how to get home. Her subway line was a few long blocks away and it was cold and snowing. There was no taxi to be had. She spied a line of horse-drawn carriages across the driveway. She'd lived in New

York for ten years and had never ridden in one. She wondered how much it would cost to be driven home in a carriage. Big, thick snowflakes, the kind that stuck, landed on her hair, her nose, her eyelashes. Subway, carriage, subway, carriage? She couldn't decide. Nick would take the carriage, she thought, but only if at least five other people were watching him be spontaneous.

"I bet I know what you're thinking." It was Alex Drake, the shoulders of his navy blue cashmere coat already thick with snowflakes. How long had he been standing there? "Jane pointed you out to me inside, but you disappeared before I could make my way over to you. Where are you headed?" he asked.

"Way Upper West Side," she said. His birthmark a single inadvertent brushstroke.

"Me too," he said, grabbing her hand and pulling her toward the horses. "It's on me. I've been dying to do this for years, but the karma never felt right until this moment." They climbed into the back of the carriage and sat side by side, not touching, on a red leather seat. There was a strong odor of horse manure. Alex told the driver, a ruddy short fellow wearing a frayed overcoat, to take the Park Drive up to 110th Street. The driver handed him a blanket and Alex spread it across their laps. As the horse's hooves clip-clopped against the asphalt, the driver and his top hat formed a silhouette against a gray-black sky of flickering snowflakes. Veronica knew with all her heart that the Alex Drake who was the father of her sister's baby and the Alex Drake sitting next to her at that moment in a horse-drawn carriage on a wintry night were one and the same. If he wasn't the same guy, *that* would qualify as uncanny. No, it was he and Veronica was instantly tempted to do something she would deeply regret, something that would make even Sisyphus grateful for his rock.

Two

VI

Lillian arrived at the Hungarian Pastry Shop well before Veronica. It was early spring and, appropriately, raining. She ordered, then sat at a table in the back where she flipped through a semi-soaked copy of *The Village Voice* she had grabbed to cover her head during her dash across the street from the hospital. The smell of wet baked goods combined with trying to read in dull gray light aroused in Lillian the stirring of nausea. She wondered how many of the bibliophile types who frequented the café had suffered vision impairment due to the low lighting. Glancing around the room she noted that most of the other customers wore glasses, their noses buried in words. As readers, she thought, they should know better.

The stirring was now a wave. She kept

her eyes still, focusing on the door's horizon. She had made a point of being early, since she'd been late the last two months and the consistency of it bothered her. She had also been feeling, aside from the nausea, out of kilter lately, and seeing Veronica would help ease her dissociation. She wasn't sure why Veronica had this effect, since most of the time her sister seriously annoyed her. But Veronica was still the only person in Lillian's life who passed the serial killer test: Even if Lillian had chopped up the bodies of hundreds of small children and made hamburgers out of them, Veronica would provide her with an alibi. Lillian felt the strong urge to throw up. She was about to go to the bathroom when the waitress called out her name and brought over her black coffee and croissant. Instead of vomiting, Lillian decided to try eating.

Lillian was three years old when Veronica was born. Their mother, Agnes, brought home this screaming, needful, ratlike animal, causing Lillian to have a lifelong distaste for infants, and in time she had decided never to have one of her own. Thirty-two years later, she had a six-week-old life inside her with a beating heart no bigger than a poppy seed. It had the beginnings of a nose, retinas, kidneys, a liver, limb buds, and the neural tube connecting the brain and spinal cord was in the process of closing. When Lillian had suddenly reversed her long-held resolve and set out to get pregnant, she repudiated the idea that some biological alarm clock had gone off in her body. Rather, she concluded, she had a deep fear of motherhood — a kind of maternal vertigo — that was spurring her on.

The latest art exhibit at the Hungarian Pastry Shop was comprised of found-object box collages. Lillian was staring at a Zabar's coffee cup overflowing with colorful crack-vial tops when Veronica walked in the door, her red umbrella dripping all over the floor. She had a guilty glow about her that immediately told Lillian she had a secret. Lillian would have to determine in a few quick strokes if it was a secret Veronica wanted her to know or didn't want her to know. She wished for diversion's sake that it was the latter kind. If it were the former, it would be something boring like a promotion or that she'd finished a draft of her musical, something Veronica's martyr complex wouldn't allow her to boast about outright but would force her to hide humbly, admitting to it only when probed. How exhausting, Lillian thought, nibbling on her croissant. By the look of Veronica — cheeks flushed, eyes glossy and quick moving, the red umbrella — her secret was something sexual, which meant that even Veronica probably didn't know about it. Extracting that kind of secret would be far more entertaining.

While Veronica placed her order for one of her revolting Eastern European pastries, Lillian speculated that Nick had a rival. She couldn't understand why her sister hadn't gotten tired of Nick and his circus act long ago. Lillian had encountered him only occasionally, but it was more than enough to enable her to pass judgment. When she saw him in action she could almost hear the circus barker: "Come see Nick the Great: all charm and no substance. Step right up for your opportunity to see a completely superficial human being. Come see the man who can not only seduce a rock, but be proud of it, too." He was entirely self-absorbed and self-indulgent, seriously believing that because he "made art" the world should tolerate his every foible. He had an acute case of the Great Man syndrome. Lillian was sure that as long as he was sleeping with her sister, there wasn't a chance that Veronica would ever finish her musical. The Great Man syndrome — which could also afflict women, the most famous of whom was Gertrude Stein — did not permit the Great Man's sexual other to have any overt inklings toward greatness herself. If any greatness was to be garnered by the help-meet, it was to be by reflection only — and then it was allowed in abundance as, for example, in the case of Adam and Eve, Gertrude and Alice, F. Scott and Zelda, Bill and Hillary, and so on. Nick aside, however, her sister's life ambition to write musicals was beyond Lillian. Musicals, like Veronica, were relentlessly, even aggressively positive and hopeful, often to the point of oppression. And syrupy sentiment set to music was the one thing that truly embarrassed Lillian. Therein, Lillian thought, may lie the reason.

"This art is sheer derivative dreck," Lillian said, by way of greeting as Veronica sat down. "It makes Nick's stuff look like sheer genius."

"I don't know. I kind of like them," Veronica said, glancing around the room at the box collages.

Lillian decided she was wrong. Whatever Veronica's secret was, she couldn't possibly be having an affair. She just didn't have it in her — she was too upstanding, too moral, too in touch with her guilt to betray Nick.

"It's facile," Lillian said, pushing away her croissant. "And unoriginal."

Veronica shrugged, started to speak, stopped, started again. She pursed her lips and blew upward at her bangs. She had done this gesture since childhood in moments of self-censorship.

"Sorry to sound Zen, but isn't everything repetition?" she finally asked.

Lillian had the distinct feeling that this wasn't what Veronica had intended to say, that she had been close to divulging her secret but had at the last second changed her mind, opting for the safety of vague, indirect discourse.

"A spiral galaxy," Veronica went on, "looks uncannily like a satellite photograph of a hurricane, which looks identical to an amoeba cluster in a microscope. The first line of part II of Eliot's *The Waste Land* is almost verbatim the opening to Shakespeare's description of Cleopatra on her barge in *Antony and Cleopatra*, which is nearly word for word taken from Plutarch's life of Marc Antony."

Already feeling more herself than she had in a while, Lillian regarded her sister.

Whatever it was, something big had gone down. "Random repetition isn't operative here," she responded. "There is nothing 'uncanny' about the symmetries of nature, which are described by a number called phi. Your second example is a case of literary theft across time, and *not* some sort of cosmic echo."

"Veronica," a waitress called out, and Veronica jumped, her expression apprehensive as if she had just been accused of being herself. Lillian waved to the young woman standing in the middle of the room peering around for Veronica.

"You think Shakespeare and Eliot were thieves?" Veronica asked as she used her spoon to scrape a huge dollop of whipped cream off the top of the Viennese coffee that had just been placed before her.

Trying to ignore Veronica's gelatinous, bright-red-cherry-and-cheese strudel, Lillian wondered just what it was that Veronica thought *she* had stolen. Probably something completely ridiculous like an idea or a line or two for her musical. What a lame excuse for a guilty secret, Lillian lamented.

"Everybody steals," Lillian said. "The more obvious it is, the greater the genius. Scientists are constantly stealing each other's ideas, fiddling with them, making them more beautiful. I'm sure, eventually, even $E=MC^2$ will be gloriously transformed."

Veronica ate a bite of her strudel. When she had finished she said, "Just the other night at a dinner party Nick suggested, as a sort of game for the dinner guests, that they imagine a scenario in which they had to choose between the existence of Einstein's $E=MC^2$ and Eliot's *The Love Song of J. Alfred Prufrock*. Half the table chose $E=MC^2$ and half the table chose *Prufrock*. In the end the deciding vote was Nick's, who declared that he would keep *The Love Song of J. Alfred Prufrock* because no one else besides T. S. Eliot could have written that poem whereas sooner or later someone else besides Einstein would have come up with $E=MC^2$."

"You really have to get rid of the guy before his ego exceeds the size of the universe," Lillian said, trying to be encouraging on the off chance there actually was someone else.

"C'mon, Lillian, he has a point."

"Neither a poem nor an equation, both of which can be extraordinarily beautiful, emerges from one brain in isolation," Lillian said, glimpsing Veronica's half-eaten pastry and beginning to feel sick again.

"Unlike any of our other organs, the brain is dependent on human interaction not only for its initial development but for its sustained functionality. The inevitability of all things — a poem, an equation, a child — is determined only in retrospect."

"Oh, my God," Veronica exclaimed. "I almost forgot you were pregnant. How are you feeling?"

Several people at tables nearby lifted their heads to stare. Pregnancy, Lillian thought, freakish and miraculous, equally revered and feared. As absurd as it was, especially since Lillian was a doctor, she was glad Veronica had forgotten she was pregnant, as it was a measure of how well Lillian was repressing the reality of her own present physical state. Lillian consciously refused to connect any physiological or psychological oddities she had with the high-energy guppy flapping about her womb with webbed fingers and toes. Although Lillian was well aware of the incredible damage that could be wrought by denial, she was a great believer in its efficacy. With the innumerable body changes she was undergoing at every minute, she felt the more reasonable approach, at least initially, was simply to ignore their truth.

"Nauseated," Lillian answered.

"Morning sickness?" Veronica asked.

"Morning sickness is a term made up by men," Lillian snapped. "They see their wives in the morning feeling sick from being pregnant and then don't see them the rest of the day, so they assume that they are sick only in the morning." She shook her head, her long blond hair rippling around her face like sunbeams or snakes. "Women can't even be pregnant without men describing the experience for them."

"Oh," Veronica said, looking sheepish. "So you don't feel sick only in the morning?"

"Nausea from pregnancy comes at any time of day or night, affects sixty to ninety percent of women in the early weeks but can last the entire pregnancy. There is no definitive explanation for it. Any combination of higher estrogen levels, enhanced sense of smell, excess stomach acids, and increased fatigue could be the cause." Lillian was feeling much better, her nausea receding, herself solidly back in kilter. "Or, it is equally plausible," she went on, "that the nausea and vomiting are the somatic expression of an emotional response to the fantasy that an alien has invaded your body and will grossly distort it over the following months."

"Are you worried about that?"

"About what?"

"Your body, you know, changing shape. You're so tall and thin, the prospect of having a huge belly must be really disturbing."

Here was a perfect example of how annoying Veronica could be, like a mosquito buzzing in your ear, in need of swatting, but if you slap at it, you slap your own head.

"The true drag, Veronica, will be this: I will see in the eyes of every man who looks at me envy for the man who made me pregnant." Veronica's mouth ribboned in discomfort. Lillian had no sympathy. "Alright. Out with it. What's the secret?"

"The secret?" Veronica asked, flush turning to blush.

"You have a secret," Lillian stated.

"I do?" she asked, blew again at her bangs, caught Lillian's eye for half a second, then, looking away, added, "No, I don't. You know I don't keep secrets from you."

Veronica had never been able to lie.

"I sincerely hope, for both of our sakes," Lillian said, "that you keep countless secrets from me." One thing was sure, Lillian concluded, Veronica definitely had a secret and it was one of the kind she didn't want Lillian to know about.

Veronica finished her pastry. "Any word from Bryan Byrd?" she asked, then giggled. "That sounded like one of my song lyrics."

"Nope," Lillian answered, draining her coffee even though she knew its acidity would probably bring back the nausea. "I don't think our case is a high priority for him. But I did come across this." She shoved *The Village Voice* across the table. It was open to a page of ads for jazz clubs. She pointed to one that read: "Bryan Byrd and the Low Blows at Smoke, 1350 Broadway at 105th Street. Sundays at 9 and 11 p.m."

"Is that our guy?" Veronica asked.

"You wanna go?" Lillian asked back, her question surprising them both.

VII

On the eve of her departure from Sri Lanka for New York, after having lived almost twelve months in Vavuniya, a bustling northern town making the best of war, Lillian wanted pizza. It was her thirtieth birthday. The only pizza parlor in Co-

lombo was at the Hotel Ceylon Interconti-
nental, far out on Marine Drive near the
harbor. It was quite a distance from where
Lillian was staying at the Buddhist Ladies'
College, in a posh residential area of the
city called Cinnamon Gardens, near Victoria Park. She would have to take a rickshaw, but she looked forward to the ride
across the city even if it meant careening
through traffic in a three-wheeled motorized open-air seedpod whose driver would
inevitably seem to be a thrill seeker. There
were no clear lanes or rights of way — and
cars, trucks, children, stray dogs, carts,
motorbikes all vied for their piece of the
road.

Out on the street in front of the college
and across from the town hall with its pil-
lars and dome, she waved down a rickshaw
— even after almost a year in the country
she still wasn't used to the left-side-of-the-
road driving. The sun was low, white-hot,
in her eyes. She told the driver where she
wanted to go and didn't even bother to
haggle over the price. She would pay whatever he asked, which was sure to be at least
five or six times the regular fare. She didn't
care. It was worth simply knowing she
wasn't going to have to enter into the
strain of negotiation.

Three days earlier, Lillian had returned to Colombo from the hospital in Vavuniya, where she had been working with a team of other volunteers from World of Doctors, their number constantly shifting anywhere from two to seven. As usual Lillian made no friends, but it was easy to avoid doing so, since no one stayed very long. She took a deep breath and tried to separate the fragrant scent of the frangipani trees from the strong odor of diesel exhaust. She was elated to be out of the "conflict zone" where machine guns were as common as palm trees, where bombs and land mines went off with the regularity of car horns, where the wounded soldiers brought to the hospital were, as often as not, fifteen-year-old girls. Her mission had been to help establish community-based psychosocial services for displaced people and residents in an area where the art of the suicide bomber had been perfecting itself for eleven years. She had made some headway with the clinic, but in the end most of her time had been devoted to working in the ER often without antibiotics, pain-relief drugs, or anesthetics.

The rickshaw hurtled past Victoria Park. A constellation of lotus ponds lay across well-manicured grounds shaded by ironwoods, palmyra palms, and rain trees. Lillian easily could have done without the past year in Sri Lanka. She didn't have an altruistic bone in her body, so the idea that she had volunteered to go work under impossible conditions in a country she barely even knew existed bordered on the absurd. On the other hand, the lesbian surgeon who recruited her during her last year of residency flirted with her with such abandon that Lillian signed up with World of Doctors (Veronica said the organization sounded more like a soap opera than a medical aid organization) simply in order to honor this woman's fervor. Of course, the surgeon in the end was disappointed. She would have much rather slept with Lillian than have her volunteer her skills as a doctor in the Third World, but she took what she could get. Lillian gave no preference for where she wanted to go. She found it mildly interesting that she wound up halfway to her mother in New Zealand. Talk of a visit had come up at one point, but predictably it had never happened. In the end, Lillian had experienced wartime medicine firsthand, witnessed an elephant on a rampage, touched a six-foot water monitor, eaten the sewer-smelling durian fruit, watched the sci-fi sunrise from the top of

Adam's Peak. But Lillian had no romance for the exotic — these experiences were simply the ones she'd had instead of others.

With the setting sun, the fruit bats began dropping from the trees like small bombs, then lethargically spread their wings and flapped away in search of dinner. The bats gave her the creeps, so she closed her eyes and took in the smells — burning palm leaves, cotton candy, hibiscus. The rickshaw swerved and she opened her eyes. They were just passing the Liberty Cinema, where Lillian had watched many Sri Lankan movies when in Colombo. Her understanding of Tamil or Sinhalese was minimal, but language was decidedly unimportant in these lush visual spectacles with their gleeful musical numbers. Besides escaping the war, too much inhumanity and humanity, Lillian's biggest motivation for going to the Liberty Cinema was Veronica. Lillian hated musicals, but watching the Sri Lankan renditions had led her a little nearer to comprehending her sister's desire to write one. Musicals at heart could be seen as inspiring factories of self-celebration. In musicals, as Cole Porter noted, and her father often sang, *Anything Goes*, and Lillian appreciated that. On the other hand, when

Lillian wasn't feeling homesick and was in her right mind, she considered musicals to be factories of self-ridicule and embarrassment. She had not expected to miss her sister as much as she did or in the way that she did. She missed being annoyed by Veronica, she missed ignoring her, she missed feeling her envy and awe, she missed the directness of her love, the indirectness of loving her.

Running a red light, they turned onto Kollupitiya, which would eventually become Galle Face Centre Road and then Marine Drive. "There," the driver said, shaking his head and pointing, "there Premadasa was killed." President Ranasinghe Premadasa had been assassinated by a suicide bomber two years earlier during a May Day rally. While alive he was the great hope for ending the war. Dead he had become something of a saint — his picture in every home, regular sightings of his reincarnation. Lillian had yet to drive by that spot and not have it pointed out to her. "The killer was definitely a Tiger," the driver said. "The police found his head, and his cyanide capsule was embedded into his cheek." Lillian had heard this before as well. The cyanide-tablet necklace was worn by all ranking members of the rebel army from the North, the Liberation Tigers of Tamil Eelam. Lillian had seen a few of the capsules herself around the necks of soldiers in the hospital. The LTTE, however, had denied responsibility for the president's murder.

Heading out the Galle Road, they passed the Galle Face Hotel, a tile-covered Victorian splendor overlooking the Indian Ocean and dominating the southern end of the Galle Face Green. The hotel was famous for its bar, a place you might have expected Paul Bowles or Graham Greene to walk into at any moment. The Galle Face Green — a large rectangle of lawn and a tarmac walk on the edge of the sea — was where the city's inhabitants went to get some fresh air, to hear music, to hang out with friends, to meet lovers, to buy useless doodads from hawkers, to fly kites, to eat sweets and fried foods sold by vendors, to watch the endless parade of people. The scene always reminded Lillian of an Asiatic version of Seurat's painting *Sunday Afternoon on the Island of La Grande Jatte*.

The driver hit the brakes of the rickshaw so hard that the little egg-shaped vehicle spun around three hundred and sixty degrees. During the spin, Lillian was thrown from her seat into some shrubbery on the side of the road. She was knocked out — she didn't know how long. After she opened her eyes, she saw a purple sky and heard lots of shouting. She got onto her knees, hidden by a hydrangea bush, and looked out at the street. There was a large crowd surrounding the rickshaw. Her driver was shouting and crying as he was held by several men. A small girl, perhaps six years old — although given the nutrition variables, she could easily have been twelve — was lying under the rickshaw, her head in a pool of blood. She appeared to be dead, her neck broken. Lillian thought of Veronica, her father, the accident. *How could this happen again?*

The driver was wailing, floundering around trying to free himself from the grip of the other men's hands, scanning the crowd with his eyes. She knew he was looking for her — a tall blond, white woman who should have been easy to spot. Lillian was overcome by a paranoid fantasy. If the mob found her, she thought, they would accuse her of being responsible for the child's death. They might beat her or throw her in jail. She could spend months, even years, trying to work her way through the Sri Lankan legal system. She might never be able to leave. She might spend the rest of her life in some godforsaken prison in the jungle or in a penal colony somewhere in the middle of the Indian Ocean. She stayed low, hidden by the bush. Hunched over with her scarf covering her hair and face, she slipped along the edge of the crowd and then blended in among the people on the tarmac walk. She headed back in the direction from which she had come in the rickshaw. She moved fast but not so fast as to attract attention until she reached the other end of the green and the Galle Face Hotel. On the majestic front steps leading to the entrance, a doorman dressed in a white jacket and ankle-length lungis welcomed her with a broad smile and a small bow. She stood up to her full height, lowered her scarf, and turned to look back at the scene of the accident. The sky had turned opal: blue, yellow, orange, green, brown, ten shades of violet. The crowd was even larger now. She heard sirens. She turned away, walked through the lobby and out to the bar on the veranda. She sat on rattan and teak furniture beneath whirling punkahs, ordered the first of a series of double whiskeys, and stared out at the sea shimmering with infinitesimally discrete hues of green.

VIII

On her first visit as a pregnant woman to the Park Avenue offices of Kate Cornell, Lillian's ob-gyn and former medical-school roommate, she was told by the receptionist, a blonde named Betty, to urinate in a small container found in the bathroom and to write her name on it.

"We're verifying that you really are pregnant and checking your blood-sugar levels for diabetes," the receptionist explained, "but your peepee tells us all sorts of things about you and your baby." She smiled. "You'll need to get in the habit of giving us a sample every visit, but I'll remind you if you forget."

She gently pushed Lillian off toward the Laura Ashley–decorated bathroom, where she did as she was told. No matter how much Lillian liked and respected Kate professionally (they had always remained acquaintances simply because Lillian did not have friends), she knew the medical aspects of this experience were going to be a challenge. Already Lillian had delayed coming to see Kate. She had let not only one but two periods pass before making an appointment in order to avoid things like having her urine referred to as "peepee." Doctors, Lillian thought, become doctors because we hate being patients.

When she had finished peeing, she washed her hands, labeled her cup, and placed it next to other cups filled with various shades of yellow liquid ranging from amber to daffodil to consommé. One cup containing particularly bright urine was labeled with only a first name, *Muffy*, followed by a drawing of a happy face. Lillian thought Muffy was either supremely funny or insufferable. Over the coming months of visits to the Park Avenue office she sincerely hoped she would avoid finding out which. She had no intention of "sharing" the pregnancy experience with other mothers-to-be. She saw no reason why having a baby — even though the experience was probably like being under one long military siege — should become some ubiquitous excuse for women to be forced to bond with each other. Glancing back at the grouping of cups on the bathroom counter, she was puzzled by her doctor's rather primitive system for taking urine samples. But then Lillian realized that the cups probably reminded Muffy of snack time at nursery school, and it became clear to her that the cups were just one more example of society's plot to infantilize pregnant women and strip them of their sense of individuality and power. Kate would no doubt suggest that these feelings were just the slightest bit paranoid, but Lillian knew the truth. There was nothing more awesome, and therefore onerous, than a pregnant woman. Even God was invented to contend with her.

A chandelier bloomed from the middle of the ceiling in the waiting room. Four plush armchairs were flanked by marble-topped side tables vaunting a neat display of fashion, parenting, and business magazines. One table was usurped by an enormous bouquet of fresh-cut flowers, including cat's eyes and purple thistles. All four of the plush armchairs were occupied, which meant that Kate was running late — a bad habit of hers but one that Lillian was sure Kate's patients easily forgave her because when she was finally with you, either in the examination room or afterward in her office, she had a way of making you feel as if she had nothing she would rather do than listen to you. She would gossip about famous people (those who were not among her clients), discuss current events or a book she'd just read, or ask you about the last movie you'd seen, as if she didn't have a couple of patients over at the hospital in various stages of labor, a scheduled cesarean later that afternoon, and a packed waiting room.

Lillian did not like to wait, so for her yearly Pap smear she usually made sure to get the first appointment of the day, before Kate's eloquent bedside manner had a chance to catch up with her. But Lillian had made this appointment on relatively short notice, and, since Kate was ranked by *Time, Newsweek, USA Today, Ms., Bust,* and the American Board of Obstetrics and Gynecology as the best in her field, only an afternoon slot had been available. With Lillian's own clients (she avoided the word *patient* — the rubric undoubtedly deriving from the fact that a person had to be exceedingly patient in order to get any care), Lillian was always scrupulously on time. This was more for Lillian's sake than out of any concern for her clients. If she began on time, she had no wounded egos to contend with and she felt no obligation to extend an appointment beyond its appropriate time. An exception was a client named Charlotte Taylor, whom she had been with right before coming to see Kate. Seeing Charlotte, any hint of rules and routines had long since flown straight out the window.

Lillian had first met Charlotte about six months before. An auto insurance company had hired Lillian to give her professional opinion whether Charlotte's aphasia was due to a precondition or head injury sustained in the car accident. When Lillian met Charlotte — a blond, blue-eyed six-year-old with a nose full of freckles — she seemed in every way to be a normal child, playing with the toys and dolls in Lillian's office, smiling, giggling, but instead of talking she made odd guttural and cooing sounds. And she gave no indication that she understood anything that was said to her. Just before her sixth birthday she had gradually stopped talking. At the time her parents could identify no event, no trauma, nothing that might have triggered their child's silence, her retreat from the world of words. Her father, a math professor at a community college, had diligently interviewed her teachers, the parents of her kindergarten classmates, and janitors and cafeteria workers at the school, but came up with nothing. The report was always the same — Charlotte was a perfectly normal, outgoing, sunny, personable child. They took Charlotte to various specialists, who were mostly mystified but mentioned dreaded things like "a possible mass" and Landau-Kleffner syndrome. Before they began the series of imaging tests necessary to make a diagnosis, Charlotte and her mother were in a car accident. Charlotte's mother was killed, and Charlotte suffered a blow to her head that left her unconscious for several hours.

According to Ben, Charlotte's father, his daughter's condition deteriorated radically after the accident. Many things had changed, but the most disturbing was that Charlotte, who had been very attached to her mother even during the nonspeaking phase, gave no indication that she was at all aware of her mother's absence, "as if," Ben had said with evident pain, "her mother had never existed." He described to Lillian how, soon after the accident, Charlotte began to go through long periods in which she would "zone out." She would sit in a chair, her eyes open but blank, for hours, as if she were a zombie. At other times she would weep continuously and scream if touched. The symptoms all indicated a temporal-lobe disorder, but her EEGs were consistently normal. Lillian scanned them again and again for spikes, dysrhythmia, slow waves — any kind of low-grade electrical muttering — but found nothing. Landau-Kleffner syndrome seemed like the obvious diagnosis, but the telltale signs of the disease — abnormal brain-wave patterns in the temporo-parieto-occipital regions during sleep — were entirely absent.

Medically, it seemed that Charlotte had a motivational disorder ("the only motivation Charlotte could possibly have is that she somehow foresaw her mother's death," Ben told Lillian) rather than an organic disorder, which meant that Lillian, right from the very beginning, should have told the insurance company her findings. Yet she didn't. She led the investigator to believe that there was some indication of neurological damage due to the accident, but she wanted more time with the client. She convinced Ben that it was in his best interest to continue to bring Charlotte to her at least twice a week for evaluation. At the very least, Lillian should have been consulting with a pediatric neurologist. Just why Lillian had developed her obsession with Charlotte wasn't clear. The parallels with Veronica and her father's accident were there, but Lillian regularly saw children with head injuries from car accidents — it was, after all, her professional specialty — but she had never felt this intensely about any of them, much less any one, before. In every sense — professionally, personally, spiritually — (if there were such a thing) — Lillian found herself utterly engaged.

Charlotte, during her first several visits, had not acknowledged Lillian's presence in the slightest — playing or mumbling or laughing to herself in a corner of Lillian's office — but in that first month Lillian also never witnessed Charlotte in her catatonic state. Then for one visit, Lillian, due to an emergency, was late. When she finally arrived, Charlotte was sitting in Lillian's office chair staring at the wall, her eyes fixed but apparently unseeing. She remained in exactly the same position without moving until the time when she was normally supposed to leave, at which point she snapped out of her trance and promptly left the room. For the next few visits, she repeated the same behavior, sometimes coming out of her trance only to rock and sob. It was during these weeks that Lillian finally felt that Charlotte was trying to communicate with her.

Slowly, over the following months, although Charlotte had made no outward signs of "improvement," Lillian had developed a nonverbal understanding with the child that she found singularly intimate and meaningful. What passed between them was a kind of emotional telepathy. Lillian had no idea what was going on in the child's mind but she thought she was attuned to Charlotte's emotional state and vice versa. When Charlotte walked into Lillian's office, Lillian immediately sensed if the child was depressed, elated, content, frustrated, angry, sad. She tried to keep her own emotions well hidden, but several times Charlotte had come into the room in a relatively happy mood but soon had begun to sob. Lillian believed that Charlotte was empathizing with her.

In addition, the mutual empathy was not related to sight. Charlotte almost never looked directly at Lillian and Lillian had followed suit. She now automatically looked away when Charlotte entered the room, and would not look in her direction during their entire session. Charlotte would settle down somewhere in the room and the two of them would just sit silently together for an hour. After their visits, Lillian would be unable to remember what Charlotte had been wearing but could recall the exact vicissitudes of the child's emotional state — not to mention her own. The bond between them was so seductive and overpowering that if for some reason they had to skip a session Lillian would go through a kind of depressed withdrawal and begin to live for the moment when she would see Charlotte again. Lillian also began having brief anxiety attacks during which she was stricken with fear that her relationship with Charlotte might change, that the child might get "better," and Lillian would no longer have direct access to such a vivid and profound emotional experience. Lillian found all these nuances, shifts, and dynamics fascinating. Now that Lillian was pregnant, however, things between her and Charlotte would inevitably change — just how remained to be seen.

Kate's assistant, Tina — a plump brunette wearing a baby blue hairband, a white polyester pantsuit, and comfortable shoes — appeared in the waiting room and motioned to Lillian to follow her. In the examination room, Tina gave Lillian a pink cotton bathrobe and told her to strip. A few minutes later, she came back into the room and said, "Congratulations, you were right. You are indeed pregnant. Is this your first?"

"That I know of," Lillian said.

"Let's take your weight and blood pressure then, shall we?" Tina said. Lillian got on the scale, then sat silently as Tina Velcroed the black band around her upper arm and pumped, declared a fraction, then added, "Perfect, just what we like. We're getting off to a healthy start for the little one."

Not many women, Lillian concluded from this patter, came to Kate for abortions. Tina took from her pocket a calendar in the shape of a wheel. "So what was the date of your last period?"

"I'm eight weeks pregnant," Lillian told her. She gave her the date of her last period.

Tina gave her a conspirator's wink and said, "It must have been a great night if you're so sure." She fiddled with her toy then said, "You're right, eight weeks, wow, to the day. It certainly must have been some night. Shall we just confirm that date with the ultrasound and see if we can find a heartbeat?" It wasn't a question that expected an answer. "Just lie back. The gel will feel cold."

The ultrasound machine, made by General Electric and called Logiq, hummed into action, the screen becoming a pattern of tiny gray-and-white dots. Cold goo entered her vagina on the end of a mushroom-shaped stick, and pressed up against her uterus. She stared at the screen and saw a lima bean–shaped blob with a small pulsing center.

"There we are," Tina said. "Very easy. You've got yourself an accommodating little fellow." She began clicking away on the mouse with her left hand, and added, "or gal. Too early to tell yet, of course. I'll just take a few measurements and then you can have a picture."

Lillian stared again at the screen where the tiny mass was pumping away alone in a sea of gray. Where was the *logiq* in that, she wondered. A single tear left the corner of her eye and fell on the examination table. She quickly moved her body to cover it.

"I'm sorry, dear, did I hurt you?" Tina asked, adjusting the stick. She didn't look away from the screen, clicking an *x* here and an *x* there, presumably measuring the placenta. She then printed an image, handed it to Lillian, and said, "For your baby album." As she left the room, she added brightly, "Dr. Cornell will be here lickety-split."

Lillian's first impulse was to show the picture to Veronica — and Charlotte. Lillian considered the possibility of telling Veronica about Charlotte. For the first time in her life, Lillian had the remote worry that her relationship with a client might be inappropriate. Lillian was even more bothered by the fact that she had the concern at all. She based her approach to her work on the premise that all relationships, if they mean anything, are inappropriate. She couldn't figure out why her connection with Charlotte was suddenly causing her to doubt herself. One explanation was that it had something to do with her recent visit to Bryan Byrd. Evidently, there was something far more unsettling than she had anticipated about the detective's probe into her father's past, his hunt for a possible other family, his quest for the location of her father's body. She had an incipient feeling that the whole Bryan Byrd idea was a mistake. *Let sleeping dogs lie.* She and Veronica were going to the jazz club Smoke on Sunday to hear the detective play the tuba. She would convince Veronica that they should call off the investigation and leave well enough alone.

"My assistant, Tina," Kate said, walking in the door, "was scared to tell you that your due date is Halloween." As usual, Kate looked as if she were on her way to a dinner party — Armani suit, high heels, hair spray, mascara, lipstick. She didn't bother to put on the white cotton doctor's coat hanging on the back of the door. "I told her you most likely had planned it that way since the father is probably a descendant of Count Dracula." Kate placed her hands on Lillian's abdomen and pressed. "Any pain?" Kate had, in her way, opened the father door.

"No." Lillian closed it.

"May I see your souvenir?" she asked.

Lillian handed her the printout of the ultrasound image. Kate gave it a cursory glance and said, "Adorable, much cuter than Madonna's. See you in my office."

Kate had a Queen Anne tiger-maple desk with three matching chairs, her own and two in front of the desk, presumably for expecting couples. On a corner table was a flower arrangement, the twin of the one in the waiting room. Floor-to-ceiling bookshelves lined the wall behind her desk and were haphazardly filled with novels, gardening books, bound professional journals, and reference books. A couple of shelves were devoted to framed photographs of her nieces and nephews.

"I'm sure I shouldn't tell you this," Kate said, closing her office door after Lillian had taken a seat, "but if there is anyone on earth who would understand, it's you." She sat down at her desk, leaned her chin on her hand, and looked directly into Lillian's eyes as she spoke. "At odd moments — sometimes when I'm very stressed, sometimes when I'm on vacation or reading a book, sometimes in the operating room, sometimes while making love — a refrain I hear in my head again and again is the line from the movie *Gone With the Wind* when Butterfly McQueen, who plays a slave girl named Prissy, has bragged that she is an experienced midwife and is perfectly able to deliver Melanie's child, but when the moment comes and Melanie is having a terrible labor she turns to Scarlett, who is demanding that she perform and whimpers, 'But Mizz Scarlett, I don't know nothing about birthing babies.' So I say to you aloud and in fair warning, Mizz Lillian, I don't know nothing about birthing babies."

As Lillian knew she would, she relaxed. She was in excellent hands.

IX

If Bryan Byrd spotted Lillian and Veronica in the crowd, he gave no indication of it. They were sitting at a back table in Smoke, a small swank neighborhood jazz club with couches, velvet curtains, and a carpet. Bryan Byrd was onstage playing his tuba, and more than once had stared straight at their table and neither waved nor nodded. There were a few stage lights, but mainly the tiny room was lit by short cylindrical white candles in square glass ashtrays on each of the tables. Veronica, wearing a hard-to-miss yellow dress with huge sunflowers all over it, was sipping a vodka martini. Lillian, all in black, had ordered a glass of milk she had not yet touched.

After getting off to a late start, the show featuring Bryan Byrd and the Low Blows was now in full swing. In the all-male ensemble was a second tuba player, a piano player, a bass-guitar player, and a drummer. Bryan Byrd was wearing a loose fitting cream-colored linen suit, an olive green ascot the color of his eyes, and burgundy wing tips. At the start of the performance, his bald head shining, he announced that they would begin with "Eubie Blake and Gershwin songs, move on to New Orleans jazz and Tuba Fats tracks, then to Howard Johnson and Mississippi blues, winding up with funk, drum and bass, and maybe a little math rock." It was all meaningless to Lillian. Music was a language she did not speak and barely heard. What she had listened to so far sounded like a chorus of extraterrestrials on a trading floor and the tuba in particular sounded like the farts of some celestial body.

"Don't you think he looks a little like Orson Welles in *Citizen Kane*?" Veronica had whispered during the first set.

"*Touch of Evil*," Lillian responded, almost without thinking.

During the group's first break, Lillian had told Veronica that at the end of the show she wanted to fire Bryan Byrd. She explained that engaging him was a waste of money and whatever he did find out would be something they already knew or were better off not knowing. Veronica had immediately agreed with her, which surprised Lillian, given how keen her sister had been on "knowing the truth." So Veronica *was* hiding something.

True to its name, Smoke was smoke-filled, and Lillian was perversely enjoying Veronica's struggle not to smoke. When the band took a second break, Lillian said, "Go ahead, smoke. But just remember when you're dying slowly of asphyxiation, gasping for every little bit of air, I will be standing by your bedside saying, 'Hate to say I told you so.' "

"I'll pass," Veronica said, the candlelight flickering across her face.

"How's Nick?" Lillian asked, for the first time ever actually wanting to know in the hope that he had finally been booted out of the picture.

"Oh, he's really great," she answered, with forced enthusiasm. "He sold a couple of pieces last week and has a commission to do a mural for the mausoleum of a wealthy collector."

She went on endlessly listing Nick's recent professional accomplishments, his increased visits to the gym, his improved sleeping patterns. It was soon quite clear that Veronica had entirely forgotten that Lillian despised Nick.

"Are you alright?" Lillian interrupted. "Do you remember who I am?"

"Sorry," Veronica said, looking down at her hands. Lillian waited. "I think he was having an affair."

"Nick?" Lillian asked.

"No, no, no," she said, shaking her head, as if the very idea were impossible. "Our father. I think Charles really was having an affair. I've been meaning to tell you. The other day, I remembered — at home once when I was seven or eight — picking up the phone and hearing Charles talking to a woman."

"Oh," Lillian said, a little disappointed that Veronica's upset was based on something that may or may not have happened a quarter of a century ago. "It was probably the operator. Listen, I thought we'd decided to leave that story alone. Who cares now if he had an affair then?"

Lillian couldn't actually remember her father very well — mostly because he wasn't home much, so there wasn't a great deal of material. Also, from what she understood of the way in which memory functioned in the brain, it was unreliable as the source of any fixed truth about the past, so she was never sure if the few memories she did have of him were actual memories or stories her mother had told her or stories she had made up about him so as to have him seem more real to her. In any case, her overall impression of him was the same as her overall impression of memory: unreliable and therefore useless. In the end, both personally and professionally, when it came to memory, Lillian tended to side with the lotus eaters — the strange islanders in *The Odyssey* who feasted on lotus leaves in order to forget their pasts and their family ties.

"But what if Charles did have another family?" Veronica asked. "Wouldn't we want to know our relatives?"

Lillian sighed. "What for? Most people try to avoid their relatives. Aren't I enough for you?"

Veronica, in the candlelight, appeared anguished.

"It was a joke," Lillian said. "So we're agreed. Tonight, after the show, we'll tell our musician-detective to call it a day."

Veronica nodded just as Bryan Byrd stepped up to the mike. "Before we begin our last set of pomo-rock, I would like to dedicate a song to Lillian Moore, who is here in the audience tonight."

Veronica let out a little gasp. Lillian was less surprised. She felt he was up to something, suspecting her plan to sack him, and this was a preemptive strike, or worse, he'd become fixated on her. She stared straight at the detective without moving a muscle in her face or body. She had always found paranoia, in the right doses, to be one of the most exhilarating emotions. Feeling paranoid, however, in regard to a brass-blowing, Orson Welles–impersonating gumshoe was not exactly her idea of a challenge. But then again, why not?

"It's a little composition for the tuba put

together by the great Arnold Jacobs called 'Programming the Brain: In Search of the Source of Vibration.' "

Standing, he played a short solo riff on the tuba. Lillian imagined he was showing off, showing range, showing her once again that he was brain-obsessed. Did he really think this would impress her or was he, as her paranoia fancied, up to something else? She didn't really hear the tune at all and found it hard to watch his cheeks inflate and deflate as spittle flew off him like sea spray. She was glad when it was over. She didn't clap. Before returning to his seat with the band, he told the audience that the next set would include some Drums and Tuba songs, starting with "Open Case," "Shut Case," "In Case," and "Brief Case" and ending with their classic "The Adventures of Poo-Poo and Pee-Pee." That last song, Lillian thought, reflecting on her doctor's visit, should have been the one he dedicated to her.

Remembering that she was pregnant, she suddenly realized why she didn't want the detective to find out about her father. It was inconsistent. She was having a baby who would never know its father, while she, at the same time, had hired a professional to find out about her own father. It was unfair, contradictory, paradoxical, un-reasonable, indiscriminate, and therefore thoroughly worth pursuing. These con-flicting desires — to have a child without a father, to know more about her own father — had been at war in her preconscious. Now that she was aware of what was going on, according to the eminently reliable Freud, everything should right itself — in-cluding, she hoped, her relationship with Charlotte. She felt very relieved and even a little grateful to Bryan Byrd, for it was, no doubt, his dedication that had eventually triggered her revelation. As soon as the set was finished, she would have to let Ve-ronica know that she had changed her mind yet again and now wanted Bryan Byrd to continue with his investigation.

After an encore — another Drums and Tuba song, entitled "Does It Suck to Be You?" — Bryan Byrd headed for their table.

"I'm flattered," he said, "or were you here to spy on me? Your disguises are ex-cellent." He eyed their clothes. "I take it Veronica is the sun and you, Lillian, are the eclipse."

Veronica giggled, another annoying ner-vous habit of hers, and then launched into a guilt-induced soliloquy that Lillian enjoyed too much to interrupt.

"Actually, we're here to fire you," Veronica began. "We both live in the neighborhood and thought it would be nicer if we did it in person. You see, we just don't think it's worth the time and money to pursue this silly idea I have invented about my father's double life. But" — and here she put a hand on his arm — "I want you to know that we came here tonight first and foremost to hear you play. And I'm so glad we did. You and your band are truly splendid, alternately contemplative and boppy, airy and dense. The darker compositions seemed at once freewheeling and metronomically precise and in general you were all technically amazing."

"Veronica," Bryan Byrd said when she had finished, placing his hand on her arm. "You fired me, you didn't castrate me. I'll get over it."

Lillian suppressed a smile.

"Oh," Veronica said. She blew on her bangs. "I think I'll have that cigarette now."

"If we owe you anything more than the one hundred fifty dollars," Lillian said, knowing full well she was going to call him later and tell him they were calling the calling-off off (a favorite Gershwin song of her father's — she did actually have a semireliable memory or two), but she was presently appreciating the moment too much to sabotage it with her latest truth. "Just send me the bill."

"Case closed," Bryan Byrd said, and Lillian thought she detected a glimmer of relief cross his face. He had discovered something, she concluded, something troublesome about their father and was glad to be unburdened of his messenger role.

"But since you're here and you suffered through my playing, may I at least buy you a drink?" he asked.

"Sure," said Veronica.

"No, thanks," said Lillian.

Bryan Byrd sat down at their table and motioned to the waitress. "Another round here and I'll have whatever she's having," he said, indicating Lillian and her glass of milk.

Three

X

Hurrying up Amsterdam Avenue on a brisk, bright April morning on her way to the Hungarian Pastry Shop, Veronica was determined to tell Lillian about Alex. She had put it off for weeks now and the effort of hiding him from both Nick and Lillian was driving her crazy. She had no idea how Lillian would react. Her affair with Alex, however, would be over, which would be for the best but made Veronica feel as if she were subjecting herself to an elective lobotomy.

How could she have possibly known that her dangerous little flirtation would turn into a full-blown affair? After riding home that snowy night, she and Alex had kissed. It was a lingering kiss but nothing to feel overly guilty about. Veronica watched herself with interest as she reinvented the

111

past. It was true that relative to what subsequently happened the kiss could be regarded as guilt free, but at the time she had been consumed by guilt not only for the kiss itself but for her strong desire for more. She had taken a certain pleasure in how bold and daring she was to kiss this man her sister had also kissed. Had Lillian and Alex actually kissed? Veronica wondered. And she had been rather surprised by how secretly satisfying it felt to think she might betray Nick, the darling of dinner parties, the man at whose feet the New York art world fell. Nevertheless, she had had every intention of ending the whole thing right then and there with Alex, or rather of not beginning anything.

The trouble was she lost an earring, a ruby-and-diamond earring that had been in Nick's family for generations, passed on to Nick by his mother on her early deathbed. Nick had never actually given Veronica the earrings (nor, of course, the matching necklace and bracelet), but on certain occasions, and especially on evenings when he would not be with her, he liked to extract the jewels from their gray velvet box and put them on her, with the greatest of care, himself.

When Veronica discovered that the heirloom was missing, she had been frantic, and took the earring's loss as a sign of her treachery, a punishment for her inexcusable behavior. She spent a sleepless night of karmic fretting, interrupted only by the spinning of fantastic tales of woe to offer Nick as excuses. Early the next morning the phone rang and it was Alex, hopelessly muddying her now interstellar-scale confusion. She was impressed that he had somehow procured her number, but before he had a chance to say more than his name she broke in: "The most terrible thing has happened. I lost my boyfriend's dead mother's earring and it is all your fault."

"Let me help you find it," he said.

She was stunned speechless by his kindness and immediately became lost in a fantasy in which Alex found the earring and was her savior.

"I'm very good at finding things," he said. "It's one thing I do well. I'll be right over."

She realized, once he was off the line and she could no longer object, that Alex coming over was not a good idea. At the same time she was worried he didn't know where she lived, but then she remembered he had been with her when the carriage dropped her off the night before. She considered not letting him up, but she didn't think it would be fair of her to be so rude. None of this, after all, was really his fault. Besides, she reasoned, perhaps he actually would help her recover the earring, which Nick would be expecting to find snug in its little gray velvet box.

When Alex arrived they searched the apartment to no avail. He remembered that she had been wearing both earrings when they first met outside Tavern on the Green and suggested that they go find the horse-drawn carriage. In the cab ride down Central Park West, Veronica asked Alex if this was his first soap-opera job. He said he'd had parts on just about all of the soaps, mostly playing doctors, although on *The Bold and the Beautiful* he had played a priest who moonlighted as a hit man. His characters were inevitably killed off (the hit man actually committed suicide), so he was hoping his stint on *Ordinary Matters* might lead to something more lasting, unless reincarnation became a soap-opera staple.

When they got to Tavern on the Green, their ruddy-faced carriage driver was not at the stand. Veronica described him to the other drivers, who determined that she was talking about someone called Liam, but they hadn't seen Liam for days now — his horse could be on another bender, they said, laughing. They directed her to the carriage stand at Fifty-ninth Street near the Plaza Hotel where, in fact, Liam was sitting in his carriage reading the *Post*, his horse quite sober. He scowled at Veronica and Alex but got down from his seat and let them search the carriage. Alex found the earring buried between cushions. Veronica invited Alex to celebrate by having a champagne breakfast at the Plaza. One thing led to another, and they had a second bottle of Veuve Clicquot sent up to them in a suite. Oddly, such extravagance reminded her of Nick, but it was exhilarating for her to be the doer rather than the done-to.

Having arrived at the Hungarian Pastry Shop and feeling ill from kaleidoscopic guilt, Veronica hesitated while placing her order. She ordered Viennese coffee and a goosefoot, even though she wasn't the slightest bit hungry, so as not to arouse Lillian's suspicions. This bizarre and furtive behavior made no sense if Veronica indeed was going to confess to Lillian, who was sitting at a table in the back, her long blond hair cascading over the book she was reading — probably some neuroscience journal — with the aid of a flashlight.

Veronica had decided to tell her sister that she had gone to an *Ordinary Matters* party to welcome the actor who would be playing Dr. Night Wesley, Paramount Medical Center's new resident neurosurgeon. She had flirted heavily with him in what she believed to be an unconscious act of revenge against Nick (Lillian would sympathize here) and his controlling behavior toward her. After the party, she would explain, the new actor and Veronica ended up sleeping together, throwing her life into upheaval (Nick, work). Only later did she put two and two together and realize the awful coincidence: The actor was Alex Drake, father of Lillian's unborn child. By then it was too late to undo what had been done. She would avoid revealing to her sister that the affair had continued, and lead her to believe that it had ended immediately. Nervous but prepared, Veronica was heading over toward her sister, when she felt someone tugging on her arm.

"Your name, miss, you forgot to tell me your name." The waitress was short and thin, her dark hair wrapped in a red bandanna like a Gypsy's. Veronica wondered if she was actually Hungarian.

"Alex," Veronica answered, then panicked as she watched the woman write "Alex" on her order pad. She glanced over at her sister to see if she had been observing the exchange, but Lillian was still engrossed in her book. "Correction," Veronica whispered, jabbing her finger at the order pad, "the name is Veronica. Have you got that? Veronica." She realized there was a serious flaw in her story — Lillian didn't believe in coincidence.

"Sure," said the woman. "Veronica."

As Veronica approached Lillian's table, she took in the art on the walls. The Joseph Cornell–ish box collages had been replaced by black-and-white photographs of a variety of single-occupancy office interiors. Some were strewn with papers and books, others print-free, some messy, others clean, some ultramodern glass and chrome, others Victorian, some with desks, some without, all with chairs, couches, or chaises. In each photograph, Photoshopped in color and somewhere in the room was a shiny red child's sled — behind a couch, under a desk, in the middle of the rug, hanging on a wall, behind the door.

"Sorry I'm late," Veronica said, a little breathlessly, dreading what she had to do.

"No problem," Lillian said, clicking off

her flashlight and smiling at Veronica with a warmth that Veronica rarely saw in her sister's face. "I've been late myself quite a bit recently. Besides, I had some pretty fascinating reading."

Veronica sat down at the table and cleared her throat, readying herself to make her confession. She glanced at Lillian's book, expecting a title like *Effective Neuroscience* or *Anatomy of the Human Brain.* Instead Lillian was reading *What to Expect When You're Expecting*, the Fodor's of pregnancy books and not exactly a text Veronica would have expected to find even the expectant Lillian perusing. Veronica, however, was now more convinced than ever that the only thing in life to be expected was the unexpected. But her sister's reading material had reminded her of a fact she found herself frequently forgetting — there was a baby involved in this story — and Veronica was overcome by her own brand of the complicated mixture of hope and fear every adult feels about a new life.

"Lillian," Veronica asked, "are you alright?"

"I was just about to ask you the same thing. I'm fine. No nausea for days now. This document," she said, tapping the book, "is riveting reading in sociohistorical terms. Not long from now it will be of huge historical significance as it scrupulously illustrates our complete ignorance and terror of childbirth. And once natural childbirth becomes obsolete with cloning and artificial wombs, the book will become a quaint and nostalgic classic much like *Little House in the Big Woods*."

She sounded like Lillian, she looked like Lillian, but she still wore that grossly incongruous beatific expression. She was even wearing some new, though eerily familiar, sweet creamy talcum scent. Veronica decided it wouldn't hurt if she waited to tell Lillian about Alex until after she had finished her coffee.

"Listen, Veronica," Lillian said, putting her book and flashlight away. "I have something I need to discuss with you."

Thrown momentarily into the clutches of paranoia, an embrace she was now too familiar with, Veronica was certain her sister knew of the affair with Alex and was about to confront her. Strangely, she felt more resentful than alarmed — beaten to the punch. She wondered how Lillian had found out, if she'd seen them somewhere, how long she had known, what she was going to say.

"I wanted to talk to you about the zygote's future," Lillian said.

Veronica felt foolish but still couldn't help suspecting that Lillian might be up to something. After all, it was a little early for them to be discussing where this child was going to college. Maybe Lillian did know about Alex — that they had spent some part of every day together since they met at the party, that she had become entirely obsessed with him, that she could no longer carry on a coherent conversation for very long without being interrupted by thoughts of him, that she'd been avoiding Nick, complaining of too much work (he hadn't seemed to notice) while barely managing to churn out the *Ordinary Matters* scripts. If she wasn't with Alex, the only thing that interested her was *Quid Pro Quo.* She had written pages and pages in the last three weeks, all the while imagining reading it to him from a heart-shaped bathtub in the honeymoon suite at the Ritz-Carlton or from atop a bearskin rug in front of a roaring fireplace in a Swiss chalet — wearing nothing but panties.

"Since our father is dead and Agnes is, well, Agnes, I was wondering if you would agree to be the baby's guardian if anything should happen to me?" Lillian asked.

"Alex, Alex," Veronica heard the gypsy waitress calling out.

"Why, of course, Lillian," Veronica gushed, trying to drown out the woman's voice while avoiding all eye contact. "There is nothing I would love more in the world than to be the mother of your child." Veronica paused. The corners of Lillian's lips twitched upward. "But nothing will happen to you, Lillian. Why be so macabre?"

"Alex, Alex." The voice was moving closer. Veronica dropped her wallet onto the floor so she could hide for a few seconds under the table, hoping the waitress would give up and go away.

"Veronica, don't be such a nitwit. Focus." Lillian had become much herself again causing Veronica to think that maybe the world had miraculously righted itself while she was under the table. "This isn't something you can be sentimental or even noble about. It's just plain reality. I'll have a lawyer draw up a legal document for you to sign. Are you willing to do that?"

"Really, Lillian, I can't believe you think I would hesitate even for a moment," Veronica said, rising from beneath the table. The waitress was standing smack in front of Veronica, her order balanced on a tray.

Veronica contemplated diving back onto the floor.

"Veronica?" the waitress asked.

"Yes, yes, that's me. I am Veronica." She nodded vigorously at the waitress, entirely unsure if she, in fact, had been calling out Veronica's name all along.

"I don't doubt you," Lillian continued. "But I do want you to know that I am serious about this."

"And what about the father?" Veronica blurted out, her lips white with whipped cream.

"Oh, him." Lillian shrugged. "I kept a copy of his hospital record in case the zygote ever wants to find out about him. Other than that, as far as I'm concerned, he's served his purpose. I doubt I'll ever see him again."

Veronica nodded in agreement, mumbling things like "of course," "sure," "yes," and "you're so right," to the point where Lillian stopped what she was saying and asked, "Are you sure you're okay? I know my request might be overwhelming, and I'll understand if you'd like a few days to think about it."

Veronica, treacherous specimen of villainous and base humanity, couldn't believe the scale or scope of what she had gotten herself into by falling head over heels for Alex. She would have to end it with him immediately. She would quit writing for *Ordinary Matters*. She would move to Europe or South America. In any case, she couldn't possibly agree to her sister's request. No child would be safe in the same room with Veronica, much less under her guardianship.

"Rosebud," Veronica said. "It's been bothering me ever since I walked in here. The photographs are of psychiatrists' offices and the sled is Rosebud from *Citizen Kane*."

"The show is called *The Rosebud File*. I can't decide if they're funny or trite, but I like them," Lillian said.

"I don't need to think about anything, Lillian," Veronica said. "I'll sign."

XI

"Who was here?" Agnes asked Lillian. Veronica, aged eight, had fallen asleep on the low sectional black-and-white checkerboard couch in front of the television in the living room. She awakened when she heard her mother come home from work but had kept her eyes closed. She did not, however, squeeze them shut. Lillian had told her that if she squeezed her eyes shut everyone would know she was faking. Veronica thought her older sister, who was eleven, knew everything there was to know in the world.

Other than simply for the sake of practice, Veronica was pretending to be asleep to avoid being snapped at. Their father had been away for more than ten days now and, as usual, around day five Agnes had entered snapping-turtle mode. Now Agnes stopped mentioning him at all — no more "when your father gets home . . ." or "you'll have to ask your father" — and she snapped regularly at anyone available, especially her daughters. Veronica — stirring slightly on the couch, her face resting on a black cushion, her legs on a white cushion — realized with pleasure that her feigning sleep was going to lend her the added benefit of hearing her mother snap exclusively at Lillian. Lillian, though, wasn't bothered by Agnes's turtle behavior. Veronica wasn't sure how she did it but was determined to learn by studying her sister, by listening to her every word and intonation.

"I know someone was here. I can smell her perfume. Tell me who it was, Lillian. It's alright."

Veronica too had smelled a sweet tal-cumy scent when she had come home from school and had wondered why her sister, who had stayed home with a fever, had opened every window in the house. She wished Lillian would just tell her mother whatever it was she wanted to know. She could hear in Agnes's voice that sound, like a doorbell or the buzzer on the oven timer, that indicated something was about to happen. If Lillian would just answer, then maybe that something wouldn't have to happen, and then her sister could notice how good Veronica was at pretending to be asleep.

"No one was here, not even Charles. The perfume is mine," Lillian answered.

Lillian and Agnes were in the kitchen. Veronica heard her mother open the refrig-erator, probably to get the milk for her reg-ular after-work bowl of cereal. Lillian had been sitting at the kitchen table reading *Breakfast of Champions* by Kurt Vonnegut when Veronica had gone into the living room to watch television until Agnes got home.

"He has you lying for him now?" she said. "The 'not even Charles' part gave you away, Lillian. That tells me he was defi-nitely here. You still have a lot to learn."

Veronica couldn't imagine that her sister had anything more to learn but was glad to hear there were still a few things she didn't know. The fridge door shut with a thud.

"If it's your perfume, then show me the bottle," Agnes demanded.

"I can't. It broke," Lillian said.

"That's convenient. Is the bottle in the trash then?" Agnes said this with her mouth full.

"No, I put it down the sink."

"And where did you get this disappearing bottle of perfume?"

"From Veronica."

Veronica was amazed. Such a flat-out lie wasn't like Lillian. Something was wrong. Charles must have been at the house with someone and Lillian didn't want Agnes to find out because she was already red-hot mad at him all the time. Veronica was glad she had been pretending to be asleep. Now she would know exactly what to do if her mother asked her about the perfume — lie. She could say she got it from a friend at school whose mother sells Avon. Veronica almost hoped Agnes would wake her up and ask, so she could show Lillian how good she too was at lying.

"If I wake your sister up right now and ask her if she gave you a bottle of perfume, will I find out you were lying?"

The sound of a kitchen chair scraping against the linoleum floor thrilled Veronica. She would get her chance to lie. She realized she was squeezing her eyelids tightly shut and quickly relaxed them.

"Sit right back down, young lady. Where do you think you're going?" Agnes demanded.

"Back to bed. I think I still have a fever." Veronica was disappointed.

"You're not going anywhere, young lady. Sit down and listen to me."

At least, Veronica thought, she was not going to be the one at whom the inevitable rant was aimed. She even felt a little sorry for Lillian.

"Your father is a failure," Agnes began. "Don't ever be a failure, and what I mean by that is don't ever *think* you're a failure because if you *think* you're a failure you *are* a failure even if you win the Nobel Prize. But the same is not true of success. You can't just *think* you're good at something. You have to actually do it, and do it a lot, to ever be any good."

"Agnes, I'd really like to go to bed," Lillian said, sitting back down.

While for some time, between themselves, the girls referred to their mother as

Agnes and to their father as Charles, only Lillian dared to use their first names in their presence.

"He wishes he were Bob Dylan but actually *believes* he is Wallace Stevens. Well, he got the insurance salesman part right, but he has yet to put pen to paper. Someone should inform your father that Wallace Stevens was a poet because he wrote poetry, not because he thought about writing poetry. You can't just think you're a poet. You have to write the poems."

Lillian yawned loudly. This was a B-list rant, one they'd heard many times before.

"Agnes," Lillian said again. "It's late and I'm sick."

"Not sick enough to lie for your father. Go wake up your sister."

Veronica was ready but a little less certain now that lying would be the right thing to do. If Charles had been home, shouldn't Agnes know about it? What if he was in trouble? If Agnes didn't know, she couldn't help him. Veronica would have to tell the truth, even if it meant Lillian would hate her guts forever. If only she hadn't pretended to be asleep, but had really been asleep, she would never have known she even had a choice to tell the truth. This faking sleep thing wasn't turning out to be as great as she had thought.

"It's late."

"Wake her up."

The kitchen fell silent. Veronica heard the clink of a spoon, the rustling of pages. She tried to keep pretending to be asleep, but the real thing was so alluring.

"I don't really care about the women," Agnes finally said. "For all I know, he has another family. Maybe even more than one. He certainly wouldn't be the first. I tell you I wouldn't care, I wouldn't give a hoot, if I didn't think he did it to get at me, to hurt me. He's getting me back, making me pay for —" She hesitated, took a bite of cereal.

Now this, Veronica thought from the faraway place sleep was pulling her toward, is an A-rant and new, too. She made a feeble attempt to come back in order to listen but soon gave herself over to that other world.

XII

On the billboard across the street from Veronica's apartment, the image of the plush coffin reserved exclusively for dead smokers had been removed. In its place was a black-and-white photo of a woman's darkly nail-polished and strappy-sandaled foot sneaking up a man's trousered leg. Next to a full-color bottle of Chivas Regal, the slogan read: "CAN I BUY YOU A DRINK?" IS JUST ONE WAY TO START A CONVERSATION. This message, in its Gatsbyesque way, was clearly a comment on Veronica's moral degradation, but at least the latest communiqué from the Billboard Arbiter was now titillating, not morbid.

Veronica lit her first cigarette of the day. Having repeatedly failed to tell Lillian or Nick about Alex, she had decided to change her strategy for putting an end to their lurid fiasco. She would break it off with Alex definitively when he called from the set, as he had every morning since the start of their affair. If she ended their trysts now, she might never have to tell her boyfriend or her sister about it. Granted, such a solution was a step down in the moral hierarchy, but, if efficacious, did it matter? In time, the transgression would fade and, with luck, even disappear from memory.

Veronica wondered what percentage of life got corrected in this manner. If it hadn't been for the scent of Lillian's unusual new perfume, Veronica probably never would have remembered that long-ago conversation in the kitchen between her mother and sister. Now it was clear that there had been another woman. What Veronica wasn't at all sure about was whether Lillian remembered this event from their past or not. Veronica contemplated calling her sister to ask, but given her own situation she wasn't too keen anymore on digging into her father's extramarital affairs. Staring at the telephone, it occurred to Veronica that a tendency toward betrayal might be inherited, like alcoholism or obesity.

She turned from the billboard to the computer. It was likely that her descent into perfidy had more to do with her musical than with anything genetic. For the past few weeks she had been immersed more than ever in 1870s' New York City. During the reign of the Tweed Ring, the metropolis had fully abandoned itself to vice and crime. From the mayor down to the newest immigrant off the boat, a crudely Darwinian ethos ruled: survival of the craftiest. The city's population was near a million, fifteen thousand orphans roamed the streets, and one in ten New Yorkers had a criminal record. If you were honest, you were stupid. Immigrants could become citizens in less time than it took to ride the Ferris wheel at Coney Island. All they had to do was to promise to vote — at least once — for anyone "Boss" Tweed told them to.

If Veronica had met William Marcy Tweed, she was reasonably sure she would have thought him repulsive. But the distance of time tended to soften things, and she found Tweed, his Ring, and their political carnival an endless delight. She loved dreaming up scenes between the three-hundred-pound, sad-faced Tweed and his brilliantly named cronies in corruption — city treasurer Peter Barr "Brains" Sweeny (a.k.a. $weeny); comptroller Richard "Slippery Dick" Connolly; and Mayor Abraham Oakey, "The Elegant Oakey" Hall (a.k.a. Mayor Haul). She tended to look upon their outrageous behavior as bold rather than brash, their dishonesty as cunning, their ruthlessness unfortunate. They stole about $200 million from the city during their five-year tenure, but Veronica saw the Boss as a large-size, Machiavellian Robin Hood, a man who was democratic in his debauchery and believed, in his way, in sharing the wealth as long as he got the largest share of the pie. There was no elitism attached to the Ring's brand of corporate and political corruption — everyone, down to the street cleaner and the prostitute, was encouraged to grab a bite. What she loved most about the Boss and his crew were their prodigious imaginations. Songs about them and their wildly inventive grafting schemes flew off her pen. The material was so rich, Veronica couldn't believe that a musical about these guys had not already been done.

Big Bill Tweed got his start in politics when he joined the Americus Volunteer Fire Company No. 6, known as "The Big Six," whose emblem was a Bengal Tiger. The Big Six, with Tweed at the helm, would race other fire companies through the streets of the city. They became so famous for getting to fires first that they eventually toured the country, stopping off in Washington, D.C., to meet President Millard Fillmore.

In a fire engine, limo, or hearse
I'm going to get there first.
President and Prostitute all aboard!
With me, there is nothing you can't afford.

Veronica envisioned Tweed's first solo as a dance number with firefighters, policemen, street cleaners, prostitutes, and street urchins. And lending itself just as well to spectacle was the Council of Sachems at Tammany Hall. Their members were called braves, their clubhouse a wigwam. They regularly dressed up as Indians, smoked peace pipes, and held powwows.

> We are the natives
> and financially creative.
> Some call us knaves
> instead we are braves.
> We smoke for world peace
> and our incomes increase.

She was working on the climax of Act I, set in May of 1871 at the supremely lavish wedding of Boss Tweed's daughter Mary Amelia in the still-under-construction County Courthouse in City Hall Park. The courthouse was the Boss's most extravagant graft scheme and was nicknamed the "Palace of Plunder." Bill Tweed may have been the grandson of a poor Scot, but in his appetite for luxury he was descended from the likes of Hadrian, Cosimo de' Medici, and Louis XIV.

In Veronica's vision, the curtain would be a replica of the courthouse's majestic neoclassical façade that opened to reveal a set suggestive of the actual building's five-story octagonal rotunda, with arches made of Tuscan-red polychrome brick and columns of gray-green granite rising toward a brilliant stained-glass skylight. The construction of the highly ornate iron-and-marble palazzo (never one to pass on an opportunity to steal, Tweed had bought himself a marble quarry) was supposed to cost 250 grand, but due to the astronomical kickbacks the Tweed Ring was extracting from the contractors, the total cost of the courthouse at the time of the wedding had already risen to $13 million. Tweed was at the height of his power.

You need paper, books, or pencils?
Do not stress, I own the press.
You need marble, don't be sorry!
It so happens, I own the quarry.
You need plaster, no disaster!
Andrew Garvey is quite marvy.
We've got it all, even justice.
We don't know what the fuss is.
We're here now to stay,
So join us or go away.

She imagined working on a duet between "Lucky" George Miller, a carpenter who received $360,000 for a month's work, and Andrew Garvey, also known as "The Prince of Plasterers," who charged $2 million for his part of the job.

> In the Palace of Plunder
> There is much cause for wonder.
> The price tag's so high
> It rivals Versailles.
> The plaster is perfect
> The walls straight and tall.
> But after we're done here
> on whom shall we call?
> We need right beside us
> another King Midas!

Meanwhile, Mary Amelia was to be married off to the son of one of her father's colleagues, her future just another of his *quid pro quos*. She was actually in love with Matthew O'Rourke, an aspiring journalist on *The New York Times*, the city's most virulently anti-Tweed paper. In the Act I finale, Mary Amelia decides she will say "I do" after her father sings a solo: "Why So Much Ado About I Do?" She also decides to take revenge by helping Matthew infiltrate the Tweed Ring, which he does, eventually getting himself hired as their chief bookkeeper, which gives him ample access to the evidence necessary to bring about the Ring's ultimate downfall. Apart from the love story between Mary Amelia and

Matthew, and Mary Amelia's betrayal of her father, most of the material in Veronica's musical was more or less historically accurate, but she wasn't too concerned with accuracy as every account she read about the Tweed Ring contained glaring contradictions with the others. Even with his biographers, Tweed continued his subterfuge. In any case, London's *Oliver* and Paris's *Les Misérables* were such theatrical successes, Veronica mused, why not New York's *Quid Pro Quo*?

Staring out the window at the conversing feet on the billboard, Veronica wondered what was happening to her. She put out her cigarette, and wanted to light up another immediately. She was having delusions of grandeur instead of deciding what excuse to give Alex for ending their affair. Guilt about Nick's lack of professionalism? A spent spark? Nick's opening was days away and he was fully expecting her to go *and* to wear his dead mother's jewelry. If Veronica had a decent bone in her body, she would break it off with Alex before then. Bringing her hands to her face, almost in an attempt to stop the question, she thought, What if Alex readily agreed with her? *I was thinking the same thing myself,* he might say. *Better to stop before we get in too deep. This way no one will get hurt.*

She picked up the phone and went into the bedroom. She lay down on the neatly made bed, the sheets and duvet cover a plain silvery gray. The room was spare and generic — a bed, a chest of drawers, a small mirror, a bookcase, a chair. There were no photographs or paintings on the walls, no doodads or knickknacks accumulating on top of the furniture. Her childhood room, which she had shared with Lillian, had been much the same. Her side was tidy and uncluttered, while Lillian's side was piled high with crumpled clothes and books. On Veronica's wall there had been a poster she had always found comforting — Holly Hobby with a teardrop in the corner of her eye. Nick had given her a painting of his for her bedroom, but somehow it still hadn't made its way from his studio to her apartment.

They had met at a show of paintings in a mutual friend's apartment in the East Village. They went home together that night and five years later were still together. Despite his insatiable need to charm, Veronica had never suspected him of infidelity. He was too sentimental and possessive to cheat. She wondered if over the last few weeks he had ever had a flicker of doubt about her. If he had, he certainly gave no indication of it. When they met for dinner or a movie, neither of them asked what the other had been up to, assuming that if anything interesting had happened, it would be mentioned. At first, she had been convinced that if she told Nick about Alex, Nick would break it off with her on the spot, but now she wasn't so sure. He would certainly be hurt and angry and hold it against her forever, but she was beginning to think her affair might make him more interested in her, more challenged by her. She asked herself how much lower it was possible to sink.

Veronica desperately wanted another cigarette, but she allowed herself to smoke only in her office and if she went back in there she would have to get back to work on the script due for *Ordinary Matters* — the story of which was, at the moment, quite simply unbearable. It was the episode in which nymphomaniac Eve White's heretofore barren younger sister Faith, who has been having an affair with Eve's husband, Dr. Trent White, finds out she's pregnant. Faith wants to keep the baby, so she decides to seduce Dr. Night Wesley, the new neurosurgeon, at the party welcoming him to Paramount Medical Center, and then claim the baby is his. Older sister Eve, of course, is already devouring the fresh meat, but that is certainly no deterrent to Faith. The last lines Veronica had written were:

Faith: Operating on the brain must bring you that much closer to God.

Night (chuckling modestly): I'm just a doctor doing his job.

Faith: They say you're the best in the country, possibly the world. I can see you have amazing hands. (She takes his hands in hers.)

Veronica, who had little to do with coming up with the plot line for *Ordinary Matters* — that was Jane Lust's territory — found even the suggestion of parallels between the soap opera and her own life unsettling. She consoled herself with Aristotle's claim that there are only five possible plots, and that we keep repeating them throughout our lives and art. Most people find one and simply stick to it. Given the story lines of her musical, of *Ordinary Matters,* and of her present life, she was beginning to gather that her plot of choice centered around betrayal.

Veronica looked down at her hand. Her knuckles were white. She was gripping the receiver as if squeezing it hard enough might make it ring. She told herself she was so anxious because she wanted to get the phone call with Alex over with, but it was also true that Alex had never called this late and the little lapse in attention worried her. Was his interest in her already beginning to wane? The weird thing about the betrayal theme popping up everywhere in her life recently was that it seemed to come out of nowhere. The most perplexing thing about her illicit liaison with Alex was that there was really nothing seriously wrong between her and Nick. She was happy. She liked their life. She was intellectually and physically very attracted to him. Everybody always said that an affair is a symptom of deeper problems, and though she could easily start construing her relationship with Nick as somehow unhealthy (all she would need to do was consult Lillian), she would be dishonest if she started to blame her affair with Alex on an unhappy relationship with Nick.

Perhaps, she reasoned, her affair with Alex had nothing to do with her relationship with Nick and everything to do with her relationship with Lillian. All her life,

Veronica had been perceived by family and friends as the nice sister, the moral sister. Not that Lillian was thought of as immoral, but she was seen as the sister who was, say, less kind to stray animals, more inclined to get into trouble with teachers and boys. Unlike Veronica, Lillian was just not someone you looked at and assumed that if faced with a moral dilemma she would automatically do the right thing. Perhaps Veronica just wanted to know what it felt like to be bad.

There was yet another way to look at the situation. And Veronica was pretty sure that this would be Lillian's interpretation: Veronica had felt so sorry for the poor guy Lillian had conned into fathering her child, whom she had used and then discarded without the slightest consideration for how he might feel about Lillian or about being a father, that Veronica had decided to make amends for her evil sister by giving him the next best thing, herself. Veronica was simply righting a wrong, setting things straight, taking care of Lillian's casualty. If Lillian were to discover her affair with Alex, most likely she wouldn't be angry, she would simply find Veronica tedious.

And then there was one last way to look at the matter: Veronica and Alex were destined to meet and fall in love one way or another, and this was simply the set of circumstances under which it had come about.

The telephone rang, the staccato blips rising from her palm. Between rings, she made a decision. She would not be able to break it off with Alex on the phone. She would have to see him one last time.

XIII

If she and Alex were to get married, Veronica fantasized as she sipped her San Pellegrino at the Café Luxembourg, he would be both father and uncle to Lillian's child. Would that be so awful? At the moment, Alex was studying the menu and she in turn was studying his face. Soft and symmetrical, warm and vibrant. Jane Lust and her sister were not mistaken in their assessment — he was a very beautiful man. Golden brown hair, ivory skin, ice blue eyes, and the most perfect imperfection: a tiny rose petal birthmark beneath his left eye.

Alex's beauty was of the retail kind. Before landing soap opera gigs, he had supported his acting career modeling clothing

143

for catalogs. Nick, on the other hand, was handsome in a rough-hewn, not-so-starving-artist way. He was tall and thin and wore his shoulder-length dark curly hair in a loose ponytail. His sharp chin was graced with a perpetual five o'clock shadow. Veronica felt vile as she realized she had begun the inevitable peccadillo of comparing lovers.

A tall blond waiter, who looked like he could be Lillian's twin brother, took their order.

"A warm beet salad with artichoke hearts," Alex told him, then he smiled at Veronica, his expression adoring.

Nick would have ordered steak frites, she thought. Would she rather be with someone who ordered steak frites or a warm beet salad? Consumed with guilt, she ordered a steak, remembering too late that Alex was a vegetarian. He would never say anything, just as he had never mentioned the fact that she smoked. She had yet to light a cigarette in front of him — quite a feat — but she knew he knew she smoked. Alex was not one for many words, but in the past weeks she had learned some things about him. He meditated several times a day, never ate anything from a package, and kept at the forefront of his consciousness the desire for harmonious continuity in what he called the "spirit-body-environment triad." He loved nature. His idea of a vacation was two weeks hiking in Maine's north woods. He practiced Ansura yoga two hours a day, and on the weekends he went trapezing in upstate New York as a regular participant in a total mind-body therapy retreat. With the exception of that one trip to the emergency room at St. Luke's — which was beyond his control because the yoga teacher called 911 — he never went to a doctor, preferring healers. Whenever possible he took their workshops. He had long since given up on psychotherapy (and he had tried most variations) as it didn't take seriously enough one thing he held very dear: mental telepathy. He was a great believer in telepathy, convinced that just as the world was made up of all sorts of energy fields — electromagnetic, gravitational, and so on — there were also "thought pattern" fields through which people across rooms, cities, countries, and continents communicated unconsciously. On the ceiling of his apartment in large gold letters was a line from William James: "The breach from one mind to another is perhaps the greatest breach in nature." This detail, Veronica had noted, had not been included in Lillian's description of Alex's apartment.

Veronica found Alex fascinating and inspiring, even if participating in any of his activities was unthinkable. She smoked, drank, never exercised, and ate almost everything from a package. Her conversations with Jane Lust were as close as she came to spiritual exploration, and, as for the environment, her idea of a trip to the great outdoors was walking out of her apartment building. There was not much harmony in her triad. In truth, Veronica sighed — glancing around the restaurant at the neo-1950s' diner decor — she and Alex were just having one of those passionate flings in which the two people have very little in common but their mutual and pressing desire to have sex. All the more reason to end it, she concluded, entirely unconvinced.

Café Luxembourg was a renowned actor hangout and, appropriately, mirrors covered the walls, so that no matter where you were seated you could see yourself and everyone else in the room. It was close to the *Ordinary Matters* studio and no one she or Nick knew was likely to be there, but it had occurred to Veronica that they might run into someone Alex knew. He, however, had nothing to hide. Lately there had been "no one serious" in his life. Lillian, Veronica surmised, was in the "no one serious" category, along with who knows how many other women. Veronica had lied to Alex, saying that she and Nick had a "don't ask, don't tell" policy. Alex had pointed out that the military policy of the same name was a colossal failure.

But then again so was monogamy, Veronica thought, as her gaze leapt from mirror to mirror, couple to couple, trying to determine how many of the duos in the room were illicit. Her eyes landed on a familiar face she couldn't quite place, at a table not far from theirs. She was momentarily worried that he was a friend of Nick's, but then she realized he was probably an actor. The woman he was with — a pretty redhead — was also someone Veronica had seen before and she was sure it was on the screen. She turned back to Alex. Father and uncle. Funcle. She was reminded of Faye Dunaway's famous scene in *Chinatown* in which she reveals the paternity of her daughter by declaring her own relationship to the girl — "Mother, sister; sister, mother" — but this situation wasn't nearly as bad as that, she reassured herself. In any case, she figured she had better get the difficult conversation started.

"Alex," Veronica began, "have you ever wanted to be a father?"

A look of surprise and embarrassment swept across his face. Veronica was horrified by her own question. She *was* losing her mind. That was certainly not what she had intended to say. He was sure to get the wrong idea.

"Are you . . ." he began gently. He didn't need to finish the sentence.

"No, no, no, no. That's not what I meant at all. I was thinking about the subject of fatherhood recently" — she was scrambling — "and I was wondering how you felt about it hypothetically. . . ."

"Hypothetically, I would like to have a whole brood." He smiled his scintillating J. Crew smile. "I was an only child, and I always wished for brothers and sisters."

This was a subject in desperate need of changing. She had so far successfully avoided talking about siblings. "You'd have to give up trapezing," Veronica said, wondering what the hell she was doing.

The blond waiter brought them a basket of bread.

"There's nothing dangerous about the

148

trapeze," Alex said. "There are always nets beneath us. And it is a profound lesson in developing trust — you trusting someone, someone trusting you. I would love to do it with you sometime." He paused. "You look gorgeous. The color of your hair makes me think of chocolate truffles."

"You're just hungry," Veronica said, nibbling on a piece of focaccia as she pictured herself flying through the air, her arms outstretched toward Alex's. In her mind's eye, Alex became Nick, Nick became Lillian, Lillian became Charles, Charles became Lillian's unborn baby.

"Would you like to have a child?" Alex asked.

Somehow Veronica hadn't foreseen the question and it threw her into momentary confusion. Nick brought the subject of children up every so often, but only in terms of offspring as some kind of aesthetically pleasing and original idea, as in Happy Artist with Children as opposed to the more usual Lonesome Brooding Childless Artist. He had never asked her simply and directly, as Alex just had, if she wanted children. The waiter resembling Lillian seemed to be hovering around the table waiting for her answer.

"No," she said finally. "I don't want children. I feel it's irresponsible." She was starting to enjoy lying. She thought of Boss Tweed and how stealing must have been like a drug for him. "Why bring another child into this world?" She was on a roll, flying high, thinking, Who needs trapezing when you can simply lie to the same effect? "There are so many needy children already here. If anything, I would adopt."

The waiter brought their food and Veronica was mortified. Alex had before him a colorful, healthy, reasonable lunch. In front of her was a large, gray, sizzling, odorous, instant infarction.

"Having been adopted myself," Alex said, his voice soft and sweet, "I'm very curious to have a child who is related to me. But I'm scared I might not be a good father. I still don't trust myself or my triad. That's why I do things like trapezing, to try to find trust."

Veronica, who for some time had been feeling mentally unstable, was now seriously doubting her sanity. She had completely forgotten Alex had been adopted. She was feeling very insensitive, not to mention baffled, by his triad talk. The actor she had recognized earlier at a nearby table was gesticulating wildly and speaking in Italian. The redhead was laughing proudly, indulgently, as a mother does with her child, and Veronica realized that he was Roberto Benigni, the comedian and actor-writer-director of *Life Is Beautiful*, a movie set in a death camp about a father who pretends the Holocaust is a game to protect his son from the truth. The woman he was with was his wife, Nicoletta Braschi, who played his wife in the film. Veronica was about to point them out to Alex when she remembered that she had hated the movie. She had felt grossly manipulated — the victim of a cheap trick. Using a colossal real-life tragedy, Benigni easily triggered deep emotions in the audience, then made them laugh and cry, threw a child into the mix and — presto, whammo — the artistic endeavor became Profound Oscar Material. Of course, that's more or less what an entertainer is supposed to do, so why did she have such a viscerally bad reaction to the movie?

"I trust you," Veronica said, feeling very untrustworthy. She looked down at her untouched steak.

"Trust for me is simply being willing to allow for the possibility that anything is possible," Alex said. "I trusted I would meet the most glorious woman in the world and, see" — he reached over and slid his finger down her nose — "I did."

Veronica couldn't believe that Alex actually said things like this. She wanted to laugh or tell him to get real, but mostly she just wanted to believe him.

"Let me tell you a story that explains what I mean about anything being possible," he began. "When I had a toothache recently, I went to a dental healer. He was a huge, heavily tattooed guy with a large scar across his cheek who used to be a member of the Hell's Angels."

Veronica stared at her steak and wondered if somewhere along her downward spiral of a life she had contracted mad cow disease and the symptoms had begun to manifest themselves.

"While feeling around my mouth," Alex continued, "brushing my tongue with a peacock feather, and checking out my oral-energy field, he told me that one day an elderly woman had come to see him. She had been having terrible trouble with her dentures. They constantly fell out of her mouth, they hurt her gums, gave her headaches. She preferred not to wear them, but this drove her family crazy. They couldn't stand to be around her if she wasn't wearing dentures. She'd been to see five or six different dentists and had ordered three different sets of teeth made, which was extremely expensive. Her son and daughter were seeing her less because she traumatized the grandchildren when she took her teeth out of her mouth at odd moments. While shopping in a boutique for a birthday present for her best friend, she sneezed and her teeth fell into a window display."

Figuring that she already had mad cow disease, Veronica went ahead and ate her steak. She glanced back at Benigni to make sure he was still there, that she wasn't hallucinating this whole event. He was still there, and she decided she had been too harsh on him. All careers had weak moments. Jerry Lewis, for example, wrote, directed, and starred in *The Day the Clown Cried*, a film about a circus clown who entertains children in concentration camps on their way to the gas chambers.

"Her life was falling apart," Alex went on. "The friend for whom she'd been trying to buy a birthday present told her about the dental healer. The dental healer felt her oral field, which was like nothing he had ever come across before. He tried to manipulate it as best he could, then sent her away. The next day she called and was in unbearable pain. Her jaw, she said, felt as if it were going to break. He told her to come back immediately, which she did. Again, he felt a very bizarre field and did what he could to put it back into some kind of shape. She left feeling a bit better. The next day she called crying. Not only did her jaw ache as if it were in a slowly closing vise, but her gums had become raw and bloody."

Veronica's steak could not have been more delicious. Red, juicy, soft on the inside, just a little crunchy on the outside.

"The ex–Hell's Angel dental healer saw her and again was stupefied by what he thought was happening but couldn't quite believe it. The following day, the elderly woman called in agony several times, leaving messages on the answering machine, to which the dental healer did not respond. Two days passed. She called. He answered the phone, and she told him that she had awakened that morning with a whole new set of teeth, her very own. She had grown a new set!"

"Wow," Veronica said, reassuring herself that whatever was wrong with her might not be as drastic as mad cow disease. It could be just the onset of schizophrenia. She would have to consult Lillian. "That's quite a story, Alex. Do you believe it?"

Alex shrugged. "All I know is that since

he told me that story I haven't had a toothache."

Again, Veronica looked over at Benigni
and his wife. They were talking and
laughing, eating each other's food. Alex
was right, she thought, an audience does
not expect a story to be literal. In fact, an
audience desires — even demands — to be
emotionally and intellectually manipulated. So why, Veronica asked herself, did
Life Is Beautiful bother her so much? Was it
the conceit of horror as a game? Or was it
quite simply that she just didn't believe the
story? It wasn't that she felt manipulated,
it was that she hadn't been manipulated
well enough. And because she didn't believe the story, she didn't trust it. She
thought of Mel Brooks's *The Producers*,
which also used the horror of Hitler as
comic material and had a story far more
outlandish and preposterous than
Benigni's, yet for Veronica it had been con-
vincing.

"I have to get back to the set," Alex said,
reaching over and caressing her cheek.
"What was on your mind that was so urgent?"

Veronica herself had entirely forgotten.
She looked over again at Benigni and
Braschi, fully absorbed by each other. She

had read somewhere that they had been together for over ten years. And Mel Brooks and his wife, Anne Bancroft, had been together for nearly fifty years. That stunt was even harder to pull off than a senior citizen growing a new set of teeth.

"Oh, there's always tomorrow," she answered, and as they left the restaurant she was sure the waiter winked at her.

Four

XIV

On a brisk Monday morning in early May, dogwoods and cherry blossoms in full, resplendent bloom, Lillian was waiting for Veronica at the Hungarian Pastry Shop when she was almost sure she felt her baby kick for the first time. It wasn't exactly a kick, it was more like a fluttering, a butterfly kiss, the belly surge of a sudden loss of altitude. But then again, it could have been indigestion. Lillian was fourteen weeks pregnant and could still button her jeans without even an intake of breath. So far she had gained only two pounds. She had never paid much attention to her weight, because her height and her high metabolism always kept her slim. Kate had told her that after the first trimester she should gain a pound a week, which is exactly what had happened. She was stunned to think she might gain twenty-four pounds. It was not as if she didn't know that pregnant women gained weight. She'd seen plenty of women in their third trimester and had marveled at their size and shape. But when it came to her own body, the whole physical transformation became unbelievable, and she felt like the foolish victim of some typical misfortune who says, incredulously, "I just thought it could never happen to me."

Although the body changes were unsettling, the mental adjustments were far more challenging. It seemed that her imagination was producing fantasies at a rate comparable to that of cell division in the fetus. In the darkest of them, her body was the host for an alien presence. She had inside her a devil child, a three-headed monster, an acid-spitting flesh eater. At times, she found herself loathing this being that depended on her for absolutely everything, and she blamed it for having the potential to cause her death in childbirth as a result of some freakish complication. She wanted to have a baby, but she emphatically did not want to die for that baby. These grisly fantasies were disturbing to Lillian, but she had a much more difficult time with the fact that since she had become pregnant she often found herself experiencing waves of love and general goodwill toward humankind. Luckily, the waves didn't last long and for the most part she was able to keep them in check — resisting any sudden urge to, say, coo over a newborn or help an old lady cross the street.

The pastry shop was particularly lively that morning. All the tables were occupied and in the normally curmudgeonly crowd everyone seemed overly cheerful, chatting away with one another like old friends. *The Rosebud File* photographs were still on display, most of them with little round red "sold" stickers. The smells of coffee and freshly baked cakes and cookies were once again tolerable. Gone were the sudden attacks brought on by random smells, the experience of which had been so offensive that she had been driven to wearing perfume to keep other odors at bay. Unfortunately, the perfume sample she had lifted from a copy of *Vogue* in Kate's waiting room had elicited a far more complicated response. Minutes after applying the scent, not only did she become profoundly nauseated but also the smell caused her to remember suddenly a painful episode with her father not long before his death.

Of all the senses, Lillian knew, smell is

the only one that takes a direct route to the cerebral cortex without stopping off at the thalamus, the forebrain's air-traffic-control room. We see a mountain and the thalamus makes sure we don't simply see the mountain. Signals sent to the brain's language centers have us also perceive the word *mountain,* the category of mountain, what we already know about mountain-hood, what we know about the specific mountain we are looking at. Emotion and memory centers eventually trigger associations with the particular mountain on view as well as with mountainhood, but since there is a lot else happening in the brain, mountainwise, we can easily distract ourselves from those circuits if need be. Feelings and memories associated with smell, however, are almost impossible to suppress consciously because the scent, once inhaled, directly stimulates neuronal activity in the emotional and memory centers of the brain, such as the amygdala and hippocampus. Some neuroscientists believed that the whole limbic system, the system most deeply involved in the emotions, evolved from the olfactory bulb. And one of the most startling neurobiological discoveries of the last decade was the enormous number of genes devoted to the sense of smell.

Reflexively, Lillian laid her hand over her lower abdomen. It felt as if someone had just popped open a champagne bottle in her womb. She still couldn't be positive that the internal explosion was actually a kick. Fourteen weeks was early for that. Raucous intestinal disturbances were just as likely an explanation. In any case, the sensation was at once disconcerting and ecstatic.

Lillian glanced toward the door, surprised that her sister was late again. Recently, Veronica had seemed acerbic and reticent — much more like Lillian than Lillian had been lately. Lillian was even beginning to prefer her sister's company to her own, a state of affairs she could never have foreseen. She sincerely hoped that being pregnant was not making her maudlin. For one thing, it would be devastating professionally. She could lose all credibility with clients whose fine-tuned radar detected the slightest hint of not-to-be-trusted sentimentality. She was especially concerned about the possible effect on Charlotte. Lillian believed that children knew when adults became sentimental with them. What was actually occurring was that nostalgia — i.e., a misguided yearning for their own youth — had been triggered and it had nothing to do with the actual child they were talking to. Children, she concluded, experienced sentimentality in adults as a kind of abandonment. Sometime very soon, Lillian was going to have to tell her clients — again it was Charlotte she was really thinking of — that she was having a baby. Abandonment, jealousy, anger, and resentment were all feelings she usually absorbed and deflected with the ease and precision of a superconducting magnet. But for some reason, now that she had this thing growing inside her, she was afraid of her clients' negative attitudes toward her. Inevitably, Charlotte was going to feel rejected and replaced — and would hate Lillian for it. On the other hand, things did not necessarily have to play out that way. What if Charlotte instead became excited about this new life? What if she felt included in the process of its birth, formed a relationship with the unborn baby, empathized with it, and became its protector? Lillian put her head in her hands and wondered what on earth was happening to her — she was being so blindly positive it was terrifying.

A young man with overlong sideburns sat down at Lillian's table. He was wearing a red denim jacket and carrying a copy of Kurt Vonnegut's *Slaughterhouse-Five*.

"You can't sit here," she snapped. "I'm waiting for someone."

Her father had gone through a Vonnegut phase. She remembered the books stacked on his bedside table: *The Sirens of Titan*, *Welcome to the Monkey House*, *Cat's Cradle*, *Breakfast of Champions*, *Slapstick*. She'd read them all when she was a kid, in an effort to understand her father. The dark, satiric, sci-fi morality tales had for the most part whizzed by over her head. Nevertheless, she had loved them, but they had made her worry even more than she already did about her father's state of mind.

The student — dark and handsome, if unscrubbed — scowled at her and moved off. She watched him as he surveyed the room, then aimed for another table occupied by a single woman. Definite sperm-donor material, Lillian thought, feeling stirrings of regret that she hadn't let him sit at her table. After a long spell of indifference, she had recently felt as sexually parched as an adolescent boy. Almost any male specimen, it seemed, would do to quench her thirst, and as a result she had already drunk from a tainted source: Ben, Charlotte's father. All sources are tainted in one way or another, she reasoned. There is simply no such thing as uncomplicated sex. And from Veronica's demeanor (she had just arrived and was heading toward Lillian's table looking flustered, embarrassed, guilty) she also was indulging in sex of the tainted kind.

"Hey, Lillian," she said, sitting down. She was wearing a baby-blue mohair short-sleeved sweater and navy stretch pants covered with little white daisies. Even if Veronica had become morose lately, her clothes were still happy. "I'm so sorry to be late again. I haven't been sleeping well." She blushed.

She's not sleeping well, thought Lillian, because she's sleeping with someone who is not Nick. Lillian wasn't going to insist on prying this one open. She wanted to give her sister's tryst every chance of blossoming into a full-fledged passion. Only then would Veronica have the guts to move on from her present stalled relationship. Still, Lillian couldn't figure out why Veronica had not yet told her about this affair. Veronica always had a hard time keeping a secret, believing that secrets were mean because they were exclusive.

"I realized on my way here," she went on, "what a thoughtless sister I am."

Lillian raised an eyebrow. "Do you mean airheaded or selfish or both?"

"Now what day was yesterday?" Veronica spoke to Lillian as if she were the baby, not a fully grown woman about to have one.

"Sunday. What of it?" Lillian responded, annoyed by her sister's rhetorical, school-teacher tone.

"No, silly, it was Mother's Day!" Veronica leaned over and gave Lillian a big kiss on her cheek. "And I didn't even call you. I totally forgot. I tend to block Mother's Day out of my head, but now we have a new reason to celebrate it."

Lillian was both irritated and relieved. Veronica was back to her old self, going beyond the bounds of reasonable perkiness.

"Did you call her?" Lillian asked.

"Who?"

"C'mon, Veronica."

"No, did you?"

"No."

They sat in silence for a while. A skinny waiter carrying a tray of pastries called out for Guinevere. Guinevere turned out to be a freckled brunette at Vonnegut's table. Lillian looked over and caught the youth's eye. He was still ripe for the picking, the eye told her. He'd taken off his jacket and was wearing a white T-shirt. When he wasn't reading the moral treatises of American literature's late-twentieth-century mad scientist, apparently he worked out. Lillian turned her attention back to Veronica, deciding whether or not she felt like probing the Mother subject today. It would lead to the same serpent-eating-its-tail conversation they had periodically — an endless spin of unanswerable questions to avoid the simple fact that their mother was not interested in knowing them. The toughest thing about her rejection, however, was that it wasn't total, definitive, or defined. Every so often Lillian or Veronica would receive a package from New Zealand's back country containing books Agnes had recently read and wanted to pass on, jams and chutneys she had made, a sweater or blouse she saw in a shop and thought suited one daughter or the other. She sent letters inviting them to come visit her — then follow-up postcards describing some problem with the farm or the house that needed her immediate attention, concluding that just now wouldn't be the perfect time for a visit. And every few years she promised she was coming to the United States. Once or twice she had made it as far as California before heading back home due to an emergency involving a peacock or a llama or both.

"Does she know you're going to have a baby?" Veronica asked. The same skinny waiter brought Veronica her Viennese coffee and a cherry strudel.

"No," Lillian answered, taking a sip of her black coffee. "And I don't believe in Mother's Day. It's another capitalist conspiracy to belittle women."

Even more than she had dreaded telling Charlotte, Lillian shuddered at the idea of telling her mother about her pregnancy. She anticipated one of two reactions. Agnes would either completely ignore the news, which would be fine. Or she would come to New York for the birth, which would be awful.

"You might change your mind," Veronica said with a wink, "once you become a mother." She began sniffing the air, her nose upward like a seal at the zoo waiting to be thrown a fish. "You're not wearing that perfume anymore."

"Oh, that — it was the result of a failed experiment." Lillian was surprised that Veronica had noticed.

"After I smelled it, I remembered you and Agnes having a huge fight over perfume. She thought Charles had brought a woman to the house and that you knew about it. Do you remember that?"

"No," Lillian lied. She could recall three moments in her life when she had been truly scared: when she learned of her father and sister's car accident; when the rickshaw hit the little girl in Colombo; and when her father gave her a perfume bottle.

"Are you sure?" Veronica persisted. "Agnes thought another woman had been to the house because she smelled perfume and you told her that the perfume was yours. And she said you were lying. I can't remember what happened after that, but I know you two had a big fight. I really think Charles might have had another family, or at least a lover."

"I don't remember," Lillian said. She added, "I'm sleeping with the father of one of my clients, a little girl whose mother recently died in a car accident and who may herself have neurological damage as a result of the accident."

Veronica looked shocked. But Lillian's motive in telling her sister about Ben and Charlotte was to avoid a conversation about their parents and the perfume. It was a trick she often played on herself. When something became unbearable, Lillian simply moved on to something more unbearable in hopes that the first thing would become a little less onerous by comparison. She had done something like this with Charlotte. The thought of not being a part of Charlotte's life had become unbearable, but the idea of hurting Charlotte was far more unbearable, so she had slept with Ben, Charlotte's father, making the idea of losing Charlotte slightly more bearable. Lillian knew her behavior was perverse, but perverse behavior had not worried her until recently. And it was the worry that worried her, not the behavior.

"The ways in which I am betraying this little girl are so many and weird even I wouldn't pretend to understand them. But what irks me is that I'm feeling guilty about it. I never feel guilty."

"That's true," Veronica said, taking a bite of her pastry. "What about the girl's father?"

Typical of Veronica, Lillian thought, to be first concerned with the man. "He's too distraught to know what he's doing. I just keep saying it's going to be alright. And he has no idea I'm pregnant."

Veronica put down her pastry and suddenly became very animated, almost giddy. "Might there have been some mistake and he's the zygote's father instead of the guy from the ER?" she asked.

"No," Lillian said, annoyed that the father of her baby seemed to matter so much to Veronica, who was undoubtedly rooting for Ben because she had happy visions of something resembling a traditional family in the offing. "I did consider Ben, but at the time I decided that situation was too complicated already. I wanted to keep this birth simple."

Veronica's expression disintegrated, becoming forlorn. Lillian would never understand her sister's preoccupation with the baby's father. What difference could it possibly make to Veronica who he was? Her fixation probably had something to do with memes. Richard Dawkins's theory of cultural genetics claims that the brains of humans have been colonized by memes — self-replicating culture bits, such as clichés, ideas, and fashions. Memes concerning the importance of paternity had no doubt infected Veronica's brain.

XV

The day was rainy, windy, and gray, and Lillian was home from school in bed with a fever. She didn't mind, because she wasn't throwing up and because she hated Dr. Small, her sixth-grade teacher. He had a purple nose that supported square horn-rimmed glasses, and his greasy brown hair was covered with dandruff thick as snow. He wasn't even a real doctor, and Lillian knew she was already a great deal smarter than he would ever be. Agnes had hovered around her all morning — taking her temperature, bringing her juice and toast, trying to straighten up her room. Finally, Lillian had to remind her that she was late for work. It was not that Lillian wanted to get rid of Agnes, she just didn't need her.

Lillian felt another chill coming on and looked longingly at the blankets on Veronica's perfectly made bed but couldn't muster the energy to get up and walk the three feet to wrestle the scrupulously tucked-in blankets free. Veronica loved Lillian so much, the pressure of it was insufferable, not to mention the fact that, bottom line, Lillian didn't deserve it. There was nothing about Lillian that made her worthy of such devotion. It made her feel like a fake and she wasn't even faking anything.

Lillian rolled over, her flannel nightgown twisting up around her hips, her long blond hair tangling into a hopeless "bird's nest." She reached over to the chair beside her and pulled on top of her whatever was there: sweaters, jeans, underwear, shirts, pajamas — some clean, most not. She then straightened her nightgown, back down around her ankles. She placed her palms together as if in prayer and squeezed them between her thighs, bending her knees and hunching her shoulders to keep warm. She shimmied as far as she could under the covers, waiting and hoping for the next phase, when she would stop shivering and start to sweat.

The sound of the front door closing gave her a jolt. Agnes must have forgotten something, she thought. It couldn't be her father. He wasn't expected home for another week. Maybe it was an intruder, a thief, a murderer. Body temperature no longer a concern, she held her breath and listened. Her messiness, she thought, might save her life, since she was hidden by her laundry. As she listened to noises from downstairs, she began mad and feverish deliberations — should she stay where she was and wait to be killed? Should she escape out the window? Should she sneak into her parents' bedroom and call the police?

As she heard footsteps come up the

stairs, she continued to hold her breath while reflecting on what it would be like to die. Lillian didn't usually think about death, but Veronica, from a very young age, had always asked her about it. "When I die will you and everyone else die too?" she had wanted to know. "Do we die in order to make room for other people, or do we die so that we'll feel better while we're alive?" Lillian figured that when she was dead she wouldn't know she was dead, so why wonder about it?

Unable to hold her breath any longer, she sipped the sour air trapped under the blankets with her. It would be ironic, she thought, if she died of suffocation. It dawned on her that thieves usually break into a house. Whoever was coming up the stairs had used a key to get in, which meant that in all likelihood the intruder was Charles. As she listened to the clomp, clomp, clomp coming up the hallway she wondered if she should peek out and see. Before she had time to gather her courage, the footsteps went past her room and continued to her parents' room. Silence followed. Lillian crept back to the head of the bed and peered out. The air she inhaled was cool and clean and for a second she felt out of danger. With the sound of drawers opening and closing down the hall, however, she dove back under the laundry pile. Now the intruder was at the hallway closet, where they stored suitcases. It had to be her father. She came out from under the covers again.

"Charles," she whispered.

She heard more fumbling, drawers opening, from her parents' room. Oddly, she found herself wishing desperately that Veronica were home so that Lillian would have to be brave if only to show her little sister that she was indeed brave. She looked over to Veronica's side of the room for encouragement. Her collection of Archie comics was neatly stacked on her bedside table along with her pink-and-green-striped cloth-covered diary closed with a lock. The key was hidden in an old sock in the back of her sister's top bureau drawer, and periodically Lillian read the diary, but it was always disappointing, not to mention pathetic. All her sister ever wrote about was how she wished that people liked her more, especially Lillian. Lillian eased out of bed and went to the door. She peeked down the hall but didn't see anything, just heard the abrupt sounds of someone moving around in her parents' room.

"Charles," she said louder. The noise stopped. A few seconds later a man came to the door of her parents' bedroom. For an instant, Lillian didn't recognize her father because he had a few days' beard, his sandy hair was darker than usual and greased back, his eyes bloodshot with large circles underneath them. He stared at her, his blue eyes brimming with fear, as if she were the intruder, someone who might hurt him.

"I'm sick. Agnes said you weren't coming home for another week. You scared me." As she walked toward him, he ducked back into his room.

"I had to come back to get some things," he said over his shoulder as he was haphazardly tossing clothes, books, and some papers from his desk into a suitcase. "Let me feel your head." He put the palm of his hand, swollen and sweaty, on her forehead. "Yes, sirree, you've got a fever. You ought to go back to bed."

"Are you going away again?" she asked, pointing at the suitcase.

"Not too long, just a few days, but I've run out of clean clothes," he said. He closed the suitcase and headed back down the hall toward the stairs. Lillian followed him.

"You should really get back into bed," he said.

They went downstairs. Charles left the suitcase by the front door and went into the kitchen. He opened the refrigerator, took out a carton of milk, and drank from it, some of the milk trickling down his chin. "Do you want some?" he asked, holding the carton out toward her.

"No, thanks," Lillian said, then surprised herself by asking a question she had wanted to ask for quite a while. "Charles, is something wrong?"

"Wrong? Is something wrong? Not at all." His voice wavered as if he were about to cry. Lillian was sorry she had asked the question. He put the milk back in the fridge, then turned around and stared at her, an eerie glaze in his eyes as if he weren't really seeing her. "Yes, Lillian, something *is* wrong, terribly wrong," he whispered. "Now don't be alarmed when I tell you this, but I don't think your mother is really your mother. I mean, she looks like her and acts like her, but I'm not sure she's really your mother. I know it's hard for someone your age, but if I were you, I would pack my bags and get out of here, too. If you want, you can come with me right now."

He sat down at the kitchen table and put his head in his hands.

Every conceivable horror seemed possible to Lillian in that moment. Her mother wasn't her mother. Her father wasn't her father. She wasn't herself. Everything she had believed to be true was not. Her father had lost his mind. She had lost her mind. None of this was actually happening. She was delirious from her fever. She wanted to run and hide. She desperately needed to make sense of this. Was her father telling the truth about going away again for just a few days? Or was he leaving for good? Did he seriously mean what he said about her mother, or did he mean Agnes had changed, didn't *seem* herself? Lillian was too scared to ask for clarification. Her shivers had disappeared and she now felt very hot. She wanted to open the windows. She took a deep breath and walked over to where her father sat, his forehead resting on his fingers.

"Dad," she said, placing her hand lightly on his shoulder. "Did Mom do something wrong?"

He pulled Lillian onto his lap and covered her head with kisses. "Oh, Lillian. Don't listen to me. Don't pay any attention to me. And please do me a big favor and promise not to tell your mother that I was here. It will just upset her. Promise me now."

"I promise," she said, trying to remember the last time she had sat on her father's lap.

"Good girl," he said, and he reached into his pocket. "Look here, I have a present for you," and out of his pocket he pulled a small glass bottle. "It's perfume for my best girl."

Lillian took the object in her hand. She wished she could want it and love it and hope to keep it forever. But nothing about that present was right and she knew it. To begin with, she didn't wear perfume, which made her ask herself, who did? Her mother did, but Lillian knew that bottle was not meant for her mother. And worse, it was a bribe for her silence, which might work on little kids like Veronica, but she was too old to be duped.

Lillian's father stood up abruptly and she nearly went crashing to the floor. Reaching for the table to get her balance, she dropped the perfume. Her father lunged to catch her, crushing the perfume bottle under his shoe. Instantly, a sweet smell filled the room. Her father froze, seemed almost stupefied by the scent. Tears rolled from his eyes.

"Do you smell it, Lillian? It's lilies, lilies for Lillian." But the odor didn't smell of flowers. It was a muskier smell, almost like baby powder. She stood very still while he kneeled down and used his handkerchief to wipe up the broken bits of glass. "Your feet are bare," he said, then picked her up in his arms and carried her out of the kitchen and back up to her bedroom. He glanced over at her bed and chuckled. "Still a slob like me. Let's annoy your sister a little." He yanked down the sheets and blankets on Veronica's bed and set her down. He pulled the covers up over her and said, "Don't worry, Lillian, I'll be back."

Lillian listened to his footsteps go down the stairs and out the front door. She then leaped out of bed and ran downstairs. She wanted to ask him not to leave. But by the time she got the front door open she could just see his olive-green Dodge Charger disappearing around the corner. Something wasn't right with her father. She had been noticing it for weeks, maybe even months now. He had always been moody — one minute happy, the next in some other dark world — but this was different. Her mother didn't seem to be worried by her father's latest behavior — it just made her more angry and suspicious. Lillian was always afraid to talk to her mother about Charles, because for as long as she could remember Agnes had constantly accused her of taking his side. She would say, sometimes jokingly, sometimes not, "It all began when I made the big mistake of letting him name you Lillian. He's been conspiring with you against me ever since." The smell of the perfume was overwhelming, so she opened all the windows downstairs before heading back to bed, hoping the odor would be gone before her mother came home. Feeling once again the onset of chills, Lillian crawled back into Veronica's bed and nestled deep under the covers. As she fell asleep, she smiled, thinking, 'Lilies for Lillian,' maybe the perfume really was for me.

XVI

It was a perfect day in May — warm and sunny with a gentle breeze. Lillian, Ben, and Charlotte were on the top level of the Staten Island Ferry, sitting outside on white wooden chairs fixed to the deck. The air smelled of the harbor, the winds carrying not the scent of a wild salty sea but rather a kind of stale brine, enhanced by intermittent wafts of diesel fumes coming from the ferry. Every so often, the air held no particular smell, and to Lillian that was heaven. When the John F. Kennedy — with a few halfhearted groans, a couple of gentle bumps, and a long lazy toot on its horn — docked at the Whitehall Ferry Terminal, Lillian and Ben had briefly looked at Charlotte, who was staring out over the water and humming an unrecognizable but melodic tune. Just as briefly, they glanced at each other and it was decided. They would stay on the boat for a third trip across New York Harbor. If it were up to Lillian and Charlotte, which it was, they quite possibly would remain on the ferry for the entire day. No words were spoken among them, their language limited to winks, smiles, and nods.

Promoting this lack of verbal communication, especially with a child provisionally diagnosed with Post-traumatic Aphasia After Closed Head Injury, was not particularly laudable. But even though Lillian had made the diagnosis, she was not at all convinced of its accuracy — or, for that matter, the accuracy of almost any diagnosis. Someone might be diagnosed with lung cancer but really be dying of a broken heart. Or someone might just be dying of lung cancer. It was impossible medically to tell. Not enough was known yet about the psyche-soma connection, to be sure. Such ideas were professionally heretical and she was often accused of practicing pseudo medicine, of having been brainwashed by the new-age movement, of mediocrity. It always amused Lillian that her rigorous skepticism toward established medicine led her colleagues to construe her work as "feminine." In order to keep everyone confused, she hired herself out to the ubiquitously suspect insurance companies to test for injury fraud. Now she was perpetrating her own fraud.

Charlotte may have hit her head hard, but Lillian was almost sure Charlotte had a severe form of the anxiety disorder Selective Mutism, for which the long-term prognosis was good. Lillian's reading of the situation was simple: For whatever initial reason — a slight, a prank, psychological trauma — Charlotte had trouble communicating through language. Her mother's death had added significant ballast to that difficulty. Nevertheless, Lillian should have had Charlotte evaluated by other professionals — a child psychologist, a pediatric neurologist, a speech-language pathologist, and others. She had done none of this. The child was so far under Lillian's sole care. As for Charlotte's apparent mood swings, her dissociative behavior, her crying fits, her mumbling or humming to herself, all these characteristics could be read as natural in a very sensitive six-year-old who has experienced devastating loss. Lillian looked over at the beautiful Charlotte sitting peacefully in her wooden chair on the ferry deck, the breeze fingering her flaxen hair, and hoped to God that little girl would be alright.

Over the past few weeks, Lillian had insinuated herself almost completely into Ben and Charlotte's life. She had dinner with them and slept at their apartment in Fort Greene almost every night. When she could, in the morning she walked Charlotte to school, where she had been placed in a special-needs class. The first time Lillian had stayed overnight, signs of Charlotte's mother were everywhere. Her clothes were still in her closet, her makeup in the bathroom, her handwritten notes pinned to the refrigerator. Lillian had never said anything about it to Ben, but since that night the dead woman's things had either slowly disappeared from the apartment, now replaced by Lillian's own paraphernalia, or had been incorporated into Lillian's belongings. The creepiness of it made her shiver with something akin to pleasure, as if she were performing the miraculous and bringing back the dead. She had no idea what lay in the future for her with regard to Ben and Charlotte, but she had never run her life according to potential consequences and she was not going to start now. She couldn't imagine hurting Charlotte, but then again she couldn't have imagined walking away from that little girl her rickshaw smashed into in Colombo, either. Lillian saw life as being made up of the fallout from the unimaginable — something from which not a soul could protect you, and something to which you eventually became inured.

Now Charlotte was standing against the railing, her eyes closed, her arms straight out in front of her over the sea, palms parallel and about six inches apart. One palm faced down toward the water, the other upward toward the sky. Every so often she would close them together in a strong clap, as if she were trying to capture something between them. For several weeks now, her tantrums had stopped, but Charlotte was still not talking. It was evident that she understood all that was going on around her. But she still spent a good deal of time in some absent, trancelike state, from which it was almost impossible to rouse her.

Lillian, who continued to see Charlotte twice a week in her office, tried not to intrude on this place. She was envious of this other world and had to keep in check her deep and consuming desire to find a way to go there with Charlotte. With regard to Lillian's essentially moving into her house, Charlotte displayed no opinion. Just as when her mother had died, she appeared to look upon Lillian's presence as nothing more than a meaningless alteration in her life.

Professionally, Lillian was taking some huge risks — for which she was renowned — and she knew that sooner or later one or another of them would catch up with her. Until then it was her (very unpopular) position that the psychoanalytic invention of "boundaries" was a bunch of hogwash used to stave off all possibility of "cure." She didn't hold with the idea of "cure" either. There was no such thing as "cure," just the discovery that you were deeply interested in what ails you and that it was deeply interesting. She was sure nothing at all could be gained by letting the superego run the show. She believed that the only road to self-knowledge and joy was through unanticipated transgression. Of course, it was a convenient belief, especially in her present circumstances, in which she was obsessively mining her relationship with this child for its emotional high, with the vague and self-serving hope that if the relationship was good for her it had to be good for Charlotte.

Ben was leaning back in his chair, his eyes closed, his face to the sun, which was warm though the air held a slight spring chill. He was a good-looking man — tall, dark, and slim — but there was a hesitant look in his eye and an awkwardness in his movements that made him appear bumbling and unattractive. He was the physical embodiment of his profession — math nerd. His thick-lensed black-framed glasses didn't help. Lillian couldn't quite make out what Ben thought of her beauty. At times he seemed indifferent to it. Other times he was obviously in its thrall. There was no question in her mind that life was easier, in the day-to-day practical things, for the beautiful. At the deli, in line for a movie, at the bank, women as well as men wanted to serve you first. You were automatically given the benefit of the doubt, and this had been true even in medical school, where she had thought she might have to fight the dumb-blonde stereotype, she found instead that her professors were particularly eager for her to be successful. With her peers, however, things were different.

When it came to intimacy, both men and women tended to keep their distance. Those that were willing to overcome their intimidation and engage with her soon developed some form of extreme behavior. They wanted exclusive ownership, or became exceedingly jealous or suspicious or hypercritical. Soon she no longer understood what was a reaction to her and what was a reaction to the threat of her beauty. In the end, she decided it was easier to avoid intimacy. Lillian put her hand in Ben's. She supposed he was still in shock — shocked not only by his wife's death but also shocked that this other woman had so quickly entered his life. She knew he was worried for his daughter, worried that he might not be doing enough, or, worse, doing the wrong thing without knowing it.

For the third time, Lillian watched the Statue of Liberty glide across the horizon, a trickster goddess who inspired both chaos and conformity. The ferry was full of tourists and families out for a free boat ride and a view of the unreal spectacle that is Lower Manhattan — a clump of sparkling towers, a bouquet of skyscrapers. A girl about Charlotte's age, wearing a leopard print coat and black leggings, was staring at her, her parents and brother a few paces off looking at a map. There was nothing odd about Charlotte's appearance, but she had a way of moving through space that seemed otherworldly, as if she were an alien pretending to be human and had the part down almost perfectly. Her movements were just a bit too slow-motion and her reactions were slightly delayed, as if she had to translate before understanding. Most people did not notice that she was different. The girl took a step toward Charlotte, who was still leaning out through the railing, clapping her sideways clap.

"What are you doing?" the girl asked.

Charlotte didn't answer, didn't even acknowledge the girl.

"My name's Cassandra, what's yours?"

Clap.

"It's okay if you don't want to talk to me. I'm used to it. My brother never talks to me unless he wants something and then he's all nice to me. I prefer it, actually, when he doesn't talk to me because then I

188

can pretend he's not real."

Silence.

"Are you real?" she asked, and when Charlotte gave no response she looked first at Lillian and then at Ben, the presumed parents, owners of this alien doll.

"Is she real? I mean, does she talk? Does she want a friend? If she's not real, it's okay, because I have lots of friends who aren't real too."

"Cassandra," a boy's voice yelled impatiently, "we're leaving. The boat's docking. C'mon."

She began to follow her family and then turned back toward Charlotte. She ran up to her, gently patted her on the head as if she were a baby, and ran off. Charlotte again seemed not to notice and continued her clapping. About twenty minutes later, however, once again as the ferry pulled out of the terminal, she turned toward Ben and Lillian, put both hands over the place on her head where she had been touched, and started giggling.

"I have something to tell you two," Lillian said. Charlotte continued to giggle. Ben was smiling.

"I'm going to have a baby," she said, looking into Charlotte's blue eyes. She then turned to Ben and added, "The father is a sperm donor. I'm due at the end of October." Ben's smile faded. He pulled Charlotte onto his lap, where she went on laughing and touching her head.

Lillian had no doubt handled the doling out of this information all wrong, but there wasn't a right way. She could have told Ben first. They could have talked about how best to present the situation to Charlotte. That would have been the adult, sensible thing to do. But Lillian resisted sensible and adult, concepts invented as protection from the immediacy of surprise, from the sorts of experiences children have daily. Lillian had watched parents use information as a commodity to control their children. They kept secrets supposedly to protect the children, but in the end it was just an elaborate power game called Who Knows What and Why?

Charlotte reached out and touched Lillian's head, much as the leopard-clad little girl had done to Charlotte.

Lillian repeated, "That's right, I'm going to have a baby."

"She will be real," Charlotte said in perfectly enunciated words. It was the first time she had spoken in nearly a year. "She will be my best friend."

Ben gasped. A terrifying thrill ran

through Lillian's body. She was in deep with Charlotte, deep enough to do true good, deep enough to do real damage.

Lillian said, "The baby might be a boy. I don't know yet. As soon as I know I will tell you. Whatever it is, Charlotte, he or she will be very lucky to know you."

Charlotte appeared uninterested in the sentiment. Ben, tears falling down his cheeks, was hugging Charlotte. He stared toward the Statue of Liberty. He didn't look at Lillian, and she suspected he couldn't.

XVII

Lillian was looking out the window scanning the Manhattan skyline for the Empire State Building. She did this knowing full well that she was *inside* the famous landmark, on its seventy-ninth floor. This had not happened the last time she had been here. The nervous tic, she rationalized, could be attributed to the fact that she was coming to see Bryan Byrd without her sister's knowledge, or it could be because she was anxious to find out what disturbing information about her father Mr. Byrd knew. Or it could simply be a collateral effect of the spring flu she felt coming on. But Lillian knew that the real reason she was failing to acknowledge her search for a building that couldn't possibly be seen from where she was standing had to do with something else entirely. She had come to Bryan Byrd's office that day to engage his services concerning another matter.

"I thought," Bryan Byrd said, rising from his desk piled high with neat stacks of papers and books, "that I had been, as they say in England, made redundant."

On the far left corner of his desk sat a small white vase holding a single stem of yellow orchids. He was wearing yet another linen suit, ivory this time, with fine milk-chocolate pinstripes. He probably had a whole closet of them at home, Lillian thought, and tried to guess where that might be — the Upper West Side, the East Village, Brooklyn?

"You were, but I want my money's worth," she said, shaking his outstretched hand. His grip was firm, his palm soft.

He motioned for her to sit. Lillian, who was feeling all sorts of strange disturbances inside her body, perched instead on the arm of a chair. Bryan Byrd returned to his mahogany-and-rattan desk chair. The fan was spinning very slowly overhead. It made her feel dizzy, so she tried to ignore it.

"Your alma mater?" she asked, noticing a Harvard seal stamped on her chair.

"No, no," he said, shaking his head. "I didn't go to college. I have the chairs for clients who are on the fence about hiring me."

"Although it may appear that I am sitting on a fence, Mr. Byrd," she said, rapping her knuckles against the arm of the chair, "I am not. My sister and I did fire you. I just want to know what you learned about Charles before we did." After their encounter at Smoke, she had meant to call him to ask him to continue on the case but hadn't gotten around to it, and then she had thought of something more pressing he could do for her.

"Oh," Bryan Byrd said, chuckling. "I didn't intend the chairs for you." He paused, then added, "Unless you think they would work?"

Lillian was not feeling herself. And she didn't have Bryan Byrd at all where she wanted him. She needed to get the upper hand.

"Why didn't you go to college?" she asked.

"I have a superiority complex," he answered. "I think it was developed in response to being called 'birdbrain' by my classmates in high school. Another result of that endearing epithet, I believe, is my casual obsession with the mind."

"Tell me about that," Lillian said, and she stood up, hoping that movement would make her feel better.

"Yes, well, as you know, I am a fraud," he said, his pate resembling cool marble in the white sunshine. She wanted to lean against it. "I do belong to the Center for Neural Science, the Society for Neuroscience, the Neuro-Psychoanalysis Institute, and quite a few others. I go to one of their conferences every year and pose as a neurologist. Mostly, I attend the more speculative sessions on things like neurophysics, the binding problem, and panpsychism. While I'm listening, I believe I understand more about the subjects than the speakers do, but after the talks I retain surprisingly little."

Lillian smiled. "I've always wondered who goes to those things." She walked over to the window.

"Have you ever investigated the neurobiology of humor?" he asked. Before she had a chance to reply, he said, "No, no, that's right, I remember, you haven't. You might think about it. I'm sure it would be fascinating."

Lillian wondered which of them was delirious. She sat down.

"It is incredible to me," he went on, drunk on his own enthusiasm, "how little *we* — well, really, *you* — know about the one hundred billion neurons and the one hundred trillion synapses that are contained in the three-pound melon that is our brain." He delicately tapped the top of her head. "There was even a whole decade devoted to it and still we cannot explain consciousness."

Lillian felt her baby kick, a good, solid, unmistakable punch. If she had been looking, she might even have seen the imprint of the foot on her skin. She surreptitiously opened the bottom button of her jacket. Her clothes were getting tighter by the day. She smiled at the detective and remembered that her baby's brain was generating something like 250,000 neurons per minute.

"We don't know anything, Mr. Byrd," Lillian said. "We don't know how the universe began or what it is made of, we can't explain existence or the purpose of most of our DNA." She paused, turned, and stared into the detective's hazel eyes. "What do you know about my father?"

"I mean," he went on as if he hadn't heard her, "do you think consciousness is located in a specific place in the brain or is it more like a force?"

"Well," sighed Lillian, despairing of getting to any kind of point with this man. "Poser or not, your consciousness question is very much in vogue."

"Whatever consciousness is, I'm sure we'll learn that it consists of no ordinary matter. But I honestly don't think we'll ever know exactly what consciousness is," Bryan Byrd went on, Scheherazade-like, as if, were he to stop, he might die. "I will confess to being a mysterian. It's not a club, like being a Mason or Elk or a member of Mensa. We simply believe it is impossible for the human brain to know everything there is to know about the human brain."

Lillian suddenly felt very cold.

"Now, about your father. If I told you your father was a traveling salesman who hated the fact that he had to spend so much time away from his family, that he felt trapped by a mediocre job with a mediocre salary but saw no way out, that he was quite miserable and on the verge of a nervous breakdown, what would you say?" Not pausing for a breath, he added, "Don't answer. Now, if I told you that he was also a member of the Communist Party, if I told you that he had another family in a town an hour away from where you grew up, if I told you that he had written several romance novels under a pseudonym, if I told you that before the automobile accident he had learned that he had a fatal illness, if I told you that he was under surveillance by the FBI and was a CIA operative, if I told you that he had a regular practice as a Jungian psychologist, which, if any, of these would you believe and want to know about?"

"Mr. Byrd, will you please get to the point?" She clenched her jaw as she spoke to keep her teeth from chattering.

"I just did," he sighed, fiddling with his eggplant-colored tie. "At Smoke I got the distinct feeling that you and your sister don't want to know about your father's past. In fact, I'm almost positive that's not at all why you're here."

She caught a whiff of the orchids and felt a sudden flush. "It would seem you've got more than your fair share of intuition."

"I try," he said. He stared at her, then added, "Now it's your turn to get to the point."

"While I was in Sri Lanka two years ago working for World of Doctors," she began, the story tumbling out of her quickly, feverishly, "the day before I was about to leave I was a passenger in a rickshaw that ran over a little girl. She was badly hurt. I walked away. I want to know what happened to her." She was doing what she had come to do, she had gotten what she wanted, yet somehow she felt she had been maneuvered there, like a ship into port. She took a sheet of paper from her pocket and dropped it onto his desk. "I have written down all the details."

While she spoke, Bryan Byrd rose and walked over to the window. "You want to know something spooky?" he said. "I often find myself staring out this window frantically trying to find the Empire State Building." He sat back down at his desk and picked up the piece of paper. "You know it's a long shot," he said. "And if by some miracle I do find out what happened to the little girl — that she's dead, an invalid, or just fine — what do you intend to do?"

Lillian shrugged. Like a sloth, she needed to go backward in order to go forward.

"Guilt is like gravity, the only direction it can pull you is down."

"When you're with me, Mr. Byrd, do me a favor and avoid platitudes."

"I actually hoped you would think that line rather clever," he said, with sincere disappointment.

The detective and Lillian sat in silence while a whole army of angels passed.

"So you're hiring me again," he said finally.

"I am."

"Those chairs," he said, pointing to the Harvard desk chairs, "are simply magic."

Lillian stood up to leave. "Evidently," she managed to say, even though she was seeing stars from rising so quickly.

"I cannot find a grave for your father," Bryan said. "Only a death certificate. Your mother must have had him cremated and kept the ashes."

"Or chucked them in the garbage."

"And one last thing. Call me Bryan. I would have told you sooner if I didn't love hearing you say 'Mr. Byrd.' "

She headed toward the door. Her hand on the knob, she turned around and said, "By the way, Bryan, where do you live?"

He pointed a long finger straight at her, which also happened to be in the direction of New Jersey. "Newark," he said. "In the house where I grew up. I live with my mother."

"Oh," Lillian said, almost swooning.

XVIII

Lillian was sick. Sweats and chills, nightmares, daymares, she feared she would never get out of bed again. After leaving Bryan Byrd's office she had wanted to go to Ben and Charlotte's in Brooklyn but decided it would be better all around if she just went home to the Upper West Side. If she needed anything, Veronica was only a few blocks away. Lillian had been eating Tylenol capsules as if they were popcorn, but they weren't having much effect. Wrapped in her down comforter, she stared out her window at sheets of rain and a curling fog over Central Park. Damp air was penetrating flesh to bone and a cloying dank smell caused her sore throat to constrict even more. The possibility that her virus could affect the fetus was very small but, as Lillian well knew, statistics were never a comfort to the ill. She considered calling Veronica, Ben, Kate, even Bryan Byrd. She picked up the phone and dialed.

"Hello."

"Hi."

"Oh, Lillian. I was just thinking about you. It's so nice to hear from you. What's wrong?"

"Nothing. We just hadn't spoken in a while." The sky outside Lillian's window was the color of lead.

"Honey, I can tell by your voice something's wrong. Are you sick? Have you got a fever?"

"Just over one hundred, nothing serious," Lillian said, although she felt as if she could be dying. She couldn't figure out what was really wrong with her. She was physically ill, but she was aware that her pain was emotional. Nothing in that realm was clear, and she was used to having that part of her life neat and simple. Bryan Byrd confused her, making it impossible for her to dismiss him. Instead, she was curious about him, and was, in spite of herself, absurdly enjoying his apparent curiosity about her. As for Charlotte and Ben, she couldn't get enough of them and yet she was beginning to understand, but in no way to accept, that her longing for them went far beyond what they could ever give her.

"I'm so sorry."

It had been those words, said with a tone of genuine sympathy, that Lillian had been craving. She sighed and listened to the uneven patter of the rain. She wondered if calling your mother when you were sick was genetically encoded. After all this time, all the years of not seeing Agnes, her voice could still comfort Lillian. She knew the sensation wouldn't last and she should make the conversation short. But there was something pressing, something she needed to know from her mother, or maybe it was something she wanted to tell her mother. She couldn't remember.

"Do you remember that time you came home from work and the house smelled of perfume and you got so mad at me? I think you even hit me." Was it this she wanted to ask about?

"No, honey, remind me." Lillian heard a sound, rhythmic but unlike rain, little metallic taps like a telegraph machine.

"Do you think Charles had affairs?" Was it this, she wondered, her head burning? Was it her father's extramarital affairs that she needed to know about so badly?

The sound stopped briefly, then started up again, faster.

"You're not feeling well, Lillian," Agnes said. "Thinking about those things won't help you to get better. We can talk about it some other time." The tapping was furious. "How's Veronica? Is she still seeing that nice boy Nick? I did think I might have heard from one of you on Mother's Day."

It was an old tactic. Her mother was going to annoy her off the phone.

"What's that clicking sound?" Lillian asked.

"Knitting needles."

It was possible, Lillian thought, that her mother had gotten married and had a whole new family. She'd left when she was just over forty. Or perhaps she'd married someone who already had children who now had children themselves and her mother was their grandmother who regularly knit socks and sweaters for them. She thought of asking about this large extended imaginary family but didn't. She thought of telling her mother she was pregnant but didn't.

"You knit?" Lillian asked.

"Oh, goodness, there's the doorbell," Agnes said.

Lillian had heard no ring or buzz or squeal and was sure no one was at her mother's door. Did people even have doorbells in rural New Zealand? And what time was it there anyway?

"I'm glad you called, Lillian. I know you will be feeling better soon. Bye now."

Lillian put down the phone and lay back on her pillow. Her eyes hurt. Her head was pounding. But she knew the worst of it was over. She swallowed a couple more Tylenol capsules. Through her window she saw a figure — no umbrella, his hat and raincoat drenched — emerge from the park. He stopped, looked up at her window, and walked on. She didn't recognize him. She closed her eyes and promised herself that when she woke up she would feel well enough to get out of bed.

Five

XIX

As she sat in the Hungarian Pastry Shop nibbling on a honey zserbo, sipping her coffee through satiny whipped cream, Veronica tried to figure out a viable excuse for why she would never again be able to meet her sister on Monday mornings — or, for that matter, any morning, afternoon, or evening. Since Veronica's affair with Alex began, seeing Lillian had become increasingly excruciating. And since Veronica had failed at all attempts to break it off with Alex, she had to devise plan B — divesting herself of her sister. She didn't count murdering Lillian as an option, so she had concluded the only thing for her to do was to get out of town. After some research, she had decided to teach English in the world's southernmost town — Puerto Williams, in

Chile's Tierra del Fuego.

Wanting someplace southern, exotic, and remote, she had first chosen as her destination the South Sandwich Islands off the tip of South America. Rugged and volcanic, mountainous with glaciers, they seemed perfect — snow and sea, sun and fun — until she learned that the islands were almost entirely ice-covered with occasional patches of moss and lichen. Needless to say, they were uninhabited. Finally, she settled on the nearby Tierra del Fuego — "the birthplace of evolution," the tourist board boasted — as the throne of her future. She even went so far as to request an application from the Chilean Ministry of Education. As fate would have it, within minutes of placing that request the Black Lagoon Theater Company (to which Veronica had sent a draft of *Quid Pro Quo* in a moment of egomaniacal self-destructiveness), had called to tell her that the book for her musical had been selected for possible production. She wasn't letting herself get too excited. It was great to have your play read, but the chance of anything happening beyond that was practically nil. With Tierra del Fuego still very much on the table, her only dilemma was whether to make a clean break with Alex or to ask him to go with her. Most days she was convinced she couldn't live without him.

The tables outside the Hungarian Pastry Shop had been set up for some time now, but Lillian never wanted to sit there even in the finest weather. It was a shame that morning, as the warm June air was fragrant, the light soft and embracing. Even the usual gloom inside the café seemed unable to take itself seriously on such a splendid day. The art on the walls that week, however, was doing its best to maintain the morose status quo and reflected Veronica's mood perfectly. A series of cubist angels painted in earthy tones hovered along the walls. The fragmented shapes and dark colors made Veronica feel that the angels were sad, even desolate, but still somehow hopeful. She thought the pictures very powerful and wondered how much they cost. Nick, she was sure, would hate them for being too cheerless, but his opinions no longer mattered, since she had broken up with him last month. She did it just before his opening rather than go through the farce of being seen at the event as his devoted other, even muse, and basking in dearly undeserved glory. He had been so stunned that she could do such a thing to him that she hadn't

207

heard from him since.

"How could *you* do this to *me?*" he had yelled at the top of his lungs over brunch at Jerry's in Soho. Heads turned, people stared. "I could have left you a million times but didn't! I can't believe *you* have the hubris to leave *me*," he repeated. She felt the whole room sympathizing with him. "I made your life interesting. I brought *you,* a soap-opera writer, to exclusive parties filled with MacArthur Fellows and Pulitzer Prize winners. I introduced you to New York's *avant* avant-garde. I took you to openings and premieres that even Mrs. Guy Ritchie had trouble getting an invitation to." He paused, swallowed. Veronica was terrified he would cry. "I even let you wear my mother's jewelry," he stage whispered. The whole restaurant was silent, devastated for him, furious at her. "There couldn't possibly be anyone else," he stated. It wasn't a question, yet he and the rest of the brunch eaters all held their breath waiting for her response. Finally, she shook her head.

"No, no, there's no one else," she had said, somehow believing this to be the truth with the rationale that Alex was a symptom, not the cause, of her troubles with Nick. Struggling to weep, her eyes no wetter than a dry martini, she had sobbed, "I'm so sorry."

Nick had stormed out of Jerry's saying that at the very least she could have had the decency to wait until after his opening to perform this abominable act, and that was the last time she had heard anything from him. Except for a very odd thing that had happened a couple of days ago. According to her super, a private detective calling himself Rudolph Saturday had been asking about her at the building. She wondered if Nick wasn't up to something — although it was hard for her to imagine him as Othello hot on some revenge scheme. He was much more likely to use his wronged-man status to seduce other women. Veronica's present guilt-ridden dilemma was whether or not she should call him and see how he was. When she had told Lillian about the breakup, her sister had said very little more than "Perhaps there is a God."

"Should I call him?" Veronica had asked.

"Cold turkey, it's the only way."

Veronica was surely in the grip of insanity, if she was listening to advice from Lillian on the subject of men. Yet so far she had followed her sister's dictum. Veronica looked back at the angels. She had no idea what Alex would think of the paintings, but it was his nature to try to like something she liked.

"I think we have to stop meeting in this place," Lillian said, startling Veronica, who hadn't noticed Lillian's arrival at the pastry shop. "I mean, the art is just so consistently bad, I'm reduced to reassessing your ex-boyfriend's talent."

"Actually," Veronica said, "I was kind of liking it. I was even thinking of buying one."

"You know what these clownish, puzzle-piece angels remind me of?" Lillian asked as she sat down.

"No," said Veronica, very aware, for the first time so immediately, that her sister was pregnant. Veronica usually didn't notice anything about Lillian's physical appearance if she could avoid it, because doing so inevitably led her to compare herself unfavorably to her gorgeous older sister — which meant, of course, that she always noticed everything about Lillian down to the last detail but worked hard to suppress it. Even with Lillian's slimming black clothes there was no mistaking her protruding middle: a small mound, a beer belly, the aftereffects of a gluttonous feast. Her breasts were swollen, not hugely, but conspicuously full, and her face seemed rounder, pinker, younger. Somehow her sister had succumbed to that gestational state commonly referred to as "maternal glow."

"They remind me of that Holly Hobby poster you had on your side of the room," Lillian said.

"Wow, I guess you're right," Veronica said, while thinking that the two images had absolutely nothing in common. Was pregnancy making Lillian nostalgic? "Maybe that's why I like them so much. I had completely forgotten about that poster. I think you gave it to me, too."

"I gave you that poster?" Lillian shook her head in disbelief. "Children can be so cruel."

The waiter called out Lillian's name and brought her mint tea and a croissant.

Veronica raised an eyebrow at the choice of beverage.

"Kate has suggested I give up coffee. I've been having trouble with indigestion," she explained.

"Speaking of children," Veronica said, "in case you haven't noticed, you're definitely showing."

Veronica didn't like to mention Lillian's pregnancy, because Lillian either changed the subject or let loose a stream of vitriol about society's nefarious treatment of pregnant women, which led to a generalized theory of a conspiracy against women spearheaded by the medical and pharmaceutical industries. Still, Veronica felt it her duty as a sister and future guardian to bring it up anyway.

"You're funny," Lillian answered, with a tone indicating that she was gearing up for a verbal takeoff, "but not as funny as my colleagues. Listening to their reactions when I tell them I'm pregnant has been like participating in *The Uterus Monologues.* The women who've had children are immediately all-knowing and slathering me with advice. They embark on endless litanies about the pain, the horror, how plain disgusting the whole physical part of the experience is, *and then,* they say, the child is born, and their litany grows even more intense — no sleep, body ruined, time sucked forever into a vacuum — *but,* they say, *it's the best thing I've ever done.* The women who haven't had children either vehemently pretend they want them or regard you with fear and trembling while they think, There but for the grace of God go I. Those who are actually pregnant go straight for the standard questions: due date, sex, name, hospital. It does not occur to any of them to ask about the father."

A sip of tea, a bite of croissant, and Lillian soared on.

"The men, obviously, provide the greatest entertainment in the Uterine Comedy. In general, for men, women are bodies from the neck down, but never more so than when they are pregnant. Any pretense that a woman is a multifaceted, complicated, ambiguous human being vanishes. She simply becomes a baby-carrier, and men assume the right to comment upon, advise about, even touch her body. In the male collective unconscious a pregnant woman is fundamentally an instrument in the greatest purpose of the human race — to propagate itself — and therefore she is public property."

Lillian was on a roll, but for once Veronica was thoroughly enjoying it.

"So when I tell a male colleague I am pregnant he performs for me a variation on the following skit: 'Congratulations,' he says, thinking Ah, she's finally realizing her biological destiny. He relaxes, feels superior. 'Such wonderful news,' he exclaims, gleefully condescending, so pleased with himself that he will never have to endure this particular physical humiliation. He then feigns interest and understanding: 'How are you feeling? It must be difficult to go through so many hormonal changes.' He pretends to set you on a pedestal: 'Women are the true heroes in my book,' he says, thinking with relief, One less rat in the race. Then ultimately, the prerequisite act necessary for my condition occurs to him and he asks hesitantly, fearfully, but compulsively, 'Who's the father?' My answer then sends him into a delicious psychosexual identity crisis from which the only exit is a door labeled OBSOLETE."

Veronica was laughing uncontrollably. Occasionally, Lillian used to make her laugh like this when she was a kid, sending her into a state of pleasurable pain she had no idea how to end.

"Which reminds me," Lillian added. "Any word from Nick?"

"No," Veronica said, getting a hold of herself. "I feel so bad about him."

One glance from Lillian and Veronica was newly dissolved in ripples of giggles.

"Have you finished that musical yet?" Lillian asked.

"Close," Veronica answered, marveling at both her sister's clairvoyance and her question. "I'm workshopping the whole thing next week and I have begun to search for a composer."

Lillian almost never asked about her musical and when she did it was always in the most disparaging and cursory fashion. One might have concluded that her sister was embarrassed by the fact that Veronica had been working on a musical for the last several years. Yet very little embarrassed Lillian. If anything, she simply wasn't interested in Veronica's pursuits. And before Veronica had a chance to crush the thought, out popped this: There was *one* pursuit of Veronica's that Lillian was sure to be interested in — Alex. Was Veronica's affair with Alex simply a means of getting her sister's attention? Veronica looked up at the angels, horrified by herself. She had remembered in that instant the hideous Bronson Hartley episode in high school. And the fact that his name arose in her consciousness from the dark and distant past had to mean that the matter then and the matter now were somehow related.

"Are you still sleeping with Ben?" Veronica asked, wanting to remind Lillian that her choice in men wasn't always the most felicitous, that she too erred, strayed, wandered from the straight and narrow — not that Lillian cared about these things.

"Yes, I am. I was even thinking of asking

him to marry me," she said, calmly sipping her mint tea as if she were talking about a man she had been with for ten years, not two months.

"Marry you?" Veronica asked, trying to figure out the angle here. "I thought the whole idea was you wanted to have a kid on your own, no father in the way."

"For the moment biology dictates that there will always be a father in the way — whether he is present or absent, he is. Even if, as corroborated by my new hero the geneticist Steve Jones, men are by far the weaker sex, male chromosomes existing mainly to traffic genes between females. Just because I generally dislike men doesn't mean that there are no exceptions. To be honest, although I am very fond of Ben I am obsessed with his daughter."

Now or never, Veronica decided. Lillian was confessing her evil ways and means of the heart. It was Veronica's chance to do the same.

"Listen, Lillian, I've been wanting to talk to you about the biological father of your baby."

"Oh, not again, Veronica. Why do you insist on worrying about him? You should have your testosterone levels checked."

"Have you ever considered the fact that

this guy might eventually have other children and that your child might have brothers and sisters that she or he won't even know about?" Veronica asked, swinging her way to the bright side of her relationship with Alex. If Veronica and Alex had children, Lillian's child would have a half sibling who would conveniently also be his or her cousin.

"For all I know, he already has a kid," she said.

Alex? A kid? Did Lillian know something? Veronica was petrified. "I guess this breakup with Nick has me wondering about what it is that keeps people connected," Veronica said. She was pulling the words out of the air, making it up as she went along. Her real concern was Alex's increasing number of offspring. "I mean, in a few years it's quite possible I won't have any idea where Nick is, much less be friends with him, but I know that you will always be in my life because you are my sister, and whatever comes up between us we're going to find a way to get around it or through it or over it. There's a lot to be said for blood." That was pretty good, Veronica thought. Sometimes, writing for a soap opera came in handy.

"You seem to be totally forgetting our

very own mother," Lillian said. "As far as I'm concerned, that blood stuff is a load of crap. There are plenty of sisters and brothers, mothers, fathers, sons, and daughters who lose track of each other on purpose and are none the worse for it. Blood is like fate, you make what you want of it and it's always open to interpretation. In neurobiology, study after study is finding that friends more than parents or siblings influence our brain structure. Studies of TV watchers have even found that they count among their circle of friends the characters they see regularly on their favorite shows or news programs. So just think, Veronica, Dr. Trent White and his wife Eve, Faith York, Crystal Clear, and Dr. Grant Monroe — all those people you make up for a living — are actually changing the brains of your viewers."

"How terrifying," she answered, wondering how Lillian was able to name so many of the characters on *Ordinary Matters*. Veronica became very suspicious. Had Lillian been watching the show lately? And, if she had, she knew Alex was Dr. Night Wesley. If she knew that, why hadn't she mentioned it?

"But Veronica, will you do me a favor?"

Lillian asking for a favor? Now *that* was

truly terrifying. "Sure," Veronica said.

"Just forget about the biological father of my child. He's history. Let's not dwell on him anymore, okay?"

Veronica nodded. Tierra del Fuego, here we come, she thought.

Lillian got up to leave.

"Oh, by the way, have you been in contact with that detective?" Veronica asked.

"Bryan Byrd?" Lillian asked, as if there were any number of detectives Veronica might have been alluding to.

"Yes, him," Veronica said.

"No. Why?" Lillian asked.

"The super of my building said a small man with a mustache calling himself a detective was snooping around my lobby, a guy named Rudolph Saturday. I was just wondering if Bryan Byrd had told you anything about it."

"As I recall," Lillian said, "we fired him." She turned to go, hesitated, turned back. "But if you'd like, I'll call him and find out if he knows anything," she offered.

Lillian offering to call someone? Another strange result of pregnancy — or could Lillian possibly *want* to call him, Veronica wondered. "I'd appreciate it," she said.

Veronica watched Lillian as she paid at the counter and thought, Even with a belly, she's stunning. Veronica sat for a long time wondering how she was going to convince Alex to go far, far away with her.

XX

"A boy?" Lillian was saying to Veronica as they stood on the edge of the playing fields behind the high school. "You are getting teary-eyed over a boy?"

Lillian was flanked by her three best friends of the week. She was enormously popular with everyone at school — the preps, the jocks, the freaks, the geeks, the greasers, the teachers. Veronica could tell that they didn't exactly like Lillian but they all wanted to be near her just the same. Lillian wasn't interested in any of them, which made them want her even more. It seemed to Veronica that Lillian hung out with whomever was the least annoying to her at the moment.

It was early June, graduation only a few weeks away, and Lillian, a senior, told Veronica daily how once she got her diploma she was never setting foot in their crazy, hypocritical, invasion-of-the-body-snatchers suburban town again. Veronica was always torn between two responses: "C'mon,

Lillian, it's not that bad" and "Wherever you go, take me with you." Lillian was actually headed for New York City. She would be one of the first women to attend Columbia College, which, she duly noted, had been built on the grounds of one of America's first lunatic asylums. Veronica, meanwhile, would have three more years of high school to get through.

Veronica had started out her freshman year with enormous clout simply because she was Lillian's sister. But it soon became clear to all that Veronica was not a means by which Lillian could be reached. Veronica had never tried to use her proximity to Lillian to gain any kind of personal advantage, knowing full well that it would backfire. Her sister was simply not someone who could be used or manipulated.

Then along came Bronson Hartley. Midyear, he arrived as a sophomore, after being expelled from his private school. He was way cute — silky light brown hair, penetrating green eyes, a full-lipped mouth that was often twisted into an amused and mischievous pout. Veronica developed an immediate crush on him, as did nearly all the girls in the freshman class, and quite a few of the girls in the school at large. Lillian befriended him long enough to obtain a large ball of hash. Then she would have nothing more to do with him. "What a sucker," Lillian told Veronica.

Bronson, at first, barely noticed Veronica, but one day he struck up a conversation with her, then asked her to an end-of-the-school-year party at his house, adding, as an afterthought, "Oh, and you can bring your sister if you want." In a complete reversal of everything Veronica knew to be safe and sound in dealing with her sister, she not only mentioned the party to Lillian, but begged her to stop by for a few minutes, telling her how much it would mean to her for the rest of her life if Lillian were to go with her to the party even briefly. Lillian responded: "One: I loathe any kind of gathering, and parties as you well know are simply out of the question. Two: If I were to make an exception at any time in my life it would not be to go to a party given by Bronson Hartley, who is rich, stuck-up, and boring. He is obviously using you to get to me and frankly, Veronica, you should be smart enough not to fall for such scum."

At the party, when Bronson saw Veronica, the first and only thing he said to her was: "Where's your sister?" As soon as he understood that Lillian wasn't coming, he moved off and didn't speak to Veronica again. At school on Monday, Bronson ignored Veronica and continued to do so the rest of the week. Leaving school that Friday afternoon, she passed him and a few of his friends in their lacrosse gear heading for the playing fields. She walked with them for a bit, asking who they were playing against and what their plans were for the weekend, when suddenly Bronson stopped in his tracks, his green eyes flashing, and said, "Do me a favor, Veronica. Pretend I don't exist, and I'll do the same for you." The other boys had laughed and, to her surprise, so had she. They continued walking, but she didn't move. After they were far enough away, she sat down, hugged her knees to her chest, rested her chin on her knees, and tried as hard as she could not to cry.

The sun was hot on her back and head, the air just barely holding on to the cool edge of spring. She stared at a line of ants marching through the thick bright-green blades of grass. She listened to the steady murmur of distant voices coming from kids standing around in groups near the school, drowned out now and again by the sound of a car engine starting, a siren, a birdcall. She wasn't thinking about what had just happened with Bronson. She was concentrating on bringing under control the overwhelming urge to cry. "Nothing's wrong, nothing's wrong, nothing's wrong," she whispered, wondering where the ants got their obvious sense of purpose. She let her mind drift to the red A at the top of the English paper she got back that morning, the fact that she hadn't had a cold sore in months. She was feeling much better when she heard Lillian's voice somewhere close by. She couldn't quite make out what her sister was saying, but her laugh was its usual knife slice and her words sticky with sarcasm. Veronica did not look up, hoping upon hope that Lillian wouldn't see her.

"What's this? My little sister in a heap?"

Veronica felt an arm around her shoulder lightly but forcefully lifting her to her feet. She could feel all her hard work trying to quell her misery vanish suddenly like a popped soap bubble. At the back of her throat, in her eyes, she felt the return of the salty sting of need. "Nothing's wrong, nothing's wrong, nothing's wrong," she said to herself, knowing that now just about everything had gone wrong. To cry at school in front of her sister and her sister's friends would be even more humiliating than what had just happened with Bronson.

"What's wrong?" Lillian asked.

Veronica had to speak. Nothing's wrong, nothing's wrong, she futilely continued to tell herself. Out loud, trying to sound tough, acerbic, carefree — like Lillian — she began, "I was just talking to that kid Bronson —"

Lillian immediately cut her off. "A boy? You are getting teary-eyed over a boy?"

Her three friends were momentarily silent — one blushed, another blanched, the other looked down at her feet, then a small chorus of giggles arose.

Lillian continued, "If you're going to be such an idiot as to cry over a boy, then, well, go ahead and cry." Her hand dropped from Veronica's shoulder and she placed a finger under Veronica's chin, lifting her face so that they were staring into each other's eyes. "In fact, I want to *see* you cry."

Tears rolled down Veronica's face. Lillian scoffed, whispered an acid "pathetic," and walked away, her friends in tow. Veronica wanted to die, but as she walked home she thought dying wouldn't earn her Lillian's respect or pity, just more disdain. She made it to her house without meeting anyone she knew along the way and she felt encouraged, as if someone was finally looking out for her (her father? She threw a look of appreciation at the sky). The front door was open, which meant her mother hadn't left yet for the evening shift at the hospital. Veronica's heart sank. She was desperate for sympathy but knew from experience that her mother's brand could, at times, come wrapped in something akin to invisible barbed wire. She was, after all, Lillian's mother, too.

Veronica saw out of the corner of her eye that, dressed in her one-size-too-small salmon-colored nurse uniform, she was in the kitchen having a cup of tea. Veronica tried to go straight up to her bedroom, but her mother put down her cup and came out of the kitchen to greet her. She took one look at her and said, "Veronica, what is it?" She put her arms around her. "What's wrong, darling?"

Without a word, Veronica immediately buried her face in her mother's shoulder and dissolved in sobs for what felt like hours. Slowly, her mother guided her over to the living-room couch. She lay Veronica down, then sat down herself, lifting Veronica's head and placing it in her lap. She stroked Veronica's hair until her sobs became whimpers. After some more time, like earthquake aftershocks, involuntary sobs accompanied by a whole body shiver would escape from Veronica without warning.

"It's so unfair. Lillian is so much prettier than I am," Veronica blurted out.

Her mother didn't answer for a while and Veronica was sure it was because she was sickened by how petty and vain her youngest daughter was, shocked into silence by such hysteria over a matter as small and mundane as physical appearance. She already deeply regretted having told her mother what she was feeling and would have done anything to take those few words back.

Her mother sighed, then said, "You are plenty pretty, Nica, but remember, nothing is fair in this world — think of that little girl next door with the harelip. Lillian's beauty and her magnetism come with severe burdens — burdens that will only get worse as she grows older. She is the kind of girl men will want to blow their brains out over. And it will be hard for her to love anyone other than you, her sister. You, on the other hand, will always love and be loved by lots of people."

"She hates me," Veronica said.

"It may seem that way," Agnes answered. "But Lillian has a terrible flaw — one I know well. She can't bear weakness of any kind, especially in the people she loves most."

Veronica felt consoled by her mother's words, but it was also possible that Agnes was just saying these things to make her feel better. There was something not quite right about comforting one sister by putting the other down. Besides, who would ever want a man to blow his brains out over you? And wasn't the ability to give and receive love the most important thing in the world? She let these questions drift in and out of her mind as she fell asleep. She barely noticed as her mother placed a pillow where her lap had been before, slipping out the front door.

XXI

Following the reading and discussion in a stuffy church attic on Eighteenth Street, Veronica and Jane found the nearest Irish bar and immediately lit up in celebration of the positive reception of *Quid Pro Quo*. Veronica blew a cloud of smoke into the air and allowed herself to believe for a moment that her musical might get as far as a Black Lagoon production. A couple of the senior members had even made suggestions for composers. Alex had also once mentioned that he knew a composer, so she was sure to find a partner soon. As they sat waiting for the whiskey to be poured, Veronica made an effort to take in Jane's gushing.

"I just loved the opening," she said in her pebbly voice, "with the Tammany Hall Sachems and Braves welcoming the immigrants off the boat — how did the refrain go again? *The only caveat: tit for tat, this for that, quid pro quo.*"

Silently, Veronica ran through the song in her mind:

Welcome to New York
Where every day is sunny
Welcome to America
The land of milk and money
The only caveat:
Tit for tat, this for that, quid pro quo

Veronica chose to believe Jane, even though she was notorious for her hyperbole.

This place is really great

You're gonna fit right in
If you do just what we say
We're sure to let you stay

Over the years Jane was really her musical's only supporter.

In this country you can vote
For whom we tell you to
We're all for democratic
But prefer the acrobatic

So when Veronica had been contacted by Black Lagoon, she was surprised that she didn't want to tell Jane, because Veronica would then have to invite her along to the reading.

The land of opportunity
Is right there in your hand
Just give us your John Hancock
(Or we'll send you on to Bangkok)

Veronica took a long drag on her cigarette.

Welcome to New York
Where every day is sunny
Welcome to America
The land of milk and money
The only caveat:

"And the scene where Big Bill Tweed goes to meet President Millard Fillmore was simply a riot." Jane was actually cackling.

The theater world, even the musical-theater world, was so different from the soap-opera world. Jane was perceived as glamorous at the *Ordinary Matters* studio, with her brightly colored Chanel suits, her made-to-match lipstick, her pumps, her curves, her deep blue eye shadow, her baby- doll blush, her dyed-strawberry-blond hair cascading down to her shoulders and rebounding in a perfect inward curl. Veronica was afraid that among theater people, Jane would just be taken as a loud old lady from New Jersey whose hair was too long for her age, who wore too much makeup, and, given her shape, would do well to discover black. For several days, Veronica had felt like a true cad as she failed to tell Jane her good news. When she finally did tell her, Veronica had insisted Jane come to the reading, and thank God she had. Veronica never would have made it through the whole ordeal without her.

By the time their whiskey arrived, Jane had finished gushing and was moving on to the "suggestions." Veronica listened, nodded, agreed. She would think about it all later, though — not right then. She was just going to enjoy the high.

"The scene with the two kids in the school playground," Jane was saying, "needs clarity. It's obvious who Big Bill is, but it is not at all clear that the kid he is bullying is Thomas Nast." Veronica sipped her whiskey as Jane told her that more could be done with the relationships among Mary Amelia and her seven siblings, and so on. But it didn't matter to Veronica. She felt she could fix anything now, because she had something to fix. The reading of her play had made it real, an object, matter that mattered.

"And the love affair between Mary Amelia and Matthew O'Rourke" — Jane seemed almost giddy — "is so complicated, so passionate, so unbelievable it feels totally believable. Obviously you want to fall in love with the one person you absolutely shouldn't. That is true love."

Veronica took a deep swallow of amber, felt her chest burn, her toes tingle, her brain numb mercifully.

"You know, come to think of it," Jane went on, "the way you look — rosy-cheeked and neat — if I didn't know you and Nick were a lock, I would suspect you were freshly in love." She threw Veronica an inquiring glance before lighting up another Pall Mall.

"Nick and I broke up."

"Hah! I thought so," Jane said, tapping her fuchsia fingernails against the bar. "I had an inkling I was playing a stand-in. Of course, I'd do anything for you." Jane took a long drag, then asked with the smooth, offhandedness of a professional gossip, "Who is it?"

"I can't tell you."

"Don't make me guess, Vera darling. It's impolite and irritating."

"Alright, but you can't fire me. Alex Drake."

"Oh, how sordid of you! You're sleeping with the help." She feigned shock and disapproval. "You dumped suave, sophisticated Nick for sensitive and soul-searching Alex? Are you nuts?"

"More than you can possibly imagine."

Jane frowned, the information having sunk in. "I don't quite get the spark here. And there is the Laralee issue, though I'm sure that's just a rumor. Nigel loves to spread lascivious stories around about Laralee's affairs, especially at key moments in their divorce proceedings."

Veronica had made a big mistake. Jane was decidedly not a good choice in confidantes. Veronica had to get out of this but couldn't imagine how. What, she asked herself, would Lillian do?

Veronica asked Jane, "How's that novel of yours coming along?"

Jane laughed, trying to hide her surprise and embarrassment. "Oh, darling, I'll never write that thing. I *think* I want to write a novel — along with four billion other human beings. Everyone wants to write a novel, but few are masochistic enough to expose themselves so fully and then endure the resulting humiliation."

"Maybe everybody *is* a novel," Veronica said, pleased she had been able to get them off the subject of Alex. "I read the other day about how they've been able to encode all of Dickens onto one strand of human DNA, and I started having a science-fiction fantasy about how our DNA is actually literature and that humankind is some other civilization's library."

"So you see, there's no need for me to write a book," Jane said, a plume of smoke exiting through her pursed pink lips. "I am a dime-store romance, read by gazillions of aliens. That's far more gratifying. Maybe that should be the subject of your next musical. I've never heard of a science-fiction musical. Or you could do a noir." Jane hesitated. "Oh, that reminds me: a woman, an attractive redhead" — she touched her own hair — "came looking for you at the office this morning. I overheard her ask the receptionist for you, so I stepped in. She said she wanted you to get in touch with her at your convenience, then she handed me her card." Jane reached into her handbag, pulled out the card, and gave it to Veronica. It read: *Sybil Noonan, Private Investigator.*

Yet another private detective? Who could have hired this one and why? Nick? Alex? Lillian? Agnes? And what was it with this sudden proliferation of detectives? Were they like ideas? Have one, and all sorts of others start crawling out of the woodwork? Her first impulse was to call Lillian. But she then remembered Alex — what if this had something to do with him? She was seeing him the following day — maybe he would give her some clue. And if he didn't, she'd get in touch with this redhead herself.

Jane's feline curiosity had her perched at the edge of her chair. "Nick," she suggested, "wanting to know what you're up to?"

"Doubtful. If he were capable of hiring a detective to spy on me, I probably never would have left him."

Jane nodded in agreement.

"Listen, Jane," Veronica said, "I need you to keep quiet about Alex. I'm sure it's just a fling. If people knew about it at the studio, it would become a much bigger deal than it is."

"Do you think the redhead might have something to do with Alex?" Jane asked ignoring Veronica's request no doubt in hot pursuit of what promised to be the better story.

"Could be," Veronica said, not knowing the answer to much of anything anymore. "But, Jane, I'm serious. Please don't breathe a word about me and Alex to anyone."

With an imaginary key, Jane locked her lips and handed the key to Veronica. Veronica completed the charade by taking the key from Jane's hand and pretending to swallow it. As she did this, Veronica reminded herself that Jane Lust was known for many things, not one of which was discretion.

XXII

For a little over two hours, Veronica had been sitting on a picnic bench in High Falls, New York, watching Alex, indeed, fall from a trapeze. The late June day was perfect — warm in the sun, cool in the shade — and Stone Mountain Farm was all bustle and commotion, not unlike a circus, but one in which the audience was the show. In addition to trapezing, the farm offered myriad activities to people of all ages, from yoga and trampoline to less conventional endeavors such as Upside-Down Language, in which students learned Japanese while standing on their heads.

As she watched Alex fall thirty feet in his umpteenth attempt to catch in midair another trapeze, Veronica feared she would disappoint him. She had promised that she would take an afternoon class that included a first swing off the ten-meter platform. She glanced again at the trapeze rig, which — with all its bars and wires, belts and nets — looked like a torture chamber designed for the delicate mutilation of large creatures. She was going to have to renege on the promise. There was no way she was going up there — not for money, certainly not for love. Besides, she'd had an idea for a love song:

> I lack the proper diction
> To tell you precisely how I feel
> You have lit me up with friction
> You've made a wiggle of my keel

During Alex's two-hour break between sessions, they had bought a couple of sandwiches and decided to take a short hike into the Shawangunk Mountains.

"They're called the Gunks," Alex said as they walked down a trail looking for a picnic spot.

Veronica nodded as if she knew what he was talking about but had too much on her mind — the detectives, Tierra del Fuego, her new song. Bringing up any of those subjects seemed as terrifying as swinging into the void on a trapeze. Breathing in the fresh pine-freshener air, she told herself just to enjoy the moment. Just as people who love the great outdoors do when they go outside — they are in the moment, they are the moment. The trouble was, however, that as much as Veronica wished she had an affinity for nature it made her very nervous, all that open space — mountains, animals, insects, grass, leaves, no people.

"Shawangunk is a pretty ugly name for such gorgeous mountains," Alex went on. "But I think the locals are being affectionate, not disparaging."

"Did you always want to be an actor?" Veronica asked, deciding that a metaphorical leap was far better than an actual one. She had barely finished asking the question when she stubbed her toe on a rock. It was quite painful, but she thought if she ignored it, the pain might go away.

Alex was walking ahead of Veronica and she couldn't see his face, just the back of his head, his wispy hair, a little too long for his role as a neurosurgeon.

"The other day I saw Julia Roberts on Fifth Avenue near Washington Square," he began. "She was with her boyfriend, the actor from *Law and Order*, and I was immediately mesmerized — as was everybody else who saw them. Even though I was late for an audition, I decided to stop and watch them. For me it was heaven; she never faltered from playing her role of famous movie actress pretending not to notice she was being noticed by the whole world. I followed them as they strolled for twenty blocks up Fifth Avenue. Of course, I missed the audition."

Feeling irrationally jealous of Julia Roberts, Veronica was missing the point of his story.

"I love actors," he went on, "but I've never really liked being one. In college, I was always asked to be in friends' movies, I modeled for money, I got an agent, and one thing led to another. The truth is, I'd so much rather watch actors. Not too long ago, I met an actress in a juice bar. She was a tall, strikingly beautiful blonde who looked so familiar. You know how that can happen with actors, you think you actually know them. Anyway, I still can't place her. I was having a smoothie at the bar, delaying going to some celebrity party my agent said I *had* to go to, when this woman sat next to me and began to totally hit on me. For whatever reason — my vibe, my aura — that kind of thing just never happens, so I was entirely intrigued by her motivation."

Seconds before Veronica had been feeling insanely jealous of Julia Roberts, now she was simply feeling insane. She actually pinched herself, but she didn't wake up. She was still somewhere far from the city in a world with only the barest hints of civilization — a deli wrapper, a beaten path, Alex — and otherwise filled with trees, rocks, and endless sky. If she made it out of here, one thing she promised herself was that she was never again leaving the island of Manhattan. She also promised herself that she would forever live either in the past or the future, never in the moment.

"At first, I thought she might be on a dare," he was saying.

Veronica was desperate to hear every last word, to read every possible meaning into what he uttered, to analyze fully his tone and word choice, knowing all the while that the result would destroy her.

Alex said, "She seemed too sophisticated for that, so I concluded she was acting out a scene, seeing how believable she could be." He stopped talking, and turned around. "Veronica," he exclaimed and put his arm around her. "Are you alright? You look so pale."

She wanted to scream at him, "Just finish the story!" But instead she stared down at her feet so that he couldn't see her face. Her toe was caked with blood, the dark red clashing with her sparkle-pink polish. "Look, I'm bleeding," she said, then added, "It's nothing," although she was nearly crying. "I stubbed my toe." But it wasn't the pain that was causing her to suffer, it was the knowledge that Lillian, much less Julia Roberts, would absolutely never have allowed herself to be on a walk with a lover and stub her toe.

"Here, Nica," he said, digging around in his backpack, "I have a Band-Aid." He had a sweet grin on his face, as if he thought her upset over a stubbed toe adorable. She wondered at his use of her long-ago nickname. How did he know it?

"Let's have lunch," he said, "right here." Alex was standing in the shadow of a boulder fifteen feet high. A number of rocks of similar size were strewn across the landscape.

"Anyway, I'm giving you a very long answer to your question," he said, handing her a sandwich and taking one himself.

"Go on, go on," Veronica said. She had lost her appetite but pretended to eat.

"I loved watching her, but I didn't want to be her. I've never felt about acting the way I feel about, well, music. With music, the struggle or tension I feel between wanting to enjoy what I'm hearing and knowing what it took to execute it gives me a huge high. It's that place where you're caught between wanting something to be done to you and wanting to do something to someone. Music catches me like that. I have always written music, I have always wanted to be a composer. You remember when I told you I knew of a composer for your musical — he's me. That's, of course, if you want to take a chance with me." Alex was beaming, and then suddenly he lowered his eyes. "I would understand if you wanted someone else," he said, almost whispering.

So that was it, Veronica thought. Alex was interested in her only because of her musical. He wanted to use her book as a way into composing. She would provide him with a ready-made musical, and he would add the dum, dee, dum, dum. Lillian was right about men. They were always just looking out for number one — no sympathies for those whom they trampled on to get where they wanted to go, their victims so many trophies of cutthroat determination.

Veronica looked over at Alex. He had turned slightly away, and from the expression on his face she realized he was embarrassed. How wrong she had been about him. He had, in fact, flattered her deeply by blindly believing in her musical while at the same time standing naked before her. What more could a woman want?

Veronica took the sandwich out of Alex's hands and placed it aside. She pushed him onto his back among all the scratchy bits of strong-smelling nature and started to kiss his face, his neck, his lips. It was all very awkward and uncomfortable and the last thing in the world she thought she would ever do was have sex in the great outdoors, but Alex didn't seem to mind, and very soon he was naked for real.

As they were rushing to meet Alex's instructor for the afternoon lesson, Veronica began fantasizing about herself and Alex as a great musical team the likes of Rodgers and Hammerstein, Lerner and Loewe, Comden and Green. "Moore and Drake," she whispered to herself. It even sounded right. As soon as they got back to Manhattan, she would give him the book and the lyrics of *Quid Pro Quo*. Everything was going to work out between them despite all the crazy complications, she just knew it.

Harry Pericolo, a six-foot bundle of muscle, was waiting for them when they got back to Stone Mountain Farm. He was with a man and a woman — both, to judge from their appearance, triathalon regulars, whom he introduced as his colleagues Dave and Gwyneth.

"Are you ready?" Harry asked Veronica.

"Ready for what?" Veronica had totally forgotten about her promise.

244

Harry smiled a big charismatic smile. "Ready to come over to the other side."

"Oh, right," she said, feeling as if she had already fallen and had the wind knocked out of her.

Dave, who was a short solid man with a mustache, said, "You will experience transcendence."

Gwyneth, who looked as if she had starred in her own set of exercise tapes, said, "You will become a connoisseur of your own fear."

Veronica hated being pressured into doing something she didn't want to do. Harry, Gwyneth, and Dave continued to try to convince her. They explained that the first swing was the most crucial, in that its real purpose was to allow you to embrace your fear and show you what it felt like to be totally immersed in the moment. For the first swing, they offered little verbal instruction. Veronica outright refused to do it, until Alex took her face in his hands and said, "Quid pro quo. You swing, I'll write you a score that would turn even Oscar Hammerstein green with envy."

Veronica looked at Alex with deep suspicion. "That's not fair. Besides, I don't get it. What's the *quo* for you?"

"Getting you to do something you wouldn't do for anyone else in the world." He kissed her on the forehead.

"I'll do it," she said, "but only if you answer one question absolutely honestly."

He agreed. But she couldn't bring herself to ask the question she wanted to ask about the blonde in the bar — so she asked about another blonde. "Is there anything going on between you and Laralee?"

Alex laughed. "Absolutely nothing. She just likes to hang out in my dressing room and gossip about healers and yoga instructors. I'm sure she likes to keep everyone guessing, but I promise there is no mystery."

Veronica climbed the scaffold feeling like Marie Antionette. What could she be thinking in suggesting that Alex write her music? She'd never heard a thing he'd composed. He was probably tone deaf. He would ruin all her long, hard work. He had a composer fantasy — did that mean she had to sacrifice her work at his altar? If she was still alive after this flight, she would seriously amend her agreement with Alex. He could try out for composer of *Quid Pro Quo,* but he was by no means a shoo-in.

Behind her, Harry was saying things like, "Jump back and up, not forward, but don't worry about any of it — whatever you do will be fine." As they neared the platform, Veronica had a chilling thought: It *was* Alex who had hired one of those detectives. He wanted to find the strikingly beautiful blond woman from the bar and in so doing had discovered that Veronica was Lillian's sister. The trapeze was his attempt to get her out of the way.

> In Tierra del Fuego
> They do not say "prego"
> Darwin says survival
> Is death to your rival

No use getting any more paranoid, she thought, as Harry was putting her into a harness and attaching her to a safety belt.

"After you jump, leave your arms and legs long," he said. "Don't bend your arms as you descend into the forward swing."

She wasn't hearing a word he was saying. She was wondering if Alex was really worth dying for.

"Leave your legs long as you swing through the bottom, then pull your legs into a tuck as you ascend in front."

She was standing at the edge of the platform wanting to know how the hell she got there and what level of shame and mortification she would cause herself by climbing back down that scaffolding. As Harry put the bar into her hands and guided her arms into a full stretch in front of her, he continued his useless instructions.

"Just like you were on a swing, push your legs at the top of the forward swing and thrust forward, then pike your legs and hold your body in a seven position as you begin the backward swing. Do it all over again, and then, when you're ready, just drop. All set?" he asked.

Veronica was by now having a full-blown out-of-body experience. She was watching herself standing on the platform, being stared at by several people from below, including the man who, until a few minutes ago, had been a strong possibility as the love of her life, and now was insisting on her doing something as deranged as this. Could that be love? She leapt, letting her body do whatever it wanted to do — no stretching, or piking, or seven positioning, whatever the hell those things meant. As her body flew up into the air, she thought, This is what it must feel like to fling yourself off the Empire State Building. At the top of the forward swing, in the split second before she would be heading into the backward swing, she heard a voice, her

248

own, say, "higher." She didn't wait for a second swing. At the bottom of the backward swing, she let go of the bar and dropped into the net. As she lay there bouncing lightly for a few seconds, she thought, If I can do that, making musicals in Tierra del Fuego will be a breeze.

Six

XXIII

The Hungarian Pastry Shop was empty,
Lillian the only customer sitting inside. A
few of the sidewalk tables were occupied by
tourists. The regulars — graduate students
and local veteran intellectuals — were long
gone, burrowing in foreign archives or taking
advantage of a relative's country estate. The
entire city, in fact, had a B-movie post-evac-
uation feel. The following day was Tuesday,
July 4th, and on the previous Friday there
had been the usual mass exodus. In truth,
Central and Riverside Parks were packed
with those who had nowhere or no desire to
go, but the streets and avenues were like
barren runways, deserted yet expectant.

The temperature outside was pushing
ninety degrees and it wasn't even eight
o'clock in the morning. The pastry shop

was not air-conditioned and there were no fans, but Lillian, now six months pregnant, had developed an aversion to direct sunlight. She wondered, as she sipped her iced coffee (caffeine having proved more crucial to Lillian's overall well-being than avoiding a little stomach upset), what the chances were that the creature who now regularly whirled around inside her was a vampire. Lillian was irritated to see that the art depicting dissected angels was still on the walls. One of the paintings had a little red sticker on the lower right corner of the frame that read SOLD. She imagined that the tasteless patron was Veronica but didn't really want to know. There was, however, one thing about Veronica that Lillian did want to know: who she was sleeping with. Since Veronica had begun sleeping with the mystery man, she had become increasingly distant. In some ways it was a relief to Lillian, but in a much bigger way, Lillian was — and she found it unbearable to admit this — hurt.

Veronica had left Nick, her boyfriend of many years, and had told Lillian about it only after the fact. Her musical was finally seeing some light of day and Lillian heard about it only if she asked. Worst of all, Veronica was obviously carrying on with some guy but didn't feel the need to let Lillian in on it. Lillian wondered if this change of behavior had anything to do with her being pregnant. Then she wondered if the fact that she cared at all about Veronica's antics had to do with her being pregnant. On the other hand, the fact that she had married Charlotte's father at city hall the previous week and had not told Veronica about it had to be taken into consideration.

Lillian hadn't told Veronica about the nuptials because, much as Lillian resisted it, she was feeling strange about, in effect, marrying her six-year-old client. As soon as Lillian and Ben had signed the papers at city hall (dragging another bride-to-be, Tula from Calabria, into the "chapel" as their witness) she knew the marriage was a huge mistake. In Lillian's opinion, marriage was almost always someone's desperate attempt to gain control over something in his or her life. And this was certainly true in her case. Ever since Charlotte began speaking again, Lillian had felt their relationship changing, which was natural and inevitable, even healthy. But Lillian couldn't bear losing what she had once had with Charlotte, so she had married Ben. Usually, Lillian enjoyed her rash acts of perverse selfishness, but this time even she felt she had gone too far.

It dawned on Lillian that Veronica's new beau must be so taboo and unorthodox that in Veronica's very restricted moral universe she was committing such a heinous crime that it had become impossible for her to tell Lillian who he was. Was he Nick's best friend, or brother, or, better yet, his father? Or was it someone work-related: a head writer at *Ordinary Matters?* the board director of the Black Lagoon Theater Company? Lillian hoped it was a Broadway producer and that Veronica was sleeping her way to success. Looking as usual sunny-side-up, wearing a yellow linen sheath and pearls, Veronica sat down across from Lillian.

"Why are you hiding in here?" Veronica asked. "You look ravishing." She reached over and put a hand on Lillian's belly. "I bet you're not even wearing one thing that is maternity."

Lillian imagined chopping off Veronica's hand with a butcher knife. In her normal incarnation, she hated to be randomly touched, pregnant she loathed it even more, yet just about everyone felt entitled to grope her freely — and the bigger she got, the more they touched. For all that, the touch was the least startling aspect of this exchange with Veronica. Never before in her life had her sister told her she looked ravishing. Veronica had never had the confidence to say such a thing. It was too hard on her, the jealousy too palpable.

"Fortunately," Lillian responded, "stretch wear is in fashion."

Veronica smiled and said, "Well, whatever the reason, you still look ravishing."

"Actually," Lillian said, "the whole idea of maternity clothes makes me sick. That bag wear is so horribly unflattering — another facet of the conspiracy to convince women that motherhood necessitates a loss of sexual identity. And have you noticed how maternity stores have been popping up like Starbucks all over the city? This is part of a subliminal campaign to induce middle-class women to get pregnant, give up their jobs, and stay home."

Veronica sighed audibly, blew at her bangs, and looked distracted, as if she were the intolerant sister.

Lillian, however, would not be deterred. "It's like the postwar years all over again, only instead of directly telling women they belong in the home and sending them there, early-twenty-first-century-economic-downturn women are being relentlessly sold the home life. Every time they see a Mimi Maternity or Pea in the Pod window display they are meant to ask themselves, Shouldn't I be wearing those clothes? I read the other day that nearly forty percent of women who buy maternity clothes aren't even pregnant."

Veronica appeared profoundly bored — beyond stimulation even by that sinister and alarming statistic.

"By the way," Lillian said, refining the subject, "I forgot to tell you I got the amnio results. He's fine — four heart chambers, spine closed, bones the right size, neurons proliferating, neurons migrating, neurons differentiating, dendrites arborizing. All systems normal, and with any luck he'll be gay."

Veronica perked up: "He? Fuck, Lillian, you never tell me anything. I didn't even know you were having amnio."

"Watch your tongue. He can hear now," Lillian said. "And he has eyebrows." She rubbed her forefingers over her own. "He's still skinny as a string bean, no fat yet. I must say it's something of a relief to know I'm having a boy. So much less to worry about, since his sex is privileged by society in every way. And the men I know are even more unnerved than ever by the news —

one of their own at such perilous risk with me as a mother."

"How was the amnio?" Veronica asked. "Don't they use some huge needle?"

"The doctor had to jab me twice. While putting the needle in the first time, he was telling me about his family's plans to do a six-city European tour this summer and on the sonogram screen we watched the baby hit the needle. Both the baby and the doctor freaked out. I, of course, was the picture of calm, thinking, Oh, well, I wasn't sure this baby thing was such a good idea anyway. He curled up way over on my right side and didn't move for about fourteen hours. My shape was so odd, I looked as if I had swallowed a gourd. It all turned out okay. The baby's fine, and the doctor by now has done Paris, Prague, and Vienna."

"Jesus, Lillian," Veronica said, fingering her pearls. "You're so angry at so many things most of the time, and then when it's appropriate to be apoplectic you make jokes. I'm livid right now, and feeling incredibly protective of that little bean. I feel *I've* been injured, as if something of mine has been hurt, and I want revenge."

Lillian shrugged. "Well, since you signed that paper, someday he might be yours and then it will be open season for Veronica."

"Can't you just for a second enjoy the fact that you have this wonderful little life inside you?"

The waitress called out Veronica's name, needlessly, since they were still the only customers inside, then brought her iced Viennese coffee and an almond horn.

"Look, Veronica, I may be on my way to having a child, but that does not mean that I am about to transform into Madonna. Women have children for all sorts of reasons, not only those prescribed by the prevailing culture."

Veronica took a large bite of her pastry, sat back, and said, "Here we go again."

Lillian, ignoring her, said, "The maternal instinct doesn't exist. It is a concept made up by men to keep women confused and ashamed for not feeling something they are told they are supposed to feel. Mothering is learned behavior, and there is no one way, much less one good way, to do it."

"*Shshshshshsh.*" Veronica put her finger to her lips and then pointed at Lillian's belly. "As you said, he can hear now and he has an entire lifetime of your sermons ahead of him. Give him a break while he's still in the womb."

A woman in her late forties wearing a white Lacoste short-sleeved shirt, a lime-green tennis skirt, and white sneakers came in the front door and walked over to their table. She had shoulder-length blond hair held back in a headband.

"I'm so sorry to disturb you," she said in a slightly southern accent, "but my wallet has been stolen and I need to get back home to Greenwich. I can't call my husband because this just seems to happen to me all the time and he already thinks I've lost my mind. You wouldn't have twenty dollars you could spare for the train? As soon as I get back home, I'll write you a check."

On closer inspection, the woman's hair had gone long unwashed, her shirt and skirt were stained and a rancid odor was in the air. Lillian had seen this woman around the neighborhood before, maybe even at the hospital. It did not take a neuroscientist to deduce that something was wrong with this woman's brain. Her sense of reality, due to a stroke or alcohol-related dementia or any number of things, had been seriously compromised. Over the years, Lillian had interacted with people with neurological deficits that ranged from things like achromatopsia (inability to distinguish color, the entire world becoming rat-gray) to Cotard's syndrome (the belief that parts of the body are missing or have putrefied). One neglect syndrome Lillian had seen not long ago involved a belief that those closest to you, especially your spouse, were imposters. Given her recent memory of her father and the perfume incident, she wondered if she was remembering that scene accurately or if she had included the imposter idea in her memory because of her experience with the neglect patient — an attempted suicide with carbon dioxide poisoning who insisted her husband and son were aliens. Her functional MRIs showed lesioning, but there was no way of really knowing which came first, her belief that her family was from outer space (which caused her to want to commit suicide) or her desire to commit suicide, which led to her belief that her family was on the wrong planet. In the months before her father's accident, his behavior had been so noticeably different, she now wondered if he was suffering from depression or worse. Perhaps this was what she had wanted to ask her mother when they had spoken on the phone the other day when Lillian was sick.

Wanting to make the repugnant smell of

old urine go away, Lillian reached for her bag, took a twenty out of her wallet, and gave it to the woman.

"Oh, you are so kind. I've had the worst luck in New York City with these hooligans. Oh my, look, you're pregnant," she said with a squeal. "Congratulations. I was pregnant three times and loved every second of it. Then I got cancer and had to have my uterus out. But I'm fine now. No need for pity here. I've got three great kids, a wonderful husband." She took the bill gently from Lillian's outstretched hand. "My health, a big house in Greenwich. I'll write you a check when I get home." The woman turned and walked slowly to the front of the shop, where she paused to speak with the waitress.

"Do you think any of what she said is true?" Veronica asked.

"Probably all of it in some form," Lillian said. "Memory has no organic sense of time. We organize our lives around time through external narratives, but the brain itself doesn't use time structurally. We really just delude ourselves into thinking we have an ordered past. Ironically, what's really wrong — or right — with Mrs. Greenwich is that her brain's capacity for coherent self-delusion has broken down."

For a moment Lillian thought of Bryan Byrd.

Veronica said, "You know, Lillian, what you do and what I do are not so far apart as one might think."

"Well, then, next time I explain the brain I'll make sure to sing," Lillian said. "By the way, I asked Bryan Byrd about Rudolph Saturday. He'd never heard of him but said that didn't mean anything, because private dicks were as common as head colds. He offered to find out for us. For a fee — the skinflint. Do you think he's Scottish?"

Veronica laughed, finished off her almond horn, and said, "Lillian, I have a confession to make."

Lillian was finally going to learn who had been sleeping in her sister's bed. She tried to appear concerned, surprised, piqued.

"I haven't been entirely straight with you recently," Veronica went on. "The weirdest thing has happened and I'm not sure why I haven't told you about it."

"Out with it," Lillian snapped. "Who is he?"

"He?" Veronica looked genuinely confused. "It's a she, a private detective named Sybil Noonan left her card at the studio. She wants to meet with me."

"Damn," Lillian said, "I entirely forgot about her. She left a message for me at the hospital and I never called her back. I thought she was from an insurance company."

"All this time I've been feeling terrible for keeping something from you and she called you, too," Veronica said. "I thought maybe it was Nick who had hired her, so I didn't want to involve you."

Lillian had to admit that her sister was actually getting pretty good at deception. If Lillian could control herself, she would let this charade go on indefinitely, if only to watch Veronica grow and improve. But Lillian doubted she could wait. Sooner or later the need to know was the downfall of all and sundry, geniuses and civilizations; it would eventually get her, too.

"I think we should find out what all of these detectives want," Veronica said. "Maybe we should hire Bryan Byrd again and have him set up a meeting to see what everybody is really looking for."

"Not a bad idea. But the meeting is going to have to wait. Ben, Charlotte, and I are going to Sri Lanka for two weeks on a honeymoon of sorts."

"Honeymoon?" Veronica asked.

"Ben and I got married last week at city

hall, no big deal, a lunch-hour thing," Lillian said, as if she were describing what she'd had for lunch. "But, before I go, there is one thing I want to know: Who is this guy you've lost your head over but can't tell me about?"

Veronica appeared terrorized.

"I cross my heart and hope to die," Lillian said, crossing her heart, "that I will not under any circumstances steal him from you."

"Oh, Lillian," Veronica said, flushed and shaking her head vehemently. "How could you? I can't believe you got married without telling me."

Lillian suddenly understood that the mystery of the mysterious lover had something to do with her.

XXIV

Whenever Lillian's father was home for more than a few days, which was rare, he would eventually suggest that the family spend an evening at Lovers Lanes, a bowling alley on the outskirts of town. Lillian, who was eleven, thought bowling was dumb — rolling a heavy ball down a wooden plank to smash into a few plastic pins — and she wished her parents would realize that they were living in the seventies, not the fifties. Her mother would wear high-waters of some pastel color and a matching cardigan with either embroidery or sequins sewn into the collar. She pulled her hair back into a high ponytail but, luckily, resisted tying a ribbon around it. Her father made a concerted effort at playing the part of the clean-cut traveling businessman — something Lillian often wondered if he managed to do while actually on the job — and was always shaking everybody's hand. He even shook the hand of the guy who took their street shoes in exchange for bowling shoes, both before and after the transaction. It was as if her parents were immersed in some mutual delusion that the 1960s had never happened.

Lillian hadn't always thought bowling was dumb. When she and Veronica were little, her parents would rent two lanes: one for themselves and one for the girls to mess around on. She used to pretend that the ball was God and the pins his congregation. She and Veronica used to take great pleasure in bowling the red kid-size ball from the top of the lane and watching it slowly gain momentum until — if it didn't go into the gutter, which it did 99 percent of the time — the colossus wreaked doom and destruction on his unwitting worshippers. They spent hours playing at Lovers Lanes, and their parents drank beer and ate French fries and bowled game after game and, much to Lillian's embarrassment, kissed long kisses between rolls of the ball.

Everything about bowling eventually become deeply annoying to Lillian. Her mother looked too old to be wearing that silly outfit, and her father's friendly-guy attitude just didn't mesh with a man who had heavy circles under his eyes and shaky hands. They were both creepy. The only good thing was that her parents absolutely never kissed anymore, so at least there was no risk of her having to endure that spectacle in front of other bowlers. Not that Lillian ever let on to anyone, even to Veronica, that she found anything embarrassing or amiss about her parents. Lillian had learned very early on that to show weakness was to be weak, to express worry or doubt was tantamount to surrendering to the enemy. As if to prove the theory true, Veronica's near total lack of confidence made her a hopelessly easy target for other kids, and most of all for Lillian. There was, however, another, more important lesson Lillian had learned: to have someone devoted to you did not ultimately elevate your power. The person who worships you weakens you. The pins are there for the ball to knock down — but the ball will miss, will fall into the gutter, will just be sent back to be heaved again in an endless cycle of defeat. True strength, she concluded, lies in apathy.

Beer had long since hit the wayside and the drink of choice for both parents was Jack Daniel's. No one bothered to eat anything at Lovers Lanes. Her mother kept score, her father chatted up the people bowling on either side of them, shaking their hands. After a few pleasantries he'd ask "What are you drinking?" and would stride off to the bar to get the drinks, his own always being refreshed in the process. Agnes frowned at each new "friend" because she knew that the drinks ultimately would come out of her nurse's paycheck. Lillian had heard over and over again about the family's financial difficulties — that the mortgage was barely met every month, that Agnes had no idea where Charles was putting the money he was supposedly making on those countless business trips, that it was at least eighteen months since she had bought a new dress.

Watching her father play host at Lovers Lanes was a pretty strong clue, Lillian thought, to where the money was going. But despite complaints and scowls of disapproval, Agnes was obviously reveling in the show. She was getting a glimpse of the gregarious, fun-loving family man whom she believed she'd married. Lillian knew it was, in fact, all an act her father was putting on for her mother to distract her. From what, Lillian wasn't sure. From their money problems? From his drinking? Or from something else? Lillian, who was not even a teenager yet, was a good deal more savvy than her mother. She was sure Charles had a lot going on in his life that his family didn't know about. And why not, thought Lillian jealously. She wished she had some secrets.

"Another round?" her father asked cheerfully, meaning another game. His glass was newly brimming.

"Oh, yes!" said Veronica.

"Sure," said Agnes eagerly.

"Lillian?" Charles said, turning to her, his blue eyes moist and happy. Lillian hated his always seeking her approval, always needing her to be on board, backing him up, pleased with his ideas.

"I don't care either way," she said, the

unmoved colossus. She wouldn't give him what he wanted. She wouldn't be weak.

"Lillian, why do you have to be such a spoilsport all the time?" Agnes asked, and Lillian knew Agnes was miffed not at Lillian's reticence but by the fact that Charles cared so much about what Lillian wanted.

Lillian said nothing. Charles threw Agnes a nasty glance. Veronica was playing with the lace on her bowling shoe.

"Let's go on home then," Charles said, before draining his glass in one long swallow. "Maybe there's a good movie on television."

Neither Agnes nor Veronica protested Charles's decision. Lillian judged the lot of them too pathetic for words. They deserved to go home, they deserved to feel bad, she thought. She shrugged her shoulders and stared first at her mother and then at her sister until both of them looked away.

The family turned in their bowling shoes and put the balls back on the rack. Charles shook a few more hands, and they were in the car on their way home — Charles driving, Agnes next to him, the girls in the backseat. Everyone was silent as they pulled out of the parking lot and onto the road heading toward town. Lillian couldn't imagine that they would make it home without a fight. Her mother was disappointed, and when her mother was disappointed about one thing she dredged up everything she was disappointed about and verbally ran through them almost without thinking, as a nun fingers her rosary.

"Charles," she began, "I didn't see a dime of your paycheck this month."

"Haven't picked it up yet," Charles answered, turning on the radio and moving the dial until he found a jazz station.

"When will you?"

"Not sure. I have to leave again first thing tomorrow morning."

Here we go, thought Lillian. She looked over at Veronica, who had her eyes closed, pretending to be asleep, and soon probably would be for real.

"How long will you be gone?"

"Unclear."

"Jesus, Charles, couldn't you be just a little more precise?" Agnes's voice was metallic sharp. "I mean, you're gone most of the time, I never know where you are, I spend my life waiting for the tiniest scrap of news from you. You could at least do me the courtesy of trying to give me a minimum of information as to your plans and whereabouts. What if something were to happen? I wouldn't even know how to find you."

"You know you can always leave a message for me at the office. Sooner or later I always get my messages." Charles's voice was slow, deep, beleaguered, as if he were too tired or drunk or sad to find these words he had so often repeated.

"That's a big comfort, 'sooner or later,' and half the time no one even bothers to answer the phone when I call. Aren't there secretaries?" Agnes trudged on through the scene, as if she didn't know what else to do.

"Cost cutting."

Agnes turned off the radio. "I can't live like this. I hate this life. I hate you, the kids, my job. I hate not having enough money all the time. I hate where we live, the house, the town. I want out."

Then get out, Lillian thought.

"What is it, Agnes, that you need to know that I'm not telling you?"

Her father was about to make all their problems her mother's fault, and Agnes would let him, but there was a new tone in his voice, a timbre that was higher-pitched, more urgent somehow.

"Your nagging, your insecurity, your wish to monitor my every move is so repugnant. It kills all fun and romance.

Every time I come home, I dread your disappointment and your anger. Every time, I pray you will have cultivated a life of your own, a life which I can be intrigued and interested by. But instead I come home to a leech, someone who sucks the blood out of life."

Lillian was impressed. His words were far more cruel than they usually were. She could tell that even Agnes was stunned, unsure how to respond. Lillian asked herself if her mother was a leech or her father just vicious? She wondered where the truth lay between these two possibilities, concluding that she would never know, so it wasn't worth thinking about. Agnes had been staring out the car window during most of this argument, and from the backseat Lillian saw the tears drop one by one off the tip of her nose. Tears should run down cheeks, Lillian thought, not off pointy noses. She did, however, admire her mother for not showing her father that she was crying.

The car stopped at a light. Suddenly her mother grabbed her bag, opened the car door, and began to lurch out. Her father's hand shot off the steering wheel and grabbed her mother's arm, his knuckles white. Her mother continued to pull herself out of the car, the sleeve of her silly sweater gnarled in her father's fingers. She had both legs out the door but Charles didn't loosen his hold. Her body position was distorted and it looked to Lillian as if her mother's arm might pull right off, a lone limb in the grip of her father's hand.

"Let her go!" Lillian heard herself scream, and she reached over the seat and punched her father's arm as hard as she could. He looked at her, fear in his eyes. He let go of Agnes. She ran off down the street. The light turned green. Cars were honking. As Charles drove forward, the front door, still open, slammed shut. Lillian was disappointed with herself for having intervened. That was against her rules of conduct. Worse, she was confused. She wasn't sure if she had made her father lose his grip in order to protect her mother or because she wanted her mother out of the car.

"I have to go find her, Lillian," he said.

Veronica had been awakened by the scuffle. She was crying. "Where's Mom?" she asked.

"Shut up, Veronica," Lillian said. "Everything is fine." Then she turned to her father. "Maybe you should just leave her alone for a while."

"That's the problem, Lillian, I leave her alone far too much." His voice now was full of longing and love, and Lillian hated him for it. She felt tricked, duped. One minute he was about to break her mother's arm and the next he was desperate for her. The inconsistency of it was unbearable to Lillian. Her father made an abrupt U-turn and drove back to the place where Agnes had jumped from the car. He turned onto the street down which she had fled, but Agnes was nowhere in sight. Charles spent the next half hour moving slowly and methodically up and down the nearby streets as if he were a cop in a patrol car searching for a fugitive.

"I love your mother very much, Lillian," her father began, and Lillian knew she didn't want to hear what would follow. Whatever he said was going to be far more than she wanted to know. She thought of escaping from the car herself, but that was more drama than she could take. "I love her more than anything in the world," he went on, "besides you and your sister. Agnes was my first love, nothing, nothing in the world can ever replace that. I will never ever leave your mother."

Lillian was right. He was saying too much. What could she do to stop him, she wondered. Nobody ever says they will never ever do anything unless they are seriously considering doing it. She suddenly felt very sorry for her mother, but quickly amended that feeling and thought her stupid and weak. Lillian realized that Charles had been acting as if he were about to leave for a while now. The only dignified thing for Agnes to do was to leave first. But her mother would never leave her father because she loved him too much, a concept that was beyond Lillian. How could she love someone who said such evil things, who never came home, who obviously didn't care at all about her? Lillian certainly didn't love him. Lillian certainly would never allow herself to be left by him.

"I wish you never came home," Lillian said, as the car continued to crawl along the street. "I wish you would go away and never come back. If I cared enough, I would even wish you were dead."

Veronica looked up at her, horrified. Charles said nothing, but soon the car sped off down the street and toward home. Lillian was proud of herself. She was just as good, if not better, than he was.

They rode in silence, except for Veronica's sniffles. Charles pulled up in front of the house and kept the engine running.

Lillian opened the car door and got out, followed by Veronica. Before she shut the car door, her father said in the same earnest tone he had used with her mother, "Be careful of what you wish for, Lillian." He took off down the street.

Lillian didn't have a key to the house with her. She and Veronica tried the back door and a few of the windows but nothing was open. They sat on the front stoop waiting for their mother. A couple of the neighbors periodically stared out their windows at them. Cars slowed as they drove by, and one even circled around a couple of times. Veronica tried to get Lillian to explain to her what had just happened, why everyone was so angry. "Did I do something wrong, Lillian?" she asked. Lillian scoffed, refusing to answer any of Veronica's questions or to become involved with her in any way. Lillian remained silent and felt very strong. After a few more cars drove by, faces peering out at them, Veronica suggested they move to the back-door steps. Lillian slipped from her silence, and said, "I don't care who looks at me or what they think." But those were the only words she uttered until, finally, after a couple of hours, Agnes walked up to them from out of the dark. She picked up Veronica, who was way too big to be picked up. She opened the door with her key and they all went inside.

"You know better than anyone, Lillian, that this is all your fault," she said, carrying Veronica up the stairs, kissing her softly on the forehead. She paused at the top of the stairs and glared down at Lillian. "We were all having such a fine time, but you had to ruin it. This was our chance to go out together like a normal happy family, but you needed to spoil everybody's fun. You had to be the center of attention. It's not enough that you're beautiful and popular at school. You need to have all of us ogling you, first and foremost your father, and when we don't do what you want, you destroy everything for us."

Lillian said nothing, staring her mother in the eye until she disappeared with Veronica into Lillian and Veronica's bedroom. Lillian stayed downstairs until she heard her mother's bedroom door close. She then went up to her room and slid into bed with all her clothes on. After a while she heard Veronica whispering to her.

"Lillian," Veronica said, "he knows you didn't mean it. He knows you really don't wish that he would go away and never come back. Everybody says things they don't mean all the time."

Lillian felt a wave of sheer loathing. In that moment, she could have strangled Veronica for her goodwill, for trying to make things better, but only making them worse. "Veronica," Lillian said, not whispering. "I meant what I said. I wish he would go away for good, and as far as I'm concerned you can go along with him when he goes."

"Goes where? Where would we go, Lillian?" Veronica whispered. She sounded scared.

"To hell," Lillian said. "That's where."

She heard Veronica hiccup, then sob. Lillian stared at the ceiling, detesting her sister's weakness, her father's inconsistency, her mother's neediness. She couldn't wait until she was old enough to leave them all behind. After a while, she got out of bed, still fully dressed, and went and lay on top of the covers next to Veronica until she was sure her sister had really truly fallen asleep.

XXV

When Lillian arrived at Bryan Byrd's office, she found it open, the secretary not at her desk, Bryan's office door ajar, his over-head fan spinning, and the private eye no-where to be found. He wasn't expecting her, so Lillian wasn't sure why she was dis-appointed, even a little offended, not to find him waiting for her. She hadn't seen Bryan Byrd since she began to show and she was curious to see his response to her pregnancy.

Lillian walked over to his desk. The yellow orchid was gone and in its place were lavender and blue oriental poppies. Running her eye over the neat amalgam of pens, notepads, an ashtray full of paper clips, a swollen Rolodex, stacks of books and papers of varying heights, her roving stopped when she found the *Journal of Neuropsychoanalysis* containing her most recent paper on empathy and conscious-ness entitled "Decoherence/anti-decoher-ence: Just How Entangled Are We Any-way?" She looked underneath *JON* and found other journals containing her arti-cles: "Functional Brain Imaging = the Death of Free Will" in the *Journal of Neurophilosophy*; "Amygdala: The Mind's Heart of Darkness" in *Cognition*; "The Journey from Intermediate Long-Term Memory to Permanent Long-Term Mem-ory: An Odyssey" in *Journal of Memory*;

and "Environment and Genome: Who Can Tell the Dancer from the Dance?" in *Brain*. At the very bottom of the pile was a copy of the obscure and long-defunct journal *Scanner Darkly* containing a paper she wrote during her first year of graduate school entitled "Aliens, Mothers, Genes, and Hollywood: Who's to Blame for the Rain Man?"

Lillian smiled, still believing that first paper was the best thing she had ever written. She was a little concerned by the detective's evident obsession with her, but she was used to such things, nothing she couldn't handle. It was also altogether possible that he was completely uninterested in her and was just being thorough. She glanced back at the issue of *Scanner Darkly* and thought, Very thorough. On the other hand, he could be a serial killer. After all, he did still live with his mother. She bumped her belly against the side of the desk and looked up toward the office door, but no one was there. She continued to examine his desk. There was a stack of letters from Norfolk Personal Insurance, the schedule for the Fifth International Conference on Neuroethology, and another for a conference on "Neuroscience, Ethics, and Survival." She saw a note written in pink saying "I quit," and beneath the words, in the place of a signature, was the pulpy imprint of pink lips. There were three guidebooks to Sri Lanka — *Fodor's*, *Lonely Planet*, and one Lillian had never heard of. Under those were copies of Steven Pinker's *How the Mind Works*, Antonio Damasio's *Descartes' Error*, and *The Emperor's New Mind* by Roger Penrose.

Just as she spied a familiar name, Sybil Noonan, and a telephone number scribbled on a slip of paper, Lillian heard steps in the hallway. She scooted around to the other side of the desk and stood leaning against the back of one of the big black chairs, her soccer-ball belly curving space.

"What a surprise," Bryan said upon seeing Lillian. She couldn't tell if he was referring to her unexpected visit or her impending motherhood. Bryan's linen suit was the color of dairy creamer with a brown silk ascot folded softly at his neck. "We didn't have an appointment, did we? My secretary has gone on to bigger and better things, leaving my schedule in disarray." He motioned for her to sit down, and did so himself. Despite the fan, Lillian felt warm. "What brings you here this fine summer day?" Bryan asked, evidently oblivious to her new shape and size. Per-

haps big people simply projected their big-
ness onto other people and didn't notice
things like major body changes, Lillian surmised.

"I'm in something of a rush to know
anything you might have learned about the
girl in Colombo." She paused, then added,
"In case you were wondering, I'm due in
October. The father's a banker of sorts —
an anonymous donor investing his sperm
in the future of the species." It was disconcerting to find herself, unsolicited, explaining, and not entirely truthfully, her
child's paternity to Bryan.

"Congratulations," he said. "I hope you
don't mind my asking what you learned
while I stepped out?"

"You're bleeding Norfolk Personal Insurance dry, but your operation is still in
the red, your secretary quit because you
won't sleep with her, you have a copy of
everything I have ever published, you've
done the Sri Lanka assignment and found
out next to nothing, your interest in the
brain is amateur and romantic, and you
know something about my father that
you're not telling me."

The detective glanced out the window.
"You're wrong about Emily, the secretary.
A couple years back her mother, who lives

in North Dakota, hired me to find her and when I did Emily begged me not to send her home and gave me reasons that checked out. I hired her as my secretary until she turned eighteen, which happened last week. And it is not your father but your mother I learned something about."

"My mother," Lillian said, annoyed. "Who ever asked you to —"

He cut her off. "I didn't. Another private eye — not Rudolph Saturday, who is still on the loose — called this morning. She found out you were clients of mine."

"What does Sybil Noonan have to do with my mother?"

"She's working for your half brother. He's a couple years younger than you, a year older than Veronica. He wants to meet you and your sister. Your mother gave him up for adoption immediately after he was born."

A half brother? Wouldn't Lillian have noticed if her mother had been pregnant and then there was no baby? Perhaps not at age two. Episodic memory doesn't begin to encode in any readily retrievable way until a child is three or four. "Half brother?" Lillian asked, talking to herself more than to Bryan Byrd. "That means my father is not his father. So who's the father?" The baby kicked.

"He was an intern at the hospital where she worked. Seems it was a one-night thing. He, however, insists your half brother is not his son. Sybil bribed someone at the adoption agency for the records."

So it was Agnes, not their father, who had another family, Lillian thought. Obviously, Charles had known about that child. So was Agnes the family philanderer and she drove Charles crazy with her infidelity? It felt impossible, even flimsy. Odd how you get certain fixed ideas about the people in your family and no matter what happens those ideas remain solid as Gibraltar. In the end, perhaps her mother was not simply a disappointed housewife, her father an alcoholic womanizer, as her memory would have it. But memory was like a palimpsest or a geologic outcropping — each line or layer told its own story, but it was the entire text or rock that made up the whole. It occurred to her that perhaps her mother had escaped to New Zealand in order to flee that family, not her own. But a second's reflection told her, No such luck. Her mother had disposed of her half brother and his father quickly and efficiently long ago. Could there have been yet another family she was escaping? Out the window, clouds were colliding like bumper cars.

Lillian laughed.

"What's so funny?" Bryan Byrd asked.

"For as long as I can remember, I swore, as daughters do, that I would be nothing like my mother. I modeled my life on that one premise, and here I am working in a hospital, married to a man I don't love, pregnant with a child who will never know his father. It's so predictable, my life a paint-by-numbers picture — yet I had an entirely different vision of how the picture was supposed to turn out. The unconscious — that thing no one, least of all scientists, has any clue about — imitates the giddy cruelty of a child pinning an insect to a wall and watching it flail."

"I guess it is pretty hilarious how we manage to have the same genes all day long. Did you say you were married?" he asked.

"Yup. No big deal. His daughter's a client of mine. We all needed a family quick and it seemed logical."

Bryan nodded. "Double congratulations to you, then."

Whatever his obsession, Lillian thought, he had a refreshing way of expressing it. "Veronica and I would, of course, like to meet our newfound relative and we would appreciate it if you would arrange the meeting through Sybil Noonan, but it will have to wait a couple of weeks. I'm leaving town tomorrow. I'm going to Sri Lanka on my honeymoon."

Bryan sighed. "I admire your efficiency." He pulled out a file from a stack on his desk. "I have the Dead-On-Arrival reports from the three Colombo hospitals nearest to where the little girl was hit. There were eighteen on that day. Two were girls under the age of fifteen. I found records for four girls under fifteen who were admitted with head traumas and lived. All of the information is extremely sketchy. Here's the paperwork. My bill is inside."

Lillian took it from him, then, pointing to the pile of journals containing her articles, asked, "What's that about?"

Bryan's slanty green eyes met Lillian's and held them. "I want to know everything there is to know about you."

XXVI

Soon after she embarked on the seventeen-hour flight home to New York from Colombo, Lillian began having Braxton-

285

Hicks contractions. Or at least she was hoping that was what they were. During the entire stay in Sri Lanka, she had periodically experienced a tightening of her uterus. She hadn't been worried, as this type of early contraction was normal and had been, so far, only mildly painful. Not until the plane was somewhere over the Indian Ocean, heading for its first stopover in Yemen, did she begin to consider that the contractions had become regular and that she could be going into false labor, not to mention the real thing. She drank more water, walked up and down the aisle, and read to Charlotte a chapter of *From the Mixed-up Files of Mrs. Basil E. Frankweiler.* Since that first utterance on the Staten Island Ferry, Charlotte had been talking like a normal six-year-old, as if her words, like De Beers's diamonds, had been, for reasons beyond simple explanation, hoarded for a while and were now flooding the market. In many ways Lillian's "honeymoon" with Ben and Charlotte had been classic: fun, romantic, exotic, exhilarating. But, in the end, more than the honeymoon was over.

When they arrived in Colombo fifteen days earlier, they stayed overnight at the Hilton, then left the city the next day by rental car. Lillian confessed to Ben and Charlotte that her choice of Sri Lanka as their honeymoon destination had an ulterior motive. Ben had asked one or two questions about the incident and let the subject drop. Charlotte said nothing.

They had headed south past Galle to a resort in Weligama just opposite the tiny island of Taprobane, refuge once upon a time to a French count, then to Paul Bowles, and most recently to Arthur C. Clarke. They stayed for a few days, sleeping, reading, watching the fishermen with crude bamboo rods perched on stilts far out in the surf. They then drove back along the coast, bypassed Colombo and headed into the hills to Kandy, the cultural capital of Sri Lanka. Lillian was eager to show Charlotte a reading room in the library of the Temple of the Tooth. An arm's-width octagon with a very high ceiling, the room was lined with glass bookcases containing leather-bound volumes written in hundreds of languages.

Sitting in the library among all the books, Charlotte was unusually quiet for her recent self. Lillian, lost in thought, was remembering how much she loved that little room, what a comfort it had been during her long year on that troubled island. She was so happy to be able to show it to Charlotte, and perhaps one day she would even consider returning there with her son.

"When I grow up, Lillian," Charlotte said, closing the book she had been riffling through, "I want to be just like you. I want to be tall and beautiful and a doctor and a world explorer."

Lillian laughed. "You know what, Charlotte? When you grow up I want you to be just like me, too. And you know what else?"

"No, I don't," Charlotte said, twirling a piece of her blond hair.

Lillian said to Charlotte, "For a long time now, I have wanted to be just like you. And as I grow up I will keep trying my hardest to be like you. What do you think about that?"

Charlotte opened another book. "I already knew that."

"So why did you say you didn't?" Lillian asked, pinching her lightly under the arm.

Charlotte gently pulled away. "I want you to want to be like me, but I think some people might think it's weird that you want to be like me."

"Weird is good."

"Does that mean you think I'm weird?" Charlotte asked.

"Are you?"

"Yes."

"Then there is a pair of us."

Kandy was halfway through its *perahera*, and in the evening a parade of elephants wearing colorful and elaborate silks marched through the streets, followed by jugglers, twirlers, dancers covered in white powder, women on stilts, men in drag, fire breathers, sprites with potbellies and foot-long tongues. The crowds lining the streets were intoxicated with celebration, and it was infectious. Lillian, however, hated crowds and felt claustrophobic. She also kept getting bumped into and, pregnant, this bothered her a thousand times more than it would normally. Charlotte held her hand tightly through it all, but at a certain point a man with a beard, his teeth black from chewing betel palm, jabbed Lillian in the belly and she let go of Charlotte's hand in order to whack him. When she turned around, both Ben and Charlotte had disappeared. Lillian looked for them for a while and when she couldn't find them she went back to the hotel. Half an hour later, they too returned to the hotel and everyone was relieved at having found one another again. But relief did not negate the fact that for whatever reasons — and Charlotte had undoubtedly identified them all — Lillian had let go of her hand.

On the plane back to New York, somewhere behind their row of seats a baby was screaming. Lillian felt another contraction. She looked at her watch — three in under an hour. Yemen had long since come and gone. Her lower back hurt, but she believed the dull pain was from sitting so long. Lillian had not allowed herself to consider that these contractions were anything but false labor. Even so, her mind was making lists of things she would need if she were to give birth on the plane: hot water, scissors, blankets, towels, an incubator. As long as there were no complications, she would be alright, but the baby technically had ten more weeks until he was out of the premature danger zone and would probably need help. If she could just hold on until their next stopover in London, she could have the baby there and her child would receive dual citizenship.

Lillian looked to Charlotte for comfort and distraction. Charlotte had headphones on and was staring at the movie screen, although Lillian doubted she was actually watching. The blank expression on her face and her empty unmoving eyes indicated that she had gone to an inner world — a place Charlotte still went to often and that was now more than ever unavailable to Lillian. On one level, language had given them a new world together, but it had become a barrier to the world they had begun to create without it. Quid pro quo, Lillian thought, everything was a trade-off. She was reminded of Veronica and her musical and remembered that they would soon be meeting their half brother, the child her mother had given birth to and had never told her about.

As her honeymoon had proceeded, Lillian, who believed she had mostly obliterated from her memory the entire year she spent in Sri Lanka, was surprised by her enthusiasm for going back to old haunts and discovering new ones. At the same time, drifting through her every hour on the island was the phantom of the rickshaw girl. She would not dissipate or become distant. She remained near always. Lillian maintained that we can only tolerate thinking about the intolerable when it somehow has already become tolerable. Still, she hadn't made even the shadow of a plan for what she was going to do with the measly information Bryan Byrd had turned

291

up. And as time went on, Lillian couldn't imagine herself spending her last days in Colombo searching through hospital records trying to find out what had happened to the girl. It would be unfair to Ben and Charlotte, and it was an absurd and futile quest. She was going to have to let the little girl go.

In Nuwara Eliya, they stayed at the Hill Club, a hunting retreat during the British raj, now a hotel, and took day trips. One morning, three hours before sunrise, Charlotte and Ben left to climb Adam's Peak. Four-thousand-four-hundred-twenty steps lead to a summit where, depending on your religion, Adam's or Buddha's or Shiva's footprint is enshrined and where for a few minutes at sunrise the shadow of Adam's Peak forms a perfect triangle that spreads over the valley and across the island toward the sea.

While Ben and Charlotte were climbing to the heavens (Lillian was too pregnant to worry about finding God), she took a walk down the wide rolling streets of Nuwara Eliya, lined with Victorian, half-timbered, mock Tudor and Gothic mansions built by the British and now owned as summer houses by Colombo's rich. As she walked, she returned to lingering questions: Having come all that way, shouldn't she at least try to find the girl? And if she did, what then? Would she apologize? Or attempt to absorb her, as she had Charlotte? If the little girl was dead, would she feel worse or relieved? Was the agony of not knowing what had happened to her easier or harder than knowing the truth?

That evening, after Charlotte had gone to bed, Lillian and Ben shot pool in the billiard room. Ben was quiet, concentrating on the precision of his game. Most of their talk had to do with logistics about the last days of their trip. During their third game, Ben stopped in the middle of lining up a shot, and said, "I'm sorry, Lillian, but this is wrong."

"I know," she said.

"What I realized walking up those endless stairs with all those pilgrims, is that I have perceived you as some kind of strange goddess sent to save me from sadness and pain," Ben said, his hands wringing the pool stick as if it were a soaked cloth. "I thought getting married was for the best. I thought I would grow to love you. But it's too soon. I still love my wife. And Charlotte — I think she knows I don't love you the way I should, the way she does."

Lillian leaned her pool stick against the

wall. She took his hands in hers.

"You and Charlotte revel in each other," he continued, "love the intensity, challenge, and fun of simply being in each other's presence. You and I don't have that."

"No," Lillian said. "We don't."

They still had two days left of their honeymoon.

A flight attendant stirred Lillian from her reverie by announcing that there would be some turbulence for the next fifteen minutes, and that they were two hours from Heathrow, where they would make the scheduled stopover before continuing to New York. Charlotte, her headphones still on, was now drawing geometric shapes in her notebook. Ben was asleep.

After Ben's revelation to her in the billiard room at the Hill Club, they had left for Colombo the following morning as planned, checking into a small hotel in the Cinnamon Gardens district. That afternoon Lillian decided to follow up on the information Bryan Byrd had given her.

Standing on Independence Avenue, Lillian hailed a motorized rickshaw. She had managed until that moment to avoid taking a rickshaw while in Sri Lanka. She could easily have avoided it then as well.

There were taxis, buses, cars. The rickshaw was not exactly her horse that she had fallen from and needed to get back on. If she never rode in another rickshaw for the rest of her life, she would be perfectly content. It was just that there was something string-tying and symmetrical about her taking a rickshaw to pursue this particular quest. In spite of the high anxiety she decided while climbing into the pod for the first time since the accident, she felt it was unavoidable. She gave the driver the address of the first hospital and off they sped.

Immediately Lillian felt dizzy and thought she would have to tell the driver to stop, or, when they arrived at the hospital, instead of asking questions about a long-ago case, she would be asking to be admitted herself. She could feel the sweat gathering on her brow and trickling down her back as she thought, entirely uncharacteristically, how she had completely fucked up her life. She had gotten married and would be divorced in a span of a few weeks, she was pregnant with a child who would never know his father, she had taken too many risks in her profession, and she had made a religion of alienating all those close to her, most of all her sister, who had made a religion of worshipping Lillian and was now faltering in her faith. She had followed directly in the steps of her flighty mother and had unfairly judged her dead father. As she sat considering what to do — get out of the rickshaw, go back to the hotel, go on to the hospital — the driver suddenly pulled the vehicle over to the side of the road and hopped into the back with her.

"It is you," he said, shaking his head. "I can't believe it's you. I have seen your face in my dreams every day for five years. After the accident, I went to every hotel to try to find you. Finally, the police made me stop — they thought I was a crazy person."

Lillian listened, disbelieving each word as the man rambled on in his rolling lollipop English. Was the world really such a fantastic place, she wondered, where this could happen? Or was she in some delusional state, like the woman from Greenwich in the Hungarian Pastry Shop?

"I needed to tell you because I saw it on your face when I caught a glimpse of you by the hydrangea bush, and I have seen it on your face for five years in my dreams — that look of terror and hopelessness. You thought she was dead, but she wasn't, isn't. I wanted to tell you, but you disappeared, poof, like a magician's dove. She's fine,

more than fine; you see, she's ours now."
He pointed to Lillian's pregnant belly as if
that gesture clarified things.

"You mean the accident on the Galle
Road? You were the driver?" Lillian asked,
although she now recognized him. She remembered the men holding him, hands
gripping his legs and arms, his wails of an-
guish.

"Yes, yes, yes. I know it's hard to believe.
But you are here and I am here and here
we are."

"And the girl?"

"Nisha is our daughter. We adopted her.
She's thirteen. You see, my wife and I, we
couldn't have children. Nisha was an ur-
chin, a Tamil orphan from the north living
in the streets. Her parents were both killed
in the fighting and a neighbor hid her in a
truck heading for Colombo."

"The girl wasn't dead?"

"Oh, no. You see, this is why I searched
for you. I knew you believed she was dead.
She had a concussion, yes. But the blood
was from her ear — her earring was ripped
off. There was a lot of blood. I picked her
up and drove her to my brother's house.
He is a doctor. She stayed in his clinic
until she was better."

Lillian put her head in her hands, then

looked up. "What happened to you? The crowd, they seemed so angry, ready to tear you apart."

"Oh, no, no, no. You are mistaken. They were holding me because they were afraid I would hurt myself, I was so distraught. I looked for you, I told them to look for you, because I was afraid for you, too."

"I thought . . ." Lillian began. "How could I have been so wrong? I thought the crowd was angry, wanted to hurt me and you for hurting that little girl."

The driver smiled to hide his confusion. "Why should they be angry? You and I, we did not intend to hurt Nisha. Sadly, animals and children are hit by vehicles all the time. Often, the driver doesn't even know it happened. And you, you were just the passenger." He gently stroked her shoulder. "I didn't mean to hit the girl, of course. Still it was my fault." He shook his head. "But you see, it was all for the best." The driver put out his hand. "My name is Anupam Puri. I know this is all very odd, but would you like to come meet my family?"

They drove back to the hotel, picked up Ben and Charlotte, and went to the Puris' home for a delicious dinner of sambols and buriyani. Nisha was a beautiful girl with dark hair in a single braid. She was dressed in jeans and a T-shirt and had tiny diamond studs in her ears and nose. She was curious to meet the woman her father had told her was part of their great good luck in gaining her as their daughter. Charlotte hardly spoke through most of the dinner, but she watched Nisha's every move with the attention of a scientist whose eye is pressed to a microscope. Toward the end of dinner, Nisha and Charlotte began to talk between themselves. Lillian tried to listen to their conversation while continuing to answer Anupam and his wife's questions about life in America. While Ben was describing the school system, Lillian overheard Nisha say, "You mean she's not your mother?"

"No," Charlotte said, "my mother died. She's just my doctor and a good friend."

"Did your mother die in a war?" Nisha asked.

"No, in a car crash. I was with her."

"Oh," Nisha said, indicating Anupam and his wife with a nod. "They're not my parents either."

The layover in London was only an hour and a half. They were somewhere over the Atlantic when Lillian realized the contractions had stopped but had been replaced by a pain in her chest. Heartburn, indigestion, the baby's feet, perhaps. She was thinking about going home, about moving out of Ben and Charlotte's apartment, about Veronica and her forbidden lover, about their half brother, about being on time tomorrow morning at the Hungarian Pastry Shop. Lillian fell asleep and didn't wake up again until they were landing at JFK. Early or late, her baby would be born in New York City.

Seven

XXVII

The Hungarian Pastry Shop was closed. A scribbled note on the door said the family had gone on vacation to Greece but had every intention of returning sooner or later, probably around Labor Day. Veronica didn't care if they returned or not, as this would be her last meeting with Lillian. It was before 9:00 a.m., overcast, and hot. She watched for Lillian from across the street in the gardens next to St. John the Divine seated on a bench in front of an enormous iron sculpture, an orgy of weird beasts entitled *Peace Fountain*. She stared at the entanglement of giant crab claws, the upside-down head of a devil, a sinister moon face, a winged dragonman, a giraffe with two heads, dreading the conversation that she must have with her sister, which promised to be even more

301

dreadful than the conversation she recently had with Alex at the *Ordinary Matters* studio.

Then as now, Veronica had been distracted by an overpowering wish for a cigarette. She and Alex had just had sex on the love seat in his dressing room. It was a double cliché, she realized, but didn't mind in the least. Sex in a soap-opera star's dressing room between takes was an event that surely merited a cigarette.

"I hired a detective," he said, "to find you."

Veronica began to put her clothes back on. She sensed impending doom and wanted to be dressed for it.

"I hired a woman named Sybil Noonan to find my birth family."

"Yes, and?" Veronica's heart was another cliché, beating jackhammer fast, breaking.

"My mother is Agnes Moore, my father Maxwell Jones, my half sisters Lillian and Veronica Moore."

"There must be some mistake," Veronica said, continuing to button her blouse. "I've never heard of a Maxwell Jones."

"He was a colleague of your mother's at the hospital where she worked at the time. He's now a neurosurgeon in Scranton. His name is on the birth certificate, although to Sybil he denied paternity."

302

Alex was still sitting naked on the leather love seat. "Don't you have to go to the set soon?" Veronica asked, hoping he would do something to cover himself. She couldn't possibly believe what he was telling her. All she could think was that this was a very peculiar excuse for Alex to invent as a reason to break up with her. But then again it was airtight.

"Veronica," he said, standing, "I love you."

"Like a sister?" she asked, then hid her face in her hands. The word *sister* had catapulted her from shock to Lillian. Did Alex know he was the father of Lillian's baby? Had the redheaded Sybil dug that deep? Or was there a medical explanation for all this? Veronica had hit her head and was in a coma.

"Alex, get dressed," Veronica insisted. "And why did you wait until after we had sex to break the news?"

Alex put on the bathrobe he had been wearing when she came to his dressing room. She had, in fact, taken it off him almost immediately after closing the door.

"I've had a bit more time than you to think about this," Alex said, pulling her next to him on the couch, his arms around her, hugging her tightly. "It's no one's fault and it's not all that bad," he went on. "Besides," he said, smiling, his tone lighter, "we could go away. In Maine or Spain we'd fit right in. And weren't Hera and Zeus sister and brother?"

"So were Caligula and Drusilla. But it's not funny," Veronica said, pushing him away.

"The truth of the matter is, Veronica, I'm okay with it. If it makes things easier, we don't have to tell anyone. I've been an orphan this long, I can remain one for the rest of eternity if it means I can be with you."

Veronica couldn't bear the outrageousness of her bad luck, the severity of the gods' revenge. In desperate need of a cigarette, she stood up and announced that she needed to take a walk. She said she'd be right back. Alex, his eyes sad, his lips trembling, kissed her on the forehead, and she left. On Broadway, she received scowls of disapproval ostensibly for her secondhand smoke, but she saw in her detractors' eyes the knowledge of her far greater crimes. She sighed, blew on her bangs, took a yoga-breath pull on her cigarette. Since her passionate love affair was now definitively over, she became practical. She would call her mother to find out how she managed to have a child between Lillian and Veronica and why she had never told them about him. She would then track her sister down in Sri Lanka with the news that not only did they have a half brother but he just so happened to be Veronica's ex-lover and the father of Lillian's baby. But this practicality could not disguise how despicable Veronica felt. She had brought this all on herself and now there was not a shadow of a doubt that she was truly abhorrent. As she passed Seventy-second Street, her mind filled with nothing but the demonic mantra: "The horror! the horror!" Just call me Kurtz, Veronica thought miserably. At Zabar's, she turned around and headed straight back to the *Ordinary Matters* studio. She decided to come clean before her voyage to Tierra del Fuego. She would tell Alex about Lillian's baby.

Retracing her steps, the heat of the day now blazing up from the sidewalk, she found herself sincerely wishing that Lillian weren't in Sri Lanka. After all, in the grand scheme of things, Lillian was as much to blame for this mess as Veronica. Wasn't it Lillian who recklessly chose Alex to inseminate her without regard for him or for the eventual questions their child might have? Lillian had thought she was so clever by choosing this guy after looking at his health records and blood tests while he was in the hospital, but she'd neglected to check out his DNA. Of course, who would have thought she needed to? What chance was there in the universe that Lillian would randomly choose her own unknown half brother to father her child? And then what chance was there that her plan would actually work? Not to mention that he would be employed by the same soap opera Veronica happened to write for. Chance, though at times mean and tricky and even downright cruel, was not, however, the real problem here. Veronica was.

At the studio, Veronica headed down a long corridor with seemingly endless doors toward Alex's dressing room. On her way, she felt as if she had landed in Alice's wonderland or in Charlie's chocolate factory. Behind each door, there was surely some person or event or thing that defied our notions of truth. Veronica's own little adventure had none of the innocence and moral rectitude of a children's story. Her tale was straightforwardly perverse. She paused, looked wistfully at those alternative doors, then soldiered ahead, wishing with all her heart she were in a fairy tale where mistaken identity and newfound blood ties led to weddings and kingdoms and universal harmony, not to incest, betrayal, and irrevocable discord.

Continuing down the hall Jane Lust had christened "Ego Alley," she read the names on the doors — Tripp Jones, Nigel Thorpe, Ashley Diamond, Melody Weaver, Laralee Lamore, Bianca McGee, Alex Drake. Veronica stood in front of Alex's door staring at a photograph of him flying in midair, the Shawangunk Mountains like great hands holding him up to the heavens. She was wondering what idiocy had driven her to pursue a relationship with the father of her sister's baby when the door to Alex's dressing room opened and a ruffled but luscious Laralee emerged. She glanced at Veronica with red-rimmed eyes and scurried off down the hall.

Veronica stepped into Alex's dressing room. Low, harmonic music filled the small space. Alex was sitting at his makeup table facing the mirror with his eyes closed. He looked so peaceful, as if he were meditating, though he was probably just waiting for his makeup to dry. She hadn't noticed earlier that he had a copy of *Quid Pro Quo* on his dressing room table. She walked over beside him and said, "Hi, I'm back."

There was nothing to do but tell him. Slowly, gently, Veronica unraveled the story, like an old woman taking apart a sweater in hopes of conserving some of the yarn. She told him about the hospital emergency room, Lillian, the pregnancy, the extraordinary coincidence of his turning up on *Ordinary Matters*. Veronica admitted to knowing who he was, but, for reasons she couldn't explain, had gone ahead and fallen in love with him. During the unspinning of her tale, Alex's eyes remained closed, his face expressionless. When she finished, ending on what she hoped was somehow a positive note — although it was difficult for her to construe anything in this skewed narrative as positive — Alex said nothing. She would wait for him to speak next, no matter how long it took.

She hadn't waited even thirty seconds, however, when the door to Alex's dressing room burst open. Nigel Thorpe stomped in, grabbed Alex with one hand, and lifted him from his chair before planting a fist in the middle of his nose. He shouted, "Stay away from my wife, you cocksucker." An audience of staff and actors collected in the doorway as blood from Alex's nose, mixed with makeup, poured down his face.

Laralee ran into the dressing room, grabbed the white surgeon's coat from a hanger near the dressing table, and used it to dab blood as she cradled Alex's head in her lap. A group of actors dressed as doctors watched transfixed as the staff nurse and then an EMS team determined that Alex's nose was broken. Veronica slipped out of the studio as if she were trespassing and might at any moment get caught for being there. Later, she had desperately tried to reach Alex — she had even waited for him outside his apartment — but he never appeared and hadn't returned her countless calls.

Now, in the gardens of St. John the Divine, Veronica's eyes scanned the dark and mangled sculpture for a body to attach to the huge free-floating claws. She felt like a character in a parody of a Greek tragedy wherein the only possible resolution to the play's machinations was a major nosebleed. It didn't immediately register on Veronica that the pregnant blonde examining the note on the Hungarian Pastry Shop door was actually Lillian. In just three weeks what had been a barely detectable little anthill had transformed into a protruding and pointy missile head.

Veronica called out Lillian's name and

waved to her from across the street. Lillian saw her and bounded out into the traffic as if her belly held nothing more than a helium balloon. Veronica closed her eyes as she watched a double-decker tour bus careen up Amsterdam Avenue toward her sister.

"Don't you think it would be rather tasteless for you and your child to be flattened by a Big Apple tour bus?" Veronica asked. Lillian appeared rested and relaxed, as if she were returning from three weeks in East Hampton, not from the other side of the world.

"Only you, Veronica, would worry about having a tasteful death. Can you believe those Hungarians? Taking vacation? Don't they know this is America?" she complained. "I'm so hot. Let's go into the church."

"How was your trip?" Veronica asked, as they walked toward St. John the Divine. She would never think badly of small talk again.

"When I left Sri Lanka the first time," Lillian said, "I swore I would never go back. This time when I left, I felt I would gladly go back anytime, so I probably never will."

They entered the cavernous stone structure and the bright world suddenly went dark and cool, dank air enveloped them, the smell mildly unpleasant. They headed down the right aisle, where the first bay they came to held Poet's Corner, a mosaic of epitaphs from the tombstones of America's greatest writers.

"I really loathe churches," whispered Lillian as she sat down on a marble step. "So much force-fed death."

"Can't be any worse than hospitals," Veronica said. Being in that soaring building suddenly gave her new hope.

" 'There were things that he stretched but mainly he told the truth,' Mark Twain," Lillian read aloud, then said, "You've heard we have a half brother."

Veronica kneeled next to Lillian. "So you know," she said, amazed at her sister's equanimity. Lillian was an emotional rock, but this was scary. "How did you find out?" she asked. As depraved as her sister was, Veronica had expected that even Lillian would be rattled that her child was the product of incest. Instead she was halcyon incarnate. At least Veronica didn't have to be the bearer of that bad news, although she did still have to confess to her own affair with Alex.

"Sybil Noonan told Bryan Byrd, and he

told me just before I left for Sri Lanka. I said I would have to wait to meet our half brother until I got back."

"Meet him?" Veronica asked, confused. "You've more than met him."

"I have?" Lillian asked. "Who is he? It didn't occur to me to ask Bryan his name, I was in such a hurry. Don't tell me it's Bronson Hartley or some yokel from high school."

Whatever relief Veronica had enjoyed for a brief second or two was now brusquely stolen away. It felt terribly unfair, like a prize awarded then rescinded, a toy finally given over only to be immediately grabbed back. Veronica spied Elizabeth Bishop's epitaph: *All the untidy activity continues — awful but cheerful.*

"Look, there's no good way to tell you this," she said, "but our half brother is Alex Drake."

For a few seconds Lillian looked at Veronica quizzically. Then suddenly her face lost all color, paled to match her blond hair, and she put her hands on her belly, a gesture Veronica rarely saw her do.

"Your amnio was fine, Lillian, remember. I read on the Internet that the chances of genetic deformity in half siblings' offspring are only a fraction higher than for those of the general population."

"Spare me the statistics," Lillian said, then stood up abruptly and started walking deeper into the cathedral. Veronica followed, slightly behind her. They passed several bays with tapestries, a New York bishop's tomb, a sci-fi model of the cathedral with a solar tower and biosphere over it. Finally, Lillian stopped in front of a two-thousand-pound, two-hundred-million-year-old giant quartz-crystal cluster found in Arkansas. A plaque read, TO HONOR THE BEAUTY OF GOD'S CREATION AND OUR SACRED STEWARDSHIP OF PLANET EARTH.

Knowing from experience that delaying the inevitable would only make matters worse, Veronica said, "Lillian, there's more to the punch line here. Alex was hired to play a neurosurgeon on *Ordinary Matters*, and I've been having an affair with him for about six months."

Lillian stared at Veronica, then broke out laughing — the hysterical laughter they used to dissolve into as children. Veronica joined in. Trying to control themselves, they just laughed harder. A priest started to approach them, and they hurried, still giggling, into St. Ansgar's Chapel, which held a sparkling new columbarium. Letters, pictures, and flowers were taped to

313

the surfaces of many of the graves. "Something reassuring about spending eternity in a file cabinet," Lillian commented, wiping the tears from her eyes. They looked at each other and began laughing again, so they left the columbarium, heading for the older and more traditional chapels. In St. Columba's Chapel they sat on miniature wooden chairs in front of a small altar and tried to focus on the seriousness of the matter.

Veronica forced words of explanation. "Right after you told me you were pregnant, an actor named Alex Drake was hired to play a brain surgeon on *Ordinary Matters*, but he had to delay rehearsals because of an accident in a yoga class. I knew it was him. Oh, Lillian," she said, trying hard not to laugh, "I'm so sorry." Veronica couldn't help thinking that her sister, sitting in that tiny chair, had something of an Alice look about her after having drunk from a vial labeled BIG.

"I always suspected you were weirder than I gave you credit for," Lillian said. "But I also don't see what the big deal is here. Me and Alex, you and Alex, Alex the long-lost brother — it's all been done before. I mean, you're the one who writes for a soap opera. It only proves yet again what a small world this is and that in the end the joke is always on us. But the mind, now that never ceases to astound me. We remember only what is convenient to our fantasy of who we are. We will allow ourselves to admit that this stuff happens all the time in, say, Appalachia or on *Jerry Springer*, but God forbid it should happen on the Upper West Side."

"Lillian," Veronica objected, "you are innocent. There is no way you could have known Alex was your half brother."

"When I die, promise me you will put on my grave what Graham Greene put on his: 'God save us from the innocent and the good.' I've been called a lot of things, but innocent is definitely not one of them. Our brains are evolutionarily hardwired to be drawn to others like us. We have invented incest taboos to control ourselves from going after what we really desire. And we have spent the last hundred years working really hard to overcome intellectually our instinctual predisposition toward total rejection of those different from us. In my own entirely egotistical desire to have a child, I happened to choose someone more like me than I could have hoped. What luck."

Veronica sighed. Lillian, as usual, would

theorize her way into coming to terms with the situation. Whatever works, she thought.

They sat in silence for a while, then Lillian said, "After all my efforts, in the end I will be on the most intimate terms with the father of my child."

Veronica said nothing, at once elated that Alex would now be permanently part of their lives, eternally crushed that he could never be an exclusive part of her life in the way she had once dreamed.

Lillian reached out and took Veronica's hand. She placed it flat against her belly and Veronica felt an arrhythmic tapping on her palm.

"Is that a foot?" she asked Lillian.

"Let's hope so," Lillian said, and they both collapsed again in laughter as St. Columba looked on.

XXVIII

In August of the year Charles died, Lillian had run away. It was a very hot summer. Most days, Veronica and Lillian sat out in the backyard under the dogwood with the sprinkler on. Veronica went inside only to get them something to drink or to watch her favorite soaps. Lillian and Agnes had been having awful fights. It was hard for Veronica to understand what the fights were really about. Lillian was always saying vicious things to her mother, like "I hate you. I wish I didn't have a mother. Go away and leave me alone."

And Agnes was always saying things like, "You are ungrateful and difficult. You make my life even more miserable than it already is. How do you expect me to do it all?"

"Who asked you to?" Lillian would respond. "Why don't you just get rid of us, give us up for adoption, put us into foster care?"

Veronica wasn't sure how she felt about Lillian making this request on her behalf. She was usually pleased whenever Lillian included her, but in this case she doubted she would want to go along with Lillian.

"Be careful of what you wish for, young lady," Agnes would threaten.

This last line terrified Veronica, as it was a line her father had often used. Did that mean her mother might die soon too? Veronica wished they would stop fighting, and at every opportunity tried to mollify both her mother and her sister, but this made Lillian only more disgusted. And Agnes would exacerbate the situation by saying things such as, "At least I have one good child," or the classic, "Why can't you be more like Veronica?"

The day Lillian ran away was so hot Veronica woke up with her hair sticking to her temples, beads of sweat across her brow and nose. Lillian and Agnes were downstairs in the kitchen shouting.

"This has got to stop, Lillian," Agnes said. "You can't treat me as if all the world's ills were my fault. You are too old for this. I need you to help me, not be some hideous harpy always complaining and making everyone's life more difficult."

"Fine," said Lillian. "You don't want me here. I'll go." And Veronica heard the front door slam.

Her mother followed Lillian out the door and yelled, "Go ahead, leave. Take the easy way out. But don't think it's going to be so easy to walk back into our lives."

Here, again, Veronica was included in her mother's statement, and, again, she wasn't entirely sure how she felt about it. Veronica believed that no matter what happened she would always want Lillian in her life.

Agnes had gone to work that morning. She'd told Veronica to tell Lillian that if she returned she would have to wait until

318

Agnes got home to ask permission to come into the house, that Veronica was not allowed under any circumstances to let Lillian inside.

"But, Mom," Veronica had objected, horrified by the implications of the mandate.

"No ifs, ands, or buts. If you let her back in here, you will be marching out yourself. Do you understand?" Agnes demanded.

Veronica prayed that Lillian would not come back before her mother got home from the hospital. She watched TV until she had such a bad headache all she could do was fall asleep. Drenched in sweat, she was sleeping on the couch in the living room when Agnes returned and woke her up.

"Where's Lillian?" Agnes demanded, as if Veronica had hidden her somewhere.

"She never came back," Veronica said. Her headache was gone, although the air was still stifling. She was hungry.

She and her mother ate a sandwich together in silence at the kitchen table, then went to bed. Agnes checked to make sure all the downstairs windows and the front and back doors were locked. Veronica lay in bed listening for Lillian and did not fall asleep until the sky began to change from pitch black to exhaust-pipe gray.

The next morning Veronica overheard her mother on the telephone with Mrs. Wilcox, the wife of the minister at the First Presbyterian Church. From what she understood of the one-sided conversation, Lillian was staying in their shelter for unwed mothers. "Well, if you don't mind," her mother was saying, "I think she should just stay there for a bit. She needs to learn a lesson. I just don't know what has gotten into that girl. When she wants to come home, she will have to ask my permission." Agnes could be very harsh, but it never lasted long and she was then always full of apologies and elaborate excuses for her "unseemly" behavior. Veronica just wished her mother would hurry up and move on to Act Two of this particular drama with Lillian.

Over the next few days, Agnes treated Veronica as if she were a princess. They went clothes shopping, out for supper, to the movies — things they rarely did and certainly hadn't done since the accident. Veronica felt guilty doing all these things without Lillian, but she enjoyed herself immensely all the same. She did wonder what would happen when Lillian came home. Would her mother bring Lillian along, too?

Or would the outings just stop? Lillian had been gone for five days when Veronica got the telephone call.

"I need some clean clothes and a book," Lillian said.

"Mom's at work," Veronica told her. "You can come get them."

There was a long pause.

"She'd kill you," Lillian said.

Veronica didn't say anything.

"Just leave the window in the kitchen open the next time you and Agnes go out, that way you won't get into trouble. She'll think she forgot to lock it."

After they hung up, Veronica went to the window in the kitchen and unlocked it. She stared out at the street and wondered how Lillian would know when she and Agnes left the house. Was she watching them? Veronica missed Lillian even if they didn't really talk much when she was there. Veronica couldn't believe that things were still so bad so long after the accident. Would their whole lives be like this? Was it all her fault? She sighed and blew on her bangs. There was no answer. She would just have to live her life and see.

That evening, Veronica and Agnes went out for a hamburger and milkshake at a local diner. Before they left the house,

Agnes checked all the downstairs windows. "Now how did I miss that one?" she asked, locking the kitchen window Veronica had unlocked earlier. Veronica's heart sank. She racked her brain wondering how to open the window again without her mother noticing. Lillian would hate her, feel betrayed, not have any clean clothes if Veronica didn't somehow leave the window unlocked. She and Agnes were in the car pulling out of the driveway when Veronica said, "Sorry, Mom. I have to pee really badly."

"Can't you hold it until we get to the restaurant?" her mother asked.

Veronica crossed her thighs tightly and said, "I don't think so. I really, really have to go."

Agnes handed her the keys to the house and said, "Well, hurry up and don't forget to lock the door on your way out."

When they got home, Veronica went straight to bed. She was trying to fall asleep, hoping Lillian had gotten what she needed, when her mother walked into the room without turning on the light and dragged Veronica from her bed onto the floor. "How could you?" she yelled, her voice deeper and raspier than usual. "How could you? I have been so good to you all week and this is the thanks I get?" Veronica put her head between her arms and curled up into a ball. Agnes kicked her lightly. "How could you betray me like this? I had my reasons for not letting her back into the house and now you've ruined everything. It was my only chance of getting her to come back home." She stood silently over Veronica for some time, then said, "I know why you did it. You pretend to be so agreeable and caring, but you're not, are you? You have a mean streak just like she does, but yours is surreptitious and festering. You don't actually want Lillian to come home, do you? You don't like your sister. You have always been jealous of her."

Veronica sobbed, "No, no, none of that is true. I wanted to help her. I wanted to make sure she was okay." Veronica fully believed what she was saying, and was sure she had opened the window for her sister in order to make things better for everyone. But there was also some truth in what her mother was saying, and that grain of truth shamed her. Veronica had imagined a world without Lillian an infinite number of times, both before and after her father's death. Those worlds contained every possible variation and combination of emotion from total bliss to utter despair. One thing they all had in common, however, was that they were safe. Veronica was aware that since her father died, their world had not been safe even if Agnes tried to pretend otherwise. Agnes didn't want to punish Lillian; she wanted her back. Agnes didn't want to punish Veronica either; she wanted Lillian back. Veronica, too, wanted Lillian back. Agnes walked out of the room, leaving Veronica on the floor. At the door, she turned and said, "Now you may just get what you want. She may never come home."

Lillian came home a couple of days later. She just showed up at dinnertime when Agnes was there and asked permission to stay. After that, life went on as usual. School started, Agnes worked long hours at the hospital. After school, Veronica watched soap operas or wrote in her diary, and Lillian did her homework or read the books from their father's bookshelves. Half an hour before the end of their mother's shift, they got into their pajamas and into bed with the lights off. Veronica didn't close her eyes until she heard her mother's footsteps on the stairs and saw the shaft of light from the hall fall on their bedroom floor. She knew Lillian was awake, too, because for as long as she could remember Lillian always waited for Veronica to fall asleep first.

XXIX

"What you did just then was actually quite difficult," Jane Lust said, staring down the lane at Veronica's gutter ball. Hips swiveling, Jane walked onto the runway and then back off, bowling a strike along the way. She was wearing tight black spandex pants and a red cotton cardigan with pearl buttons — the top three unbuttoned to reveal deep cleavage. Her strawberry blond hair was big and unmoving. Her lipstick, naturally, matched her sweater. For a second Veronica imagined she had traveled back in time and was bowling with her mother, although there was almost no physical resemblance. Oh, God, she thought, had Jane become her replacement mother? Was their relationship some kind of transference? Veronica took a deep breath and exhaled. Sophocles and Freud were right, she decided. Love in adult life is nothing more than a replay of biological family pairing-off — mother and son, father and daughter, sister and brother, and all the possible variations therein.

"Alex is going to be fired and Dr. Night Wesley is going to die," Jane said. They watched as her ball, also shiny red, was belched out of the ball-return and onto the rack. "I've been told by the producers to kill him off forthwith."

"Oh, no," Veronica gasped, feeling that she was somehow to blame. "Poor Alex. How are you going to do it?"

"Car crash," Jane said. "They don't want him back on-screen, especially with that nose. It's too real-looking. What I've come up with is this: In a fit of jealous rage, Dr. Trent White tampers with the brakes on Dr. Night Wesley's BMW. Eve will be in the car when the accident happens. She survives. Nigel wants her paralyzed for life, but even the producers agree that's not practical. I was thinking maybe she could get some rare neurological problem — in fact, I need to talk to your sister. Anyway, there will be an investigation and then a trial. I'm sorry for Alex, but every cloud has a silver lining — he's given me a year's worth of material." Jane pointed at the pins all set up again and ready to be knocked down. "Your turn."

Veronica's ball left ten of the ten pins standing.

"You just need a little warming up," Jane reassured her.

"Why did they fire him?" Veronica asked, refusing to look up at the accumulating zeros on the pink screen.

"I don't know exactly, other than his nose is broken and he's getting in the way of Nigel's divorce somehow, suggesting marital healers, things like that."

Much to Veronica's relief, her next ball knocked down more than half the pins. "Why don't they kill off Eve?" She asked. "Isn't *she* their problem?"

"Too big a fan base. They'll settle with her, but they want Alex the troublemaker gone — they were never too happy with him anyway."

Veronica couldn't help herself. "You don't think there's actually something between Alex and Laralee, do you?"

"From everything I've heard, their relationship has Plato written all over it. But, Veronica," Jane said, raising an eyebrow, "you're not considering continuing your affair with Alex, are you?"

"Oh, no, no, no," Veronica said. "I'm asking out of sisterly curiosity, that's all." She had spilled all the Alex beans to Jane on the phone that morning. Mother. Confessor. Friend. Whatever. Jane had listened, gasping and guffawing throughout the story, and then had insisted they go bowling.

"I see," Jane said, before strutting off down the runway, where she proceeded to knock down nine of the ten pins. Obviously displeased to have left one pin standing, she continued, a bit testily, "In any case, Alex should be doing something else with his life. He doesn't even like acting. He gets jobs simply because he's so pretty." She picked up her red ball and obliterated the remaining pin. "Did he ever read *Quid Pro Quo*?" she asked.

"I don't know," Veronica said. "Oliver Callow called yesterday. Black Lagoon wants to produce the musical if they can get the funding, but they want to use their own composer. I get some sort of limited final approval. I told them I'd think about it."

Jane went to her purse and pulled out her cell phone. "Call him right now and tell him you agree. You've worked too hard to let some silly ideas about integrity get in your way."

"What's wrong with artistic integrity?" Veronica asked, feeling hungry. She wanted to order a hot dog and French fries, but, like drinking alcohol, it just wasn't something you could do in good conscience before noon. Instead she lit up a cigarette.

"It's a myth," Jane answered, joining her with a Pall Mall menthol light. "Compromise has a very bad rap among artists, but they all do it because they know that true integrity is doing your work, getting it out there any way possible, and moving on to the next thing. I think that an artist's real contribution is not *what* she produces but *that* she produces. True art, for me, is the doing of the art. The rest is product, which can be sheer genius to one person and crap to another; but, bottom line, it's product, not art."

"If that's true, Jane, why aren't you writing novels? You say that you don't do your heart's work because the world doesn't need one more bad novel. But now you say the novel itself doesn't matter. I don't get it."

Jane laughed. "Ah, you're onto me," she said through a veil of smoke. "Because my theory, like all theories, is a defense. Although I truly believe my theory, there is a part of me that knows that it was devised as self-justification. Therefore, I cannot in good faith produce another bad book."

Veronica shook her head. "I'm confused."

"Yes, but I'm right." She held out the phone. "Let Black Lagoon do what they need to do and you get back to the computer."

Veronica did not take the phone from Jane's hand. She took her turn instead. Lillian had arranged to meet with Alex that day. Would they talk about Veronica? Would they fall in love? Better not think about it. She let her arm be carried back into a slow swing by the weight of the ball. As her arm came forward, she let go just a little earlier than she thought was safe and the ball shot straight down the center of the lane and sent every last pin flying.

Returning triumphant to the scoring table — Jane looking pleased as punch for her — Veronica had this thought: Just as a plumber should be familiar with his wrenches, a lawyer with legal codes, shouldn't she, as a writer, understand a good deal more about herself and therefore her parents? She knew so little about them, really. She evidently knew far less about her mother than she had believed she knew, and she had never pretended to know much about her father. Not only was she still clueless as to where her father may have been taking her on the day of the accident, she didn't even know enough about him to guess, make something up, have a fantasy. When it came to her father, she suffered the worst thing an artist can suffer: She was without material — a painter without paint, a sculptor without marble or clay. She had nothing to color the canvas, nothing to shape. She needed to do two things: ask Bryan Byrd to continue his investigation of her father, and call Agnes.

XXX

Veronica closed her office door, put a rolled-up towel along the base of the door to keep the smell from permeating her apartment, and lit up. The billboard with the coffin was long gone, but she remembered the tag line: CIGARETTES WILL KILL YOU. That and a million other things, she thought, most of which you don't even know about, like pesticides on broccoli, lead in your water, a loose brick on the roof of a tall building. At least with smoking you knew the odds, and, for some, smoking had the added characteristic of being sexy. There was nothing remotely erotic about eating broccoli. As she had been taught in her high school Sex and Substance class, a minor transgression could lead to a major one. She glanced out her window, half-expecting to see her photograph on the billboard over the line INCEST: IT'S JUST NOT WORTH IT.

She pressed the messages button on her answering machine for the tenth time since she had come home from bowling. "There are no new messages," the machine gloated. She had several competing fantasies for what had happened to Lillian and Alex, the absolute worst being that they had decided to run off together to Tierra del Fuego. The quick burn in her lungs felt good.

The buzzer rang, she stubbed out her cigarette with regret, and went to the front door. Through the intercom, she heard Bryan Byrd's voice. She couldn't believe it was already that late. Veronica had asked Bryan to stop by before going to his gig at Smoke. What *had* happened to Lillian and Alex? And what exactly did she want to say to Bryan Byrd? She opened the door to Bryan in a caramel-colored linen suit carrying a bulbous black suitcase containing his tuba. It was hot outside, and he was sweating. She asked him in and offered him some ice water. He sat on her couch and drank down the water in one swallow. He then pulled a perfectly ironed and folded handkerchief from his pocket and wiped his brow.

"So," he said, "why am I here? Is it your father, Alex, Lillian, or something my little mind hasn't yet fathomed?"

"Alex?" Veronica asked, self-censorship not even an option. "What do you know about Alex?"

"Don't worry," Bryan said, "certainly nothing more than you do."

Veronica blushed. "He's with Lillian now," she said for no reason. Of course, Bryan knew the whole story about Alex.

"What can I do for you?" he asked again.

"I've decided I want you to continue your investigation of my father," Veronica said. "I want to know who he was taking me to meet on the day of the accident. I want to know everything there is to know about him."

Bryan Byrd shook his head. "You guys are real flip-floppers. Then again, I guess it's one of those ancient questions — how well do we really want to know anyone? Sorry, Veronica, I've quit private practice. I've taken a job with an insurance company."

"Selling insurance?" she asked.

"No. Investigating claims."

"Why?" she asked, seating herself on the opposite side of the couch.

"Well, it's mostly what I've been doing anyway, and I'm getting old. I need a pension, benefits." Veronica watched as he neatly folded his handkerchief and put it back into his pocket. "Besides, I was getting jaded. Cheating husbands, cheating wives, greedy will-contesters. Men, women, and children who don't want to be found by their desperately searching relatives. When I started I liked all the stories. But after a while, I couldn't take it anymore. Scratch a little on the surface of any life and the secrets and traumas and dark ugly truths that emerge make Pandora's box look like a treasure chest. And worse, there were all these people believing I could provide the answers to their questions. It's lost its appeal. It got too lonely."

Veronica resisted lighting up a cigarette. Her private detective was having a midlife crisis right there in her living room. She had asked him over to her apartment in order for him to help her, instead she was going to have to think of a way to help him.

Bryan smiled. "I'd like to help you, Veronica, but I can't. Furthermore, I think you're asking the wrong question. In my opinion, the most pressing question for you is not Who was your father, but Did you kill your father? You want to know if you caused the accident."

In her mind, Veronica saw the third button on her father's shirt. She heard herself say "Daddy, your shirt is unbuttoned." She watched him look down, then back up at her, his expression at once sad, pained, and full of fear. She felt the car swerve off the road. Veronica closed her eyes. "For me, Bryan, there has never been any doubt. I know I killed him."

Bryan said, "No you didn't. He's still alive."

If, like dogs who resemble their owners, her life was going to become indistinguishable from her day job, Veronica was going to have to quit *Ordinary Matters*.

"Alive? How is that possible?" Veronica thought of the broken windshield, the man pulling her from the overturned car, the blood. "I was in the car with him."

"He didn't die, Veronica. Rudolph Saturday was hired, by the director of the institution where your father now lives, to find you and your sister. Your father suffered a severe head trauma and his X-ray revealed a brain tumor that turned out to be benign. He had suffered a significant aneurysm in his medial temporal lobe, but it was impossible to tell if it had been caused by the tumor or the accident. In any case, the pressure from the tumor on his brain probably caused certain neurological dysfunctions — from minor things like headaches to more serious afflictions such as depression and even delusions. The operation to remove the tumor did not go well. Your father was left with a permanent brain disorder similar to Korsakov's syndrome. It seems that he has no memory — his life newly invented minute by minute. He also has Broca's aphasia, which means that his comprehension of what goes on around him is more or less intact but his speech production is severely impaired and he is able to communicate only through automatic overused language, such as nursery rhymes and song lyrics. He is able to write. He recognizes no one but will assign each person he meets an identity, a role in one of his autobiographical fictions, but that identity too becomes another and then another almost as soon as it is articulated. He would have no idea who you are."

"Where is he?" Veronica asked, won-

dering if she were absolved or newly impli-
cated in her father's misery. Did it matter?
Her new day job would be just like her father's — setting her autobiography to
music. Just for practice, she might even
start singing her questions to Bryan Byrd.

"In a neurological institution upstate,"
he answered.

"Wasn't there a funeral?" she almost
sang. Björk could play her in the movie
version.

Bryan Byrd shrugged. "Actually, no.
Your mother just told you, your friends,
and neighbors that there had been one.
She worked in the hospital. She knew how
to make all the arrangements. It seems
your mother thought this solution would
be best for you and your sister."

"Classic," Veronica said, marveling at his
generosity toward Agnes. "How long have
you known this?"

"A while."

"Why didn't you tell us?"

"First of all, you called off the investigation. But there's another factor here. You
see, my father had Alzheimer's. In its final
stages, Alzheimer's is similar to Korsakov's
syndrome. It's a living hell for all involved.
Dante's imagination wasn't big enough for
this one. I cannot speak for the afflicted, of

course, but I can speak as the offspring of the afflicted. Death became a luxury item, something I greatly desired for my father, something I even regularly contemplated committing a crime to get. Was I going to undo Agnes's careful and no doubt painfully concocted plan to protect her daughters simply because it was my job?"

Was Agnes's motivation something as noble as Bryan evidently believed it to be? Again, anything was possible. "So what's changed?" Veronica asked.

"Lillian."

He said Lillian's name just as she had said Alex's earlier, without thinking. "Lillian? Does she know?" Veronica asked.

"No. But she must have sensed something about it at the time. She was eleven. Not much gets past an eight-year-old, the age you were, and almost nothing gets by an eleven-year-old. And look at what she chose to do for a living. It all seems so connected. I feel wrong keeping this from her. But I also feel it could wait until after the baby is born."

"So why are you telling me?"

He shrugged. "You asked."

"I suppose I did," she said. The buzzer rang. Veronica jumped up and went to the door. Lillian's voice over the intercom said,

"It's me." Veronica had just learned her father was still alive, but for the next few minutes all she could think of was Alex and what had happened at his meeting with her sister.

Lillian walked into the living room. As usual, she was wearing all black — black sunglasses, blank tank top, black bell-bottoms, white toenail polish. Nothing about her suggested anything about how it had gone with Alex.

"Hello, Lillian," Bryan said, standing up.

Lillian glanced at Veronica, then said, "Whatever are you doing here, Bryan Byrd? Was I mistaken? I thought it was me you were obsessed with."

"Nothing new on that front," Bryan Byrd said, looking at Lillian in a way that Veronica had seen before but now understood as apotheosis.

"Well, then," Lillian said, "now that that's all cleared up, what's new?"

Bryan and Veronica exchanged a look of pure soap. Should they tell her? Should they keep it a secret between them?

Cliffhang it, Veronica thought. Deal with it in next week's episode.

The phone rang.

XXXI

"Hello," she said, picking up the phone. Lillian and Bryan were standing perfectly still in the middle of her living room, frozen in time.

"Veronica, it's Agnes."

"Agnes?" Veronica asked, as if she knew of no one who went by that name.

Lillian shook her head, then sat down on the couch. Bryan looked at his watch and picked up his tuba case. "I'm on in just a bit. I'll be seeing you," he whispered, and went out the door.

Lillian lay back on the couch and closed her eyes. Veronica wanted to say to her mother, "Look here, little lady, you have got a lot of explaining to do." She wanted to hang up and pretend it was a wrong number. She wanted to scream — or better yet, sing — into the receiver, "How could you? How could you have lied to us all these years?"

"Oh, Agnes, it's you," she said. "You sound as if you're next door."

Of course, she could be, Veronica thought. For all her mother's dissembling, she could easily be anywhere. Perhaps she simply had an address in New Zealand

340

from which mail was forwarded. Perhaps her phone calls were automatically re-routed.

"I just wanted to let you know that I'm coming to New York at the end of October," she said, without a hint of guilt or apology, as if she hadn't claimed she was coming umpteen times, never to show up. "I hope that will be a convenient time for you and Lillian."

"We look forward to it," Veronica said. She politely told her mother that just now was not a good time and asked if she could call her back. She hung up and said to Lillian, "Agnes says she's coming for a visit at the end of October — just when the zygote's due. You still haven't told her about him?"

Lillian shook her head. "Well," she said, "along with being psycho, Agnes can be psychic. She comes, she doesn't come, whatever."

"What happened with Alex?" Veronica asked.

Barely stirring on the couch, Lillian asked, "Why was Bryan here, Veronica?"

Veronica realized that there was no steering clear of this conversation. She had to tell Lillian exactly what Bryan Byrd had told her. Keeping secrets was over for Ve-

341

ronica, even if it was part of her genetic code.

"Lillian, I need to tell you something."

Lillian opened her eyes and sat up. She said, "He didn't die in the car crash, did he?"

Veronica, who had been sure there was nothing that could ever again surprise her, was dumbstruck but encouraged by Lillian's words. In this world afflicted with chronic uncertainty, there was one thing of which Veronica was certain: Lillian, psycho and psychic, was definitely her mother's daughter.

Eight

XXXII

Lillian ate two bites of her croissant and gave up. She had so little room in there anymore for anything other than the rapidly growing fetus. She couldn't fathom the idea that from then until he decided to make his exit (his Halloween due date was in eight weeks) he could more than double in size. For some time now, the expression "I think I'm going to burst" had lost all metaphorical meaning for Lillian. The angel paintings were gone from the walls of the Hungarian Pastry Shop and had been replaced by Cindy Sherman-esque self-portraits of the photographer dressed up as all the different versions of Barbie — Wedding Day Barbie, Gallery Opening Barbie, Westminster Dog Show Barbie, Opening Night Barbie, Nigerian Barbie, Fashion Luncheon Barbie, Harley-

Davidson Barbie. Unlike Cindy Sherman, however, the photographer was a man. Lillian thought of making a present of Opening Night Barbie to Veronica to congratulate her on her recent success with *Quid Pro Quo*.

She was glad the café had reopened, although she wasn't sure why, since she had no great affection for the place. It had just been there so long that she thought it should go on being there. This last thought was such a Philistine concept that Lillian began to question if there was any truth in the lie that women's brains turned to mush during pregnancy. She glanced at her watch. Veronica was late. Lillian wondered if Alex had anything to do with it. Veronica had told Lillian that she and Alex had decided to remain friends, nothing more. Neither of them, Veronica had said, "could deal" with the fact that they were blood related. Lillian found this explanation lackadaisical, but who was she to tell them to disregard civilization's strongest taboo? And, to be honest, her own meeting with Alex not long ago had been, even for her, excruciating.

Lillian had requested that Alex meet her at the Thalia, a revival movie theater on the Upper West Side, whose screen, over the years, had been dark more often than alive with the light of a film. She chose the Thalia because she thought sitting in obscurity for two hours might be the easiest way to ameliorate the considerable awkwardness of their situation. And although she did want to acknowledge to Alex that she was grateful for his donation, she really didn't have much to say to him. David Lynch's *Blue Velvet* was playing as part of the Thalia's "Blue" festival and Lillian figured it was a good choice.

When Alex arrived, he appeared afflicted, as if he were a drug addict in need of a fix. He was pale and shaking, unable to keep his eyes focused for more than a few seconds. His face was puffy and his nose had a bandage across it.

Lillian handed Alex a ticket and said, "Hurry, it's already started."

And indeed Lillian had timed their meeting so that inside the theater the brightly colored, kitsch, suburban tableaux of *Blue Velvet* were already rolling. It was early afternoon, and although it was a hot August day, there were only two other people in the audience, a detail Lillian had anticipated. They sat far from the other couple.

"I thought we'd have a better chance of saying what we mean in a dark place with people on a screen telling us things they've been told to say and asking us to believe that whatever it is they are saying they mean," Lillian said. Alex stared at her blankly. "Naturally, you're an actor and know exactly what I mean," she added.

He shook his head. "No, not really. I didn't really get that at all." His voice was unsteady. "And I've been fired from *Ordinary Matters*, so I'm not an actor with a job. Even so, the term is not accurate in my case because, as you yourself have experienced, I am someone who is acted upon, rather than someone who actively acts, which I suppose makes me more of an actee than an actor."

This was not starting off well. Lillian decided to get straight to the point. "As you can see, I'm pregnant," she said.

"Veronica told me," he barely managed to say.

"I apologize for having deceived you," she said, insincerely. "I had no idea that you would ever find out."

A fireman hanging on to a shiny red fire truck smiled at them and waved vigorously from the screen.

"This was not exactly how I thought," Alex began, but then stopped to clear his throat.

Lillian prayed he wouldn't cry, and, if he did, she hoped he would try to hide it — another advantage to being in a dark theater.

"I wouldn't have chosen this way to become a father," he finally said.

His delicacy of emotion, his inability to get angry, reminded Lillian of Veronica. His hesitancy, and his apparent impulse to want everything to be right in the world, made Lillian feel as if she had known him her entire life. This was not an argument for genetics, however. There were people in one's life — not so much in Lillian's, but she knew that the phenomenon was possible — whom you met once and felt as if you had known forever. It was not an argument for past lives, either. It was just something that happened.

"As I said, I'm sorry. You weren't supposed to know," Lillian responded, trying to soften her delivery.

"Not knowing," he said, the hesitancy gone from his voice, "will never work with me as an argument, Lillian. I was adopted. All I have ever wanted was to know who my parents were, if I had sisters or brothers somewhere. I'm not sure you can imagine the joy I felt when I found out I had two sisters, and then the agony I went through when I learned I was already weirdly entangled with both."

On the screen, an elderly man was watering red and yellow tulips with a long green hose.

"So you, along with the rest of humanity, are unhappy about the incest-go-round?" She laughed, although she knew it wasn't funny. She looked down at her belly. "I guess there's not much we can do about that now. In any case, I don't think our biggest problem is the incest taboo. No one was taking advantage of family power structures to sexually abuse anyone here. For the moment, our biggest problem is that I didn't intend for the baby to have a father, and you didn't intend to have a son."

They watched a teenaged boy named Jeffrey Beaumont find a severed ear in an empty lot near his home.

"I'm sorry if I'm messing up your plans, Lillian," Alex whispered, "but I will want to know my child. I'm not going to disappear. We'll have to work something out."

There it was. Exactly what she had been dreading. A father.

At the end of the movie, Lillian rose to leave. Alex put a hand on her arm and said, "I don't think I'm ready to go yet."

Lillian shrugged and sat back down. She supposed it was the least she could do, even if she had no interest in the next movie, Kathryn Bigelow's *Blue Steel*, with Ron Silver and Jamie Lee Curtis. ("Do you think she's really a hermaphrodite?" Alex asked as the opening credits rolled. "She'd be so lucky," Lillian responded.) It was an implausible and cartoonish movie about a girl with a gun. Every once in a while, usually during the most violent scenes, Lillian would whisper to Alex things such as: "I have no expectations of you as a father. I would be more or less comfortable with you as an uncle, which you are, so that's convenient." Or, "When I was little, I used to pray nightly for a brother. Veronica was such a wimp." Or, "When you have kids with Veronica, our kids will be half siblings *and* cousins, which means double jeopardy. We'll have to keep an eye on them."

After *Blue Steel* was over, neither she nor Alex stood up to leave. The next movie was Josef von Sternberg's *The Blue Angel*, with Marlene Dietrich and Emil Jannings. Lillian had seen it before, more than once, and it always bothered her, watching a man be reduced so pathetically by his love for a woman.

"Lillian, I have an idea," Alex whispered.

"That's comforting," she whispered back. "Go on."

"Well, it's not that we would hide this half brother-father-uncle thing, but we could keep the knowledge limited to those who know now, and not let it go beyond that. It might be easier on all of us."

They listened to Lola Lola sing, *Falling in love again, never wanted to, What am I to do? I can't help it,* to the rapt professor.

"What I'm saying," Alex continued, "is that we don't exactly have to deny this thing."

> Men cluster to me like moths
> around a flame,
> And if their wings burn I know
> I'm not to blame.

"We could," he stumbled on, "just suppress it a little by not announcing it to the world. So far, who knows about this? A couple of detectives, a neurosurgeon in Pennsylvania who's got no interest in me, our mother — and even *that* limited group doesn't know the whole extent of the . . ." — he paused, searching for the right word — ". . . connection."

On-screen comes the morning after and Professor Rath rises from Lola Lola's bed fully dressed and clutching a doll.

"Alex, I'm going to tell you the awful truth. Hiding is useless. The Oedipus complex is at the heart of our humanity. Its discovery was to psychology as quantum mechanics was to physics, as evolution was to biology. Of course, all these theories are still fundamentally elusive. But the point is this: Incestuous desire is at the root of all sex. The idea is so horrific that we make great efforts, often at the expense of sex, to forget that truth. The result is that people either stop having sex altogether in order not to have to deal with their unconscious desires — an incredibly common phenomenon — or they develop kinky practices and fetishes to replace the incest impulse and have a 'normal' sex life. Freud's great conclusion about sexuality was that a 'normal' sexual life is a disturbing sexual life. As psycho-philosopher Adam Phillips has said, 'Oedipus Rex is a tragic hero because he is the most ordinary man in the world.'"

The professor and Lola Lola are breakfasting in her boudoir. Birds are chirping as she pours him tea and the two seem to be enjoying domestic bliss.

Alex said, "That's a very interesting idea, Lillian. I'm just a little worried about our kid trying to explain all that on the playground or to his friends' parents when he goes on a playdate."

The professor returns to his solitary life and tries to forget Lola Lola, but she haunts his every waking and sleeping hour. Going against all of his better judgment, he begins to frequent The Blue Angel in order to woo her.

"It should, however, be noted," Lillian said, "that Freud and his most progressive followers — Otto Rank, Sándor Ferenczi, Carl Jung — each ended up sleeping with at least one of his patients, no doubt in the name of scientific inquiry. Sleeping with your patient is the next best thing to sleeping with your mother. Speaking of the devil, I assume you've been in touch with Agnes?"

Alex said, "She's coming to New York to meet with me at the end of October. She said there were a few details she felt she should clear up with all of us."

"So she knows about . . ." Lillian's finger made a circling motion that pointed at herself, her belly, and Alex.

He nodded. He looked more serene to Lillian than he had earlier, but it could have been the lighting. "She said she found this monumental coincidence of ours reassuring," he said. "She told me that living over in New Zealand she tended to lose a sense of just how small the world actually is."

As Lillian watched the professor's ultimate debasement, she tried to determine the connections among the three blue movies. Aside from the fact that David Lynch, in his movie (the bird, the nightclub singer, bondage), was doing a lot of quoting of von Sternberg's movie, basically all three films dealt with the same thing: women, sex, and violence from a male perspective (most especially *Blue Steel*, which was directed by a woman). The leading men were, respectively, a sadist, a madman, and a masochist — all driven to their death by their desire for a woman. Of the three leading women, Marlene Dietrich seemed to create the only character who realized that her role as a femme fatale was just as much a trap for her as it was for the professor. Once the power was given her, she used it, but in full knowledge that all power was of the Faustian brand.

When the movie ended and the lights came up, Lillian turned to Alex and said, "Veronica is going to have a hard time with the fact that you are the father of this child."

"There is another way to look at it," he said. "Her jealousy of you is what led her to me in the first place, so it can only be a good thing."

Lillian said nothing. His comment was so Veronica-like — taking something negative and spinning it as positive at the expense of all reason and intelligence. Brother or lover, he and Veronica deserved each other. As they walked out of the Thalia, a larger crowd piled in. The next film was *The Blues Brothers*.

At the back of the Hungarian Pastry Shop, Lillian took a long sip from her iced coffee as she lamented not having stayed on at the Thalia for the screening of *The Blues Brothers*. She had never seen it because it was billed as a musical but she was beginning to have second thoughts about the genre. The baby gave her a walloping kick. At times, especially when kicked in the bladder, Lillian considered punching him back. He was saved from Lillian's wrath by the sound of the approaching clip-clop of Veronica's platform sandals.

"Stunning, glowing, gorgeous as usual," Veronica said, sitting down across from Lillian. Veronica was looking very pretty herself, something Lillian didn't tend to notice in her sister one way or another.

Over the past few months, though, something about Veronica had changed. It was more of an aura than anything physical, as if some switch had been flipped and she was now projecting her beauty instead of discounting it.

"You know, Veronica, you never used to comment on my physical appearance before I became pregnant."

"Could it be that motherhood becomes you?" Veronica responded, her disingenuousness impressive.

"I'm not a mother yet," Lillian said curtly. "Telling me I look gorgeous in this advanced state of pregnancy is like telling an ugly girl she's got beautiful hair. You're trying to be positive and it's so obvious it's insulting." Lillian pushed the plate with the croissant on it away from both of them.

"You're impossible." Veronica sighed.

Lillian was thoroughly sick of being pregnant. She was now seeing Kate every two weeks and soon would be seeing her once a week. She was tempted to ask Kate just to induce at thirty-six weeks, when the baby would be technically cooked, but she knew Kate wouldn't do it. She was a by-the-books kind of gal.

"If men were having babies, the artificial womb would have been invented before the wheel," Lillian said. "Unfortunately, men don't have babies, so their greatest fear — besides castration, of course — is that their reproductive role will shrink from nano to null."

Veronica rolled her eyes, blew on her bangs.

Lillian went on. "Embryos have already been created in a petri dish by inserting bits of DNA into a woman's egg. No sperm needed."

"Well, then, Lillian," Veronica said, "you've got an interesting problem on your hands. You'd like to make males obsolete and yet you're adding one more to the earth's population."

"I never said I wanted to make men obsolete," Lillian objected. "I want to make their role in reproduction obsolete. As it stands now they do this one tiny little thing and then legally, morally, and socially have a far greater claim on the child than they deserve. The truth is that not long from now, for both men and women, reproduction will be a thing entirely of choice: biological womb, artificial womb, petri dish, sperm, DNA, cloning, father and mother, two mothers, two fathers, single mother, single father — any combination you fancy."

"Hear, hear," said the small, olive-skinned, possibly Hungarian waitress. She placed Veronica's Viennese coffee and a fuchsia butter-cream-and-marzipan cake on the table, and left.

Lillian winced. "I want to go see Charles," she said.

"So do I," Veronica chimed back, with an eagerness Lillian thought more befitting a suggestion to go on a shopping spree than to make a visit to their formerly-believed-to-be-dead-for-twenty-years-severely-brain-damaged father. Veronica pointed toward Lillian's midsection. "But maybe we should wait until after he is born."

"I don't understand," Lillian said. "Why wait?" She felt an odd fluttering of her heart, probably something related to pregnancy, or, equally possible, a physiological response to the terror she felt about seeing her father.

"I just think it might not be such a good idea to undergo so much stress in your condition. I mean, from what I understand, Charles is anything but normal," Veronica said, and sank her teeth into her bright pink cake.

"I'm pregnant, Veronica, not hysterical."

Veronica licked the neon frosting from her lips. "Lillian. I'm thinking of Junior."

"Junior is just fine. In fact, it's probably better for him to meet his grandfather in utero, where he's thoroughly protected."

"You can always talk your way out of or into anything, Lillian, but you rarely think of the consequences."

"I'm going to see Charles on Saturday. I would like it if you came with me," Lillian said. "Have you seen Alex lately?"

"All the time," Veronica answered, finishing off her cake. "We play Scrabble."

"Scrabble," Lillian said, raising an eyebrow. "Right."

XXXIII

Agnes was out shopping and Veronica was having her nap. Lillian and her father were playing Scrabble for the first time. It had been his idea and Lillian was pleased, flattered, nervous with joy. Scrabble was a game her parents usually played. For some time now, even though Lillian was only six years old, she had been able to read and write with ease. She had wanted to ask her father to play Scrabble with her but was afraid of being told that it was a grown-up game, so, when he suggested they play, Lillian was overwhelmed and hadn't been able to respond.

"Oh, Lillian, we can do something else," Charles had said. "I just thought since you're such a good reader that you might have fun. We could play Trouble or Parcheesi instead. You choose."

"I want to play Scrabble," Lillian said finally.

"Me, too," said Charles, smiling. "It's my favorite game."

They sat on opposite sides of the coffee table in the living room and played for an hour and a half. Charles, who smelled vaguely of smoke and lemons, didn't light up a cigarette the entire time. Lillian got thirty-three points with *zoo* on a triple-word square and twenty-four points for *love* on a double-word/triple-letter combination. Charles added *event* using the *v* in *love* and *zodiac* using the *z* in *zoo*, but he didn't get as many points as she did because he didn't hit any special squares. Charles made words Lillian didn't know the meaning of, such as *ignoble* and *limn*. He explained the meanings to her and they talked about the fact that some words could have several meanings, depending on the context. A word like *zoo*, he explained could mean a real zoo with animals or it could refer to Lillian's room, which resembled a place where animals lived.

"And love," Lillian asked, "can that have different meanings?"

"Probably has the most in the world," Charles said. "Love means something different to everyone every time they say it."

"Oh," Lillian said, unsure if she understood him.

"For example," Charles said, "every time I say 'I love you' to you, the love is an even bigger love because I just love you more and more with each minute."

Lillian blushed. "You do?" she asked. "Is that possible?"

"Sure it's possible."

"And do you love Veronica more too with each minute?"

"Uh-huh," he said, staring at his letters.

"And Mom?"

"Yup. Your turn," he said.

Lillian believed him, but she wondered about her own capacity for love. She wasn't at all certain if she was loving her mother more and more with each minute, and she was positive she wasn't loving Veronica more and more with each anything. Her love for Veronica actually seemed to be shrinking. She was going to ask her father about this, but she thought she had better take her turn first. Adding an *x* to the *a* in *zodiac* got her thirty-one points because the *x* was on a triple-letter square.

"Next time you go away, may I come with you?" Lillian asked. "I hate staying here with Veronica and Mom. Mom just yells all the time and Veronica is so obnoxious." She paused. It was a new word she'd learned from an older kid at school and she hadn't used it yet in front of an adult.

Charles laughed and moved a lock of her hair from in front of her eyes to behind her ear. "She can be a little obnoxious, can't she?" he said. "But remember, she's still little. She's not a big girl like you yet."

"But could I, Dad, could I come with you?" Lillian asked.

"That's a lovely idea, Lillian, and maybe someday I will take you with me. But you would be bored. I talk to boring people all day about boring things — we never do anything as fun as you and I are doing right now."

"We could take the Scrabble game with us," Lillian suggested. Out of the corner of her eye, she spied Veronica coming down the stairs dragging her blanket with her. Lillian ignored her, hoping that Veronica might disappear.

"Why, look who's here! It's Princess

Sleepy Head," Charles exclaimed. Lillian did not look. She kept her eyes on her letters.

Veronica giggled and started running toward Charles with her arms outstretched. Lillian wondered how they would manage to keep playing with Veronica around. She hoped her mother would come home and take Veronica away. But she was also worried, and not sure why, that her mother might get angry if she saw Lillian playing Scrabble with Charles. Veronica jumped into Charles's arms. Her foot knocked the Scrabble board onto the floor, sending the little wooden squares flying all over the room.

"Uh-oh," Charles said cheerfully to Veronica. "I guess our game is over. Lillian, make sure to pick up all the letters or your mom and I won't be able to play. That was a great game, honey."

As Lillian picked up the letters, he tickled Veronica and made her giggle uncontrollably. Lillian was fighting hard to keep herself from crying, but not because she was disappointed that the game was over. She was terribly disappointed, but more than that, she was deeply confused. Veronica couldn't even read or write. She could barely even say a whole sentence. It didn't make sense that her father was so much more interested in Veronica, yet evidently he was. Lillian just didn't understand what it was about Veronica that her father loved so very much. Charles lit up a cigarette while Veronica played with his shoelaces. Lillian put the game back where it belonged, on the shelf under the television, then went upstairs to her bedroom.

XXXIV

When the receptionist called Lillian to say that Bryan Byrd was on his way up to see her, the baby kicked. Lillian wondered if he was objecting or if she was once again mistaking a kick for a flutter of her heart. It didn't really matter, she thought. Undoubtedly her son was already far more attuned to her physiological responses to emotional situations than she ever would be herself. A wry smile spread across her lips at the thought of yet another unforeseen feature of motherhood. Of course, a kick was just a kick, no matter how coincidental the timing. There was a tap on her door.

"Come in," she said.

Her small office was decorated with hospital-issue furniture. Nothing, not even a calendar, was on the light gray walls. Late September midday sunlight flooded through a large, rectangular window. The light was almost too strong, and Lillian considered pulling down the shade, but she liked the way Bryan Byrd's eyes sparkled. He was wearing a milk-chocolate linen suit with a clotted-cream ascot and his usual burgundy wing tips. She wondered if his intention was to look edible. Even though he always wore a variation on the same suit, she was sure he had dressed for her. She, of course, had worn black — a black halter top with black rayon wide-leg lounging pajama bottoms, revealing a sliver of her protruding belly.

She had been more than a little surprised to find Bryan Byrd on her mind as she perused her monotonal closet that morning. If she dressed for anyone, it was calculated for a very specific purpose. She wanted something. She wanted a superior to grant a request, she wanted a client to do as she said, she wanted to intimidate a suitor, she wanted better seats at the theater, and so on. She was not at all sure what she wanted from Bryan Byrd — he had become twisted up in her life in so many peculiar ways — she only knew she wanted to look good for him. This unfamiliar impulse was worrisome. First, she had never considered that she might *not* look good. Second, she was "dressing up" for an oversize, overdressed private detective who regularly impersonated neuroscientists *and* lived with his mother. Like some primordial creature slithering in the muck, the baby moved again as Bryan and Lillian made hesitant gestures in an attempt to shake hands. Finally they did, both grips firm. There was a faint smell of lemons in the room.

"Sit down," she said, pointing to an armchair whose indoor/outdoor–style upholstery had long since worn thin. She sat across from him in its twin. Although there were many things she wanted to ask him — why he had quit his job, why he lived with his mother, how long he had been playing the tuba, why he hadn't slept with his secretary, why he always wore linen suits, if he was still obsessed with her — she waited for him to speak.

"I take it the girl is fine," he said.

"You mean Charlotte?" she asked.

"No, the girl in Sri Lanka."

"Nisha. Yes, she's fine. Thanks for your help, although in the end I found her entirely by chance."

"Sometimes chance needs a plan to trump," he said, his eyes still gleaming. "In any case, no need for thanks. You paid me."

"You said on the phone yesterday that you wanted to see me about Charlotte Taylor," Lillian said. It was refreshing to note that Bryan Byrd somehow resisted staring at her pregnant belly. These days, when she had a conversation with anyone, they were forever examining her perplexing shape, as if pregnancy were some very recent phenomenon.

"The insurance company I now work for has put me on the case. I'm here to follow up."

The sun became too sharp. Lillian went to the window and pulled down the venetian blind. It made a soft metallic rustle, like spoons in a dishwasher. She was relieved to learn that Bryan Byrd was still obsessed with her but was curious as to how far he would let his obsession lead him. Had he somehow identified the insurance companies Lillian had cases with, got himself hired by one of them, and then figured out a way to be put on one of her cases? Had he just gotten lucky with Charlotte, or had he actually figured out that she was Lillian's weak point and targeted her case? Or had all of this been sheer happenstance, like her getting into the rickshaw with the same driver five years after the accident? Bryan's scheme, she decided, was a hundred percent calculated. She left the slats partly open and the room was striped with shadow and light. She sat back down in her chair.

"So you and I are now colleagues of sorts," she said.

"Yes, but since you married the father of the patient you are examining for the company, they are not convinced you can remain impartial."

"Ah, I see," she said. The detective who always seemed to know everything still believed she was married to Ben. "The marriage has been annulled by the state of New York," she told him, in spite of herself. This information, she felt sure, would make no difference to an insurance company that already questioned her impartiality. She doubted, however, that they knew anything at all about her marriage to Ben. Bryan was just trying to determine the state of her affections, and she was, for some mysterious reason, obliging him. "A divorce actually would have been easier, but Ben wanted it that way. He told the judge I was pregnant with a child who wasn't his and that was the end of it."

Bryan Byrd nodded. His expression remained neutral — no hint of relief or joy or surprise at the news of Lillian's changed status — just as it had when she told him she had married Ben. Lillian couldn't decide if this meant he was indifferent, stoic, or very self-confident. The latter, she concluded. There were, after all, fringe benefits to living in perpetuity with your mother.

"Are you still seeing Charlotte?" he asked.

"Yes. She was here this morning. We're working on a project together about the neurobiology of imaginary friends."

Bryan's mouth ribboned into a smile, his halo of blond hair glowing in a fragment of sunlight. "While you were in Sri Lanka I went to a conference in Santa Fe. This time I posed as a neuro-nutritionist who studies the effects of turmeric on the hippocampus of normals and patients with Alzheimer's disease." He leaned forward, shadows playing across his face. "It turns out the curcuminoids found in turmeric not only prevent memory loss in those who ingest it regularly, but turmeric reduces the adverse effects on neuronal functioning in Alzheimer's patients who newly introduce it into their diet."

"Turmeric is the spice that turns curry yellow," Lillian stated, wondering if she would end up marrying Bryan Byrd to keep him from interfering with Charlotte. "I ate a lot of it in Sri Lanka."

"Yes, I imagined you would," Bryan said.

"So, was my honeymoon diet the impetus for your neuroscience conference disguise?"

"I went to hear a paper on GPCR receptors," he said, not responding to her question. "I understood almost nothing, but at one point the woman giving the paper made an aside, her tone changing so that it was clear that what she was about to say was not part of her paper, causing me to listen more closely. She said, 'There are millions of receptors in the brain for which, as yet, we know no use. They are just there waiting to be stimulated by something we haven't yet conceived of.' "

Lillian nodded, and felt a slither, a flutter. "Imaginary friends perhaps?"

Bryan was silent and Lillian was afraid he had taken her question seriously and was trying to formulate an answer. Finally he asked, "How do you justify your obsession with Charlotte?"

Lillian liked the question. It was a true

question, one that was impossible to answer, therefore the kind of question that was the most fun to try to answer. "The need to explain is a property of the brain," Lillian said, thinking that Veronica would appreciate the unintended rhyme. "I could give you any number of equally plausible explanations for my special interest in Charlotte's case. Think what happens after you electronically stimulate the laughter area of a patient's brain. He will giggle uncontrollably and then immediately feel a need to explain why he laughed. He will say that the doctor made a funny face or that a cloud he spied out the window had a particularly amusing shape. In patients whose left brains have been severed from their right, it is common for the verbal left half to spin endless stories to explain the right side's actions, as in the Dr. Strangelove syndrome, wherein a patient's own hand tries to kill him by strangulation. He will explain this violence by claiming that the hand is actually his mother-in-law's, or, in the case of a woman, an ex-boyfriend's, never her own. And then there is the Stockholm syndrome, where the kidnapped or tortured comes to love his oppressor and fully believes the perpetrator is acting in the victim's best interest because that is the only tolerable explanation for what has befallen him. All this to say that we really know very little about ourselves, our motives, our world, but we use our prodigious imaginations to convince ourselves that we do know something. The human brain has evolved to be particularly prone to self-deception." An ambulance siren out on the street peaked and then fizzled.

"Your explanation is exquisite," Bryan said. "Would you mind if I offered another?"

"Go ahead."

"There is something entirely taboo about your love for Charlotte and therefore compelling to the point of obsession. It is the basis of all true love."

"Malarkey." Lillian laughed. "Obsession gets old fast, especially to the obsessee. On the other hand, there is nothing static about love. Love by definition is in a state of constant evolution. My relationship with Charlotte is evolving." Lillian knew she was getting into trouble. Not only was she allowing this man to seduce her, she was uncontrollably seducing the already utterly seduced.

"So you are still convinced of your diagnosis that Charlotte's accident has contributed to her neurological disorder even though she had a prior condition?" Bryan said, in an almost staged official tone, as if her office were bugged by the insurance company and his superiors were listening.

Lillian responded in kind. "Mr. Byrd, the girl suffered a head trauma and lost her mother due to some faulty tires the manufacturer knew about for years. Prior condition is irrelevant."

"You're biased. You should be removed from the case."

"Without bias the whole world would be phenomenally dull, not to mention nonexistent."

He stood up. "Will you have dinner with me?"

She stood up. "Yes, but only if you first take me home to meet your mother." Lillian enjoyed watching Bryan blush. She pointed to her midsection. "We could even pretend this is yours."

Bryan shook his head as he walked out of her office. He stopped at the door and said, "Nothing in my fantasy will ever compare to you."

XXXV

The Acme Neurological Institute was a set of low rectangular brick buildings extending over its grounds like a game of dominoes. In the parking lot, Lillian and Veronica sat silently in Veronica's sun yellow VW bug she'd bought used in college in an effort to get out of the city and in touch with nature but had driven mainly between the Upper West Side and Tribeca. Although the day was hot for late September, neither of them had made a move toward getting out of the small car, since Veronica had turned the ignition off some ten minutes earlier.

"I think I'm in love," Lillian said finally.

"Bryan Byrd," Veronica responded, still staring straight ahead.

"Since when did I become so transparent?" Lillian asked, shifting in her seat and thinking that with her breadth she was anything but diaphanous.

"He's in love with you, too. He practically told me that time he came over to my apartment," Veronica said.

Lillian looked over at her sister. She had pinned back her short dark hair with little butterfly barrettes. Lillian was about to lecture Veronica on how wearing those trendy, infantalizing accessories contributed to the insidious sociocultural oppression of women. But instead she asked, "Why didn't you tell me?"

"It took me a while to catch on," she said, pulling the barrettes out of her hair and tossing them into the ashtray. "I mean, it's not exactly an obvious match."

"Did it ever occur to you," Lillian asked, "that you and I might have different fathers? I mean, we look nothing alike."

"Jesus, Lillian, as if we didn't have enough to worry about. I'm not even entertaining that thought." Veronica opened her car door. "C'mon. Let's do this. What's the name of the doctor again?"

Lillian opened her door and maneuvered herself out of the car. "Dr. Brad Fitzgerald."

"Sounds like someone I made up for *Ordinary Matters*," Veronica said, slamming her door shut. "I think I'm going to quit writing for them."

They walked up a concrete path that curved back and forth like a wave for no apparent reason.

"About time," Lillian said.

Veronica pursed her lips and blew upward at her bangs.

"But why now?" Lillian asked, opening the front doors of the main building. No response from Veronica, just another blow upward. Lillian was obviously doing something wrong in Veronica's estimation — insensitive, not supportive enough, dismissive. Lillian decided not to pursue it.

Inside the building, Lillian was surprised by the smell of cinnamon. She was expecting the usual aroma of death and disinfectants. Lillian despised institutions in general but especially those dedicated to the mind. When she had even an inkling that one of her clients might eventually be headed for one, making it necessary for her to sign the order, she would prematurely terminate treatment and recommend another doctor. The problematic ethics of this had been pointed out to her by a number of colleagues, but her feeling was simply that she had to do what she had to do. She wasn't against institutions on any kind of moral grounds. Some of the best work, the greatest healing, had occurred in institutions, and without them many people would not have a hope. But that was not her issue. Lillian's darkest fear was that she would end up in one. She therefore thought it unconscionable for her to send another person into her nightmare.

Now that she knew that her father had been put away by her mother for twenty-five years, the origin of her fear seemed clear. She realized that she must have known about it all along. What she had not determined was whether she knew consciously and then repressed it or whether the knowledge had always been relegated to the realm of the unconscious. This was something she could spend years trying to decide, but Lillian was much more interested in what she was presently experiencing — something she had dubbed the Lazarus effect.

Both she and Veronica, upon learning that their father was still alive after believing that for a quarter of a century he was dead, had absorbed the information with singular aplomb. Neither had been inordinately shocked by the information, nor had they refused to believe its truth. They had rather easily accepted the fact that people can indeed return from the dead. On the other hand, they'd dealt with a number of unusual revelations recently, so one more simply had to be taken in stride.

"So," Lillian said, unnerved in spite of her rationale, "at least you know now that you didn't kill him."

"That's funny," Veronica said. "Bryan

Byrd told me almost exactly the same thing. His version, however, was slightly more delicately phrased."

Behind the reception desk sat an older woman with purplish hair, peeling and slicing apples.

A patient, Lillian thought. "Hello," she said.

"Oh, I didn't see you girls come in," the woman said, putting down her knife and wiping her hands on her red apron. "I'm so distracted. You see, today is Apple Pie Day." A slowness in the muscle movements on one side of her face indicated a stroke. "You must be Charlie's daughters. Brad said you would be coming today. Charlie will be so excited. I'll page Brad." On her right was an electronic panel containing a series of large lighted buttons with initials on them. She pressed the one that read BF. She then looked up and, with surprise on her face, said, "Oh, I didn't see you girls come in. May I help you?"

Lillian said, "We have an appointment with Dr. Brad Fitzgerald at noon."

"Oh," she said, smiling sweetly, her purple-gray curls catching the light from the window and for a moment looking almost stylish. "You must be Charlie's girls. He'll be so excited to see you. Brad told me you were coming. I'll just page him. Did you know today is Apple Pie Day?"

As she once again pressed the big white initialed button, Lillian said, "We'll just have a seat over here." She and Veronica sat down in the waiting area opposite the desk.

Veronica looked at Lillian and whispered, "Is this usual?"

"Brad Fitzgerald trained in France."

"Oh, I see," Veronica said.

"The theory is that the doctors, nurses, workers, and aides are just as neurologically unique as the patients," Lillian said. "So almost no distinction between roles is made. Art, cooking, music, theater — performance of any kind — constitutes the major form of therapy and everyone is required to participate in some way. Meds are kept to a minimum, as are visits from family members. The method hasn't really taken off in this country."

Down the hallway a door opened, and out walked an attractive man with shoulder-length dark hair and a short black beard. He wore a white T-shirt, khakis, and loafers.

Parlez-vous français? thought Lillian.

"He's gorgeous," whispered Veronica.

He glanced at Lillian and Veronica, then

headed for the reception desk. "Mary," he said, "you paged me?" He had a thick Jersey accent. New Jersey.

"I did?" she asked, smiling up at him. He nodded toward Lillian and Veronica, and Mary's gaze followed his.

"Well, when did they straggle in?" she said, in something of a stage whisper. "You would think they would have at least let me know that they were here." Then she raised her voice and said to Lillian and Veronica, who were now standing, "May I help you girls?"

"Yes," said Lillian. "We're here to see Dr. Fitzgerald."

"Well, you're in luck because he happens to be standing right in front of you," Mary said, with mock impatience. Then she turned to Brad and said, "I think they must be Charlie's girls."

"Let's ask them," Brad said to her. "Are you two . . ." and then he shouted, "bitches, witches, snitches . . . Charles Moore's daughters?"

Veronica took a step backward.

"Yes, we are," said Lillian, unperturbed. "You contacted us about coming to see him."

"I did, indeed," he said, flicking the fingers of one hand rapidly into the palm of the other. "I'm so glad you could come. Your father's a loony tune, loony moon, man on the moon, prune. I had a hard time tracking you down. Why don't you come into my office and I'll try to explain how matters stand, bland, I'm a bland hand in the sand."

He gestured for them to follow him. Mary had returned to her chair and to her apple peeling. Veronica looked at Lillian in horror.

"It's okay," Lillian explained. "He has Tourette's." She turned to Brad and said, "You might have given us a little warning."

"I'm sure you're right," he said. "I've never known what to do. Each time is different, but in your case I thought it would put me at an unfair advantage since I bet you're good in bed, good head, good thread, good dead, since you told me nothing of your syndromes. Bun in the oven, coven of sin, let me in." He turned toward Veronica and put out his hand, "Please come this way."

To Lillian's astonishment, Veronica took Brad's hand. The three of them headed down the corridor and off through a maze of passageways and doors until they came to Brad's office. Along the way — in bedrooms, common rooms, out in the garden, in a dining room — they observed many people, presumably patients and caregivers, although which was which was impossible to tell. Some of the people waved or smiled as they passed, some scowled, one spit, and another shot them the finger. Brad never let go of Veronica's hand. Every so often, with his left hand he would pat the back of her hand in a quick fluttering motion, then pat his own, all this accompanied by a slew of semicoherent mutterings.

Brad Fitzgerald's office was a large open room with windows across two walls looking out onto an expansive garden with trees and benches and swings and fountains and sculptures. There were several people in the garden, some in groups, some wandering alone. The only piece of furniture in the room was an old oak desk, and on the desk were no paper or pencils, not even a paper clip, just a pink portable Mac computer.

"Is this place state funded?" Lillian asked. Brad closed the door and let go of Veronica's hand.

Brad laughed. "Entirely private. The United States Department of Health keeps trying to shut us down, but they know that if they do most of these patients will be on their hands, so they let us slide."

"And who pays for my father?"

"Your mother."

"Does she know you got in touch with us?"

"Yes, no, maybe so," he yelled. "Slut, smut, gut."

"Why did you go to all the trouble of finding us?" Lillian asked.

"I am sorry for any pain it has caused you. Father, bother, brother, blather. When Mr. Saturday told me you had no idea your father was alive, lie, spy, cry, that your mother had convinced the hospital mortician to sign a death certificate and had staged a false funeral at the hospital chapel, I had no idea what to do, blue, sue, Loup Garou. Your mother must be a real doozy, floozy, bamboozy. Actually, to tell you the truth, in searching for you I was going against my entire ethics system, which is the same as Starfleet's. I generally follow the Prime Directive — you know, leave well enough alone. But then I realized, Jean-Luc Picard never followed the Prime Directive either, so, voilà, you're here, never fear, dear, have a beer. In fact, I was very disappointed that Mr. Saturday didn't find you sooner, as in our last theater production your father played King Lear and he was rather magnificent.

Please have a seat."

Even Lillian, who knew it took incredible financial incentive for the Board of Health to act, couldn't believe the institute was allowed to operate with a director this out there. She was very impressed by what Brad Fitzgerald was apparently pulling off at the Acme Neurological Institute. In the director's office, there was nowhere to sit — no chair, no couch, no oversize bean bag, nothing. Veronica sat on the floor Indian-style. Lillian and Brad Fitzgerald remained standing. He looked down at Veronica, pointed to his mouth, and said, "I promise this will settle down once I get a little less nervous."

Veronica nodded her head and said in a soft voice, "No problem. Please don't worry on my account." Lillian marveled at Veronica's ability to be polite even when she was totally freaking out.

"As you know from seeing your father's dossier," Brad said to Lillian, "he's suffered massive damage to the left occipito-parietal region of the brain with severe lesions to the Brodmann's area forty-four within his Broca's area. Would you like me to describe what I think it's like to be him?"

Lillian said, "No."

Veronica said, "Yes."

"Alright then," he said, sitting down across from Veronica, his legs also crossed. "In his relationship to the visual world, he sees objects as if they are under water. Nothing in the world has any clear definition for him. Things appear, disappear, melt. The world he lives in could have been created by Salvador Dalí."

Lillian leaned against the window. Sitting on the floor was out of the question, and probably would have been even if she weren't pregnant. The thought of trying to stand back up after their little powwow obliterated even the remote possibility of being one of the tribe.

"In addition," Brad continued, "he has very little sense of the right side of his body. It is quite usual for him to mistake his arm for his leg, to think his right foot is not his own, to believe his head is where his testicles are."

Lillian noticed that Dr. Brad Fitzgerald's verbal outbursts had ceased during his account of their father's state of health.

"His memory is fully compromised and he has no command of a coherent thought process. He has trouble determining the importance of details and the integration of details. In other words, if he sees an apple, the fact that it is red, round, and edible are all separate attributes that hold equal weight in significance. If he were staring at the apple and were hungry, he would in all likelihood not connect the fact that the apple is edible to his state of being hungry. From all the possibilities available for what an apple is, it is impossible for him to choose, so they all remain probable." Brad paused. Lillian smelled baking piecrust. "When he sees you, if with great effort he does arrive at the understanding that you are his grown daughters, it will mean nothing to him. And within minutes, even seconds, he will forget who you are."

Veronica looked up at Lillian and gasped. Lillian turned to her left to see a man with his face pressed hard up against the window, squashing his features, including his tongue, into a grotesque, gelatinous mask. With both hands, he had flattened against the glass a mass of pie dough. Brad jumped up, went to the window, knocked gently on the glass, and the man walked away.

"He's the afternoon outdoor supervisor," Brad explained, sitting back down. "He was just letting me know they've started cooking the pies. In some ways, the most difficult thing of all for your father," he continued, as if there had been no interruption, "yet also the most amazing, is that because his frontal lobes are intact he is fully aware of his situation and yet determined to improve it despite years and years of minimal results. He is very much like Zazetsky." He glanced toward Lillian, who appreciated the reference. Zazetsky was a patient of A. R. Luria, the Russian psychologist who founded neuropsychology and whose accomplishment was one of the reasons Lillian had decided to go into the field. "And finally," Brad continued, his hands still, his speech clear, "although the damage to his cerebral cortex has made it impossible for him simultaneously to synthesize separate parts into a complete whole and he is riddled with all sorts of aphasias, it seems that his rote memory for language, apparently located in the Wernicke's area on the right side of the brain, has not been affected. He therefore often speaks in nursery rhymes or song lyrics."

Brad unpretzled his legs and rose to his feet, followed by Veronica. "Shall we?" he said.

Veronica eagerly followed Brad through the door. Lillian was stunned by her sister's composure. Lillian felt faint. She wanted to believe it was because she was hot and eight months pregnant, but she knew otherwise. There was no way she would ever admit to Veronica that perhaps this visit had been a mistake, that they shouldn't have come. She wanted to abort the mission, put it off until never. She hadn't seen her father in twenty-five years, *why not let brain-damaged fathers lie?*

Lillian and Veronica's father was sitting at a desk in his small, well-lit room, hunched over a piece of paper, writing. A stack of clean white paper was on his left, a much higher stack of paper covered in the ripples of a small, tight script was on his right. They had last seen their father when he was thirty-five years old. He was now sixty.

"Charlie," Brad said, "your daughters are here." He clicked his fingers several times fast.

"Pussy said to the Owl, 'You elegant fowl! How charmingly sweet you sing!' " their father said, standing up and turning around. His chestnut hair was now mostly gray. Always a very thin man, he was a bit thinner. The brilliance of his blue eyes had dulled some. But he was, on the exterior, very much the same man Lillian had idolized, loathed, adored, rejected, worshipped, and feared as a child.

"Your father and I," Brad said, "have a deficit or two in common."

Veronica said, "Dad" and took a step toward him.

He turned away from her and sat back at his desk. He picked up his pen and began to write.

"Charlie," Brad said, "let's go outside and take a walk."

"Jack and Jill went up the hill," he answered, standing up again. He walked out the door, leaving the three of them alone in his room.

"What's that?" Lillian asked, pointing to the stack of paper on the left.

"He has been writing it since he first came here. When the stack reaches a certain height he throws the whole thing out."

"Have you ever read any of it?"

"Yes."

"And?"

"Well, hell's bells, this smells, it's what made me decide to try to find you."

"What do you mean?" Lillian asked.

"Most of it is words strung together meaninglessly, or at least, they are meaningless to me. But there are sections now and again, sections that seem to be written when he has stopped trying to write, fight,

388

blight, shite, that are coherent and contain memories from before he came here — from his childhood, and from your childhood. Wrong, song, ding-dong. It's how I knew he had two daughters named Veronica and Lillian. Your mother had insisted there were no children. And his paperwork indicated that she was telling the truth. It is also very common for people with attributes such as your father to invent whole families and to speak or write about them as if they were real. But I had a suspicion, an intuition, a premonition, a superstition, and I guess I just had to know the truth."

Brad headed out the door. Veronica and Lillian followed. They went out another door into the garden they had seen from Brad's office window. They found Charles standing in front of a woman who was sitting on a bench. She had on a pink blouse. With one hand she was unbuttoning the blouse and with the other she was buttoning it back up. Their father was reciting "Hickory Dickory Dock."

"Alien hands sign," Lillian told Veronica, "a neurological disorder, usually the result of a stroke, in which one hand does not trust the other and chronically undoes whatever the other does."

Brad gently took Charles's arm and they walked over to where a number of curly wrought-iron chairs were scattered around a small fountain. Each of them took a seat and watched the water cascade from the mouth of a large marble fish.

"I got that thing at an estate sale for twenty bucks. I think it's actually from Italy," Brad said.

They sat in the shade of a large tulip poplar. The air smelled slightly moldy but not unpleasant. "Charles," Lillian said. He was still staring at the water and made no indication that he knew he was being spoken to. "We were told you were dead. I am glad you are not. I would like to know you again."

He made no indication of having understood what she was saying or that she was speaking to him. Veronica got up, went over to where he was sitting and took his hand.

"Dad," she said, crying. "I'm so sorry."

"Fee, fi, fo, fum," he said, "I smell the blood of an Englishman."

Lillian leaned back in her chair and let her mind drift into a daymare while the baby did an acrobatic routine. She would run the institution with Brad, Veronica would write and direct the theater pieces, and they would never leave this place.

Charles looked at Lillian and said, "Rock-a-bye baby on the treetop, when the wind blows the cradle will rock."

"Well," Brad said, "I think that's plenty for today."

They had been with their father for less than ten minutes. Lillian was relieved, grateful.

"That's it?" Veronica said. "Twenty-five years and that's it?"

"The corn is as high as an elephant's eye," Charles said.

"And that was probably too much for everyone, but I have trouble with limits," Brad said. "Do you remember how to get out of here?"

They stood up to go, said good-bye to their father and then to Brad.

"Come back soon," he said. "Buffoon, balloon, prune. I would very much like to see you again. Maybe next month. We'll be needing help with our new production. We're putting on *Phèdre*."

Lillian and Veronica glanced at each other, and it was clear that participating in Brad Fitzgerald's production of *Phèdre* was just about the last thing in the universe either of them wanted to do. "Sure," they answered in unison.

They walked away, leaving Brad and their father seated in front of the fountain. Lillian turned back. "Why, exactly, did you want to find us?"

Brad shrugged. "I already told you. I wanted to know if the girls I was reading about in Charlie's manuscript really existed, and if they did, to meet them, eat them, beat them, sleep with them. It has been one of the most fantastic, spastic, scariest, wariest, projects of my life — and as you probably can't imagine, I've had quite a number of strange ones. But I'd never hired a detective before to find characters in a book written by a madman." He put his hand on their father's arm and tapped. "Much better than drugs. I'd recommend it. And, though not my principal motivation, I think Charlie here got a kick out of seeing his girls, pearls, swirling churls."

Making their way through the domino-game structure back toward the woman with the purple hair, the parking lot, the car, they passed their father's room. They hesitated, staring at each other. Lillian knew what Veronica wanted, because Lillian wanted it too: the manuscript. What if he threw it out before they returned in the following month? How many years did it take him to write so many pages? How long would they have to wait for him to write another? What if he didn't?

Veronica pushed the door open. "We'll just take half," she whispered. "He might not notice."

Lillian took Veronica's hand and gently pulled her away from the room. When they arrived back at the car, a freshly baked top-crusted apple pie was waiting for them on the front seat.

Nine

XXXVI

It was one of those crisp, bright mid-October days that could make Veronica feel as if anything were possible. Despite the falling leaves and the promise of decay, autumn always seemed to contain the hope of something new. A remnant from her school days, she supposed. Also, she thought, as she looked at a very pregnant Lillian sitting across from her at the back of the Hungarian Pastry Shop, this year there truly was something very new that would arrive and forever change their lives. Just above Lillian's head was a photograph of a man dressed as a blond Barbie doll wearing black leather pants, a jacket, and a cap, straddling a huge silver-and-black motorcycle. The model almost could have been Lillian dressed up as a man in drag. Veronica considered pointing out the resemblance to her sister but thought better of it.

For the past month, Veronica had been wanting to ask Lillian if she could be present during the birth of Lillian's baby. She was afraid that Lillian would object, refuse, insist on doing it alone. Veronica wanted to be there, and she was prepared to persevere. She said, "Lillian, I want to be with you when the zygote emerges."

The gypsy waitress brought Lillian a cup of black coffee.

"Fine," Lillian said, "you can be there, but just you. No Alex, no Agnes — until I feel like seeing them. This is not performance art."

"Oh, Lillian," Veronica practically sang, "really? You'll let me be with you? What a gift! I already feel so attached to that little guy. I want him to know I'm there for him right from the very beginning. I want . . ."

Lillian put up a hand. "Silence. Why is it that whenever I'm with you I feel as if I'm trapped on the set of *The Umbrellas of Cherbourg*? I reserve the right to change my mind. Besides, I think you should know I'm only agreeing to this because I can't wait to see your face when you witness the gruesome reality of the decidedly unmiraculous experience of birth. Men always marvel at women's ability to resist sex, but what woman in her right mind would ever have sex again after that experience? Not very long ago, complications in childbirth were the primary cause of death for women. And still today, six hundred thousand women die in childbirth each year, which means that every minute, somewhere in the world, a woman is dying while having a baby. This truth must have a deep and lasting effect on the evolution of the female brain, yet somehow it seems to be overlooked by all."

"You yourself have told me that forgetting is a necessary and important function of the brain," Veronica said, realizing that her sister's "gift" would not come without a price to pay.

"True, but remember: Forgetting is an art," Lillian said. "If you don't do it well, memories find a way to disturb, torture, and tease you, and very inconveniently." She reached out and took Veronica's hand, as she had in St. Columba's Chapel at St. John the Divine, and placed it flat against her belly. "Doesn't he feel like some sort of reptile?"

Veronica felt the softest little taps on the palm of her hand and she thought of the toads she used to catch in the window wells outside her elementary school. She would carry a toad home cupped in her hands and it would leap around thumping lightly against her skin. At home, she put it into a jar, and no matter where she hid it Lillian would find it and let it go. She always thought that Lillian was being cruel, wanting to hurt her, but over the years she had come to entertain the possibility that Lillian might also have been worried about the toad.

The waitress came back with Veronica's Viennese coffee and a plate of fluorescent yellow, pink, and blue petits fours.

"I called Brad Fitzgerald yesterday," Lillian said, removing Veronica's hand from her body, "to ask if he could save the manuscript for us next time Charles throws it out. After a few expletives, he told me he had saved all of Charles's manuscripts, fishing them out of the trash after Charles discarded them, and had even marked the coherent pages in case we were interested in reading them. He said if we liked he would send them to us, or we could get them the next time we visit."

Veronica sighed and ate the whipped cream off the top of her coffee with a spoon. "It's kind of creepy. I'm not sure I want to read what he wrote."

"But you nearly stole his manuscript."

"Why did you stop me? It's not like you to be so moral."

"Morality had little to do with it. I just wanted to get out of there."

Veronica could understand that. She had wondered many times since their trip to the Acme Neurological Institute how she was ever going to bring herself to go back. She nibbled on a blue petit four. "And Bryan Byrd? Are you still in love with him, or has that passed?"

"He's investigating me. He's gotten himself hired by the company that insures Charlotte, and they're questioning my impartiality, because I married her father."

"That's outrageous," Veronica said, feigning outrage.

"He's obsessed with me."

"Really?" This, too, was something new, Veronica thought, seeing Lillian so confused about a man.

"I'm supposed to meet his mother and then have dinner with him, but I'm dreading it," she said, twisting her long blond hair into a knot at the back of her head.

"Why?"

"What kind of man lives with his mother at forty-two?"

Veronica answered, "Your kind."

"And I'm about to have my half brother's baby." Lillian went on, "Something has got to be wrong with him if he's into that. Besides, he was our private detective. Isn't there something fundamentally wrong about falling in love with your private detective?"

"Wasn't it you who married the father of a patient?" Veronica laughed. "Wasn't it you who suggested I just go on sleeping with Alex? And now you're questioning the ethics of dating your private detective?"

"I don't know," Lillian said, a little dreamily. "Somehow it just seems too . . ."

"Intimate?" Veronica finished her sentence. "You know, I was thinking about Charlotte the other day and when she just stopped talking, about the car accident with her mother, and it reminded me of . . ."

"You," Lillian cut her off and finished her thought. "It had occurred to me. And as for intimacy, you must know by now that I think it is entirely overrated."

"Of course," Veronica said, knowing that it was time to change the subject.

The Hungarian waitress, who today was wearing a purple bandanna over her hair instead of the usual red, passed by their table carrying a huge piece of chocolate cake. Veronica motioned to her, and said, "I've been meaning to ask you for quite some time, are you by any chance Hungarian?"

"Iranian and Portuguese. I don't think any Hungarians work here. The owners are Greek. But the pastries are definitely made from Hungarian recipes," she said encouragingly. Then, calling out "Rocco," she headed toward another table, where a young man, several days unshaven, wearing a black-leather jacket and dark glasses, had raised his hand.

"I was thinking of that name for the baby," Lillian said.

They both looked over at Rocco, who was reading a manuscript through the dark glasses in the poorly lighted room. Veronica tried to imagine him as Lillian's grown son.

Veronica turned back to her sister. "Lillian, how scared are you?"

"Rationally, I am not worried about this birth. I mean, after all, this is New York, not Bangladesh. But now and again I find myself crazy with fear when thinking about giving birth to this child, being responsible for his life. And I can feel a compulsion to get into the deal-making. I die, he lives. He dies, I live. I haven't signed off yet on which deal I'll make. Of course," Lillian added, her lips curving into a sardonic smile, "you're taking a big risk by being with me during the birth. Who's to say that when push literally comes to shove, and I start making deals in the delivery room, I won't say, 'He and I live, she dies'?"

"In other words, you're scared shitless," Veronica said. "And that's why I want to be there, because so am I, but a little less so when I'm with you."

"As long as you know what you're getting into," Lillian said, then picked up a pink petit four and popped it into her mouth.

XXXVII

Veronica was in the hospital for two weeks after the accident. She was at home in bed for another two weeks. Finally, one day, her mother said, "Okay, little lady, enough convalescing. Off you go to school." During her convalescence, Veronica hadn't spoken much. Her mother was working double shifts at the hospital, the Polish woman who looked after Veronica spoke no English, and Lillian was consistently in no mood to talk. Veronica didn't realize just how out of practice with speaking she had become until she got back to school and everyone from the principal to the librarian to kids who weren't even in her third-grade class wanted to talk to her and ask her questions. They all looked at her with real concern and interest, and asked "How are you?" In trying to respond, she discovered that she had no idea how she actually was, so she felt it was better not to say anything. She was, however, enjoying all their attention, until she realized that it was her father's death that had made her famous. At least, she told herself, it had been a terrible mistake, an accident. She hadn't meant for him to die.

She got through her first day without saying a word. Everyone was understanding. "Don't worry, we understand," they said, nodding sympathetically. On the second and third days, the teachers and even the children, who were all fully informed about what had happened in Veronica's family, let her nontalking slide. But by the end of the week, the fact that she hadn't said a word was becoming a subject of concern among the adults, and of curiosity among the children. Meanwhile, at home, Veronica continued not to speak, and no one seemed to notice.

During her second week back at school, concern and curiosity about her antiverbal behavior evolved into frustration and anger. Her teacher threw up her hands and said, "We can't help you if you won't let us *in,* Veronica," and the children teased her and called her "Veronica Keller" and "Dumbo." Veronica had no clear idea why she wasn't talking. It upset her to see how her not speaking upset other people, but she couldn't help herself. It simply felt right to her that she should be silent.

Then one day Veronica was excused from class and sent to the principal's office. In the waiting area, she saw her mother, wearing her nurse's uniform, her auburn hair pulled back in a bun, her dark lipstick fresh. Also in the waiting area, sitting on one of the large wooden chairs, was the school social worker, Mrs. Livingston, who had made many efforts to help Veronica by telling her repeatedly how normal it was for her to be sad about "the events." "There is no right way to express grief," she told her. "This is your way. Don't worry. You are perfectly normal." Veronica didn't think there was anything normal about killing your father, and she wasn't actually feeling very sad about his death, because she was too worried about Lillian hating her for killing him. Mrs. Livingston had even come over to their house a couple of times to see Veronica and talk to her mother. Veronica sensed that her mother didn't like Mrs. Livingston, but she wasn't sure why. She thought it might be because Mrs. Livingston had bad breath. How could a social worker have bad breath? she wondered. Mrs. Livingston was also very skinny and birdlike, but this bothered Veronica less.

Veronica sat down in a chair opposite her mother, her feet dangling, reminding her that it was very unlikely that she would ever be tall like Lillian. She had long since given up wishing for her hair to change from black to blond, but she still harbored the hope that she might "shoot up" in height. Her mother smiled at her but said nothing.

After a few minutes, the principal, Mr. Allen, a white-haired man with wire-rimmed glasses, opened his office door and said, "Ladies, please come in."

Veronica and Mrs. Livingston jumped to their feet. Agnes looked the principal over, then with an almost bored expression on her face rose slowly from her chair. They went into Mr. Allen's office, and after a

404

few minutes of dragging chairs around, they all sat down, Mr. Allen behind his desk, the three visitors in front of it.

Mr. Allen took off his glasses and said, "Please accept my condolences, Mrs. Moore, on your recent tragedy."

"Why, exactly, am I here, Mr. Allen?" she responded, in no way acknowledging his sympathy.

Mr. Allen cleared his throat, put his glasses back on, and stared at the papers on his desk. "As you must be aware," he said finally, "Veronica, it seems, has lost her tongue."

Veronica pushed her tongue around inside her mouth, thinking that not only was the expression inaccurate but disgusting. She imagined searching for her lost tongue throughout the territories of her life — her bedroom, the school, the playground. And what if someone else found it before she did? What might they do with it? Veronica looked at her mother, whose own tongue was gliding delicately along her upper lip. Veronica was worried that she might mess up her lipstick. Mrs. Livingston, on the other hand, had her jaw tightly clenched.

"Mr. Allen," Agnes said, lipstick intact, "I am on my lunch break and need to get back to the hospital. If you could just let me know quickly what it is I can do for you."

"Very well then, let me get straight to the point. Veronica has not spoken a word since she returned to school. Mrs. Livingston has consulted Veronica's pediatrician and it seems that there is no medical reason for her silence." Mr. Allen was looking directly at Veronica as he spoke, although he was speaking as if she weren't in the room. "Her unwillingness to talk makes our job difficult, even impossible. I have called you here, Mrs. Moore, to see if you can shed some light on Veronica's refusal to reintegrate into normal life at our school."

Agnes stood up. "I am afraid I can be of no help. Whatever Veronica is up to I'm sure is not only necessary but constructive. In fact, I believe she deserves enormous credit for all she has accomplished recently." She winked at Veronica. "Now, if you don't mind, I need to get back to work."

"I take it, then, that you are abdicating your responsibility in this matter?" Mr. Allen said.

"Do what you like, Mr. Allen," her mother said. "Unlike my older daughter, Veronica is an exceedingly accommodating child. By nature, she does not refuse to do anything. Personally, I find her decision not to verbalize right now comforting. By doing so, she is probably saving all of us a whole lot of trouble. But if you want to worry yourself over it, be my guest. I'm sure Veronica won't mind." Dark eyes angry and proud, Agnes glanced again at Veronica, then walked out of the room. Veronica was pleased by what her mother had told the principal, but she wished she hadn't left her alone in the room with him and Mrs. Livingston. She wanted to jump up and follow her mother out, but she somehow knew that didn't fall under the definition of "accommodating."

"Well, Veronica," Mr. Allen said, "do you have anything to say to that, or for yourself?"

Veronica looked down at her hands.

"Return to class, and Mrs. Livingston and I will decide what to do about you," he said, waving her out.

When Veronica arrived at school the next day, she was sent directly to the library by her teacher. "Until you decide to talk," said her teacher, "you will spend your school days in the library reading." The librarian assigned her to read biographies of women who had overcome great odds and become famous. She began with

Helen Keller, then moved on to Florence Nightingale, Marie Curie, Jenny Lind, and Annie Oakley. About a week later, halfway through a biography of Pocahontas, the librarian told her that she was to go back to Mr. Allen's office. When she arrived, Lillian was sitting upright in a chair in the waiting area, her feet firmly planted on the floor.

Mr. Allen swiftly ushered them into his office. "Due to an inadvertent suggestion of your mother's, we've decided to try a novel approach to your hysterical ailment," he said to Veronica. "Until you find your words again, Lillian will be required to spend afternoons with you either in the library or, weather permitting, outside on the playground. You both will be excused from class, but you will have to keep up with all homework." Mr. Allen glared at Veronica. "You wouldn't by chance have anything to *say* about this arrangement, would you?"

Veronica looked at Lillian, who was staring at Mr. Allen.

"Well, then, off you go," he said.

For the next week, every afternoon after lunch, Lillian would fetch Veronica from her classroom (much to her teacher's dismay, Veronica was returned to her third-grade room for the morning hours). They would go outside to the swing sets, even if it was still quite cold in early April, and swing or not swing for the two hours remaining in the school day, saying nothing at all to each other, not a word. At first, Veronica was scared that Lillian was mad at her. But on the second day Lillian said, "Veronica, you can do whatever you like as far as I'm concerned. You can talk or not talk, cry or not cry, swing or not swing, I really don't care. And if you're worried about me being mad at you for any reason, I'm not. Besides, even though I have to be with you, being here is far better than having to go to that stupid school." Veronica relaxed, and they were silent together for several more afternoons. Every so often, the principal would call Veronica to his office and ask her questions to which she would invariably respond by looking down at her hands. One morning he called her in and asked her how she was doing, and she looked up at him and said, "Much better, sir."

"Would you like to return to class now?" he asked, peering over his glasses.

"Yes, sir."

"And you will answer when spoken to?"

"Yes, sir."

"Do you have an explanation for why you haven't spoken these past few weeks?"

"No, sir."

Mr. Allen shrugged. "Well, then, go and tell your sister that everything is back to normal and she doesn't have to babysit you anymore."

Veronica walked down the hall to the fourth-grade and fifth-grade classrooms, which, over the summer, had been made into open classrooms with no walls. The kids were allowed to do mostly what was called "free study," meaning that they could choose the subject they wanted to work on each day. Lillian hated the new configuration, and couldn't wait to go on to the middle school in the following year. Everything seemed very chaotic to Veronica in the open classrooms. There were no desks, only tables, and kids were running back and forth between the science and art areas. Teachers were talking to small groups of kids, while the rest of the students seemed to be just hanging out. Veronica found Lillian by herself in the reading area doing math problems.

"Mr. Allen told me to tell you that everything is back to normal and that you don't have to babysit me anymore."

Lillian looked up. Veronica had seen

Lillian's eyes a zillion times, but each time the intensity and fluctuation of their blue color surprised her, especially since her own eyes, like her mother's, were so uniformly black.

"First," Lillian said in her let's-set-things-straight voice, "normal does not exist. Second, I was not babysitting you. I was analyzing you."

"Doing what to me?" Veronica was relieved to hear that Lillian hadn't considered it babysitting, but this other thing sounded like it might be worse, especially given Lillian's general attitude toward her.

"Analyzing you. Understanding why you do the things you do."

"Oh," Veronica said. Lillian went back to her math problems, and Veronica turned to go, then stopped. "Did you understand why I did what I did?" she asked.

Lillian looked up from her math book. "No," she said, "it is impossible to know such things."

XXXVIII

Veronica and Jane Lust were sitting in the nonsmoking section of Smoke. Both had quit, and this was to be a true test of their resolve — a jazz club that reserved one of its ten tables for nonsmokers and the table was by the bathroom. They had agreed to meet an hour before Lillian was to join them for the first set of Bryan Byrd and the Low Blows. Jane's suit was baby blue, with black velvet piping around the collar, cuffs, and hem. She wore a string of large pearls with matching earrings. Her eyelids were the color of her suit, her eyelashes fake, her lipstick luminescent. If the lights went out, Veronica would know where to find Jane. The bottle of Veuve Clicquot Jane had ordered was brought to the table, popped, and poured.

"Congratulations," Jane said. "To every success for *Quid Pro Quo*."

Veronica would have preferred to wait to celebrate until the musical was actually staged. The Black Lagoon Theater Company had called that morning to tell her that the board had decided to produce her musical the following summer for the New York International Fringe Festival. Veronica had convinced them to give Alex a shot at the score. They conditionally agreed, giving him a month to write three sample songs. If he didn't pass muster, they would bring in someone of their own.

The room was beginning to fill up with

people, and, with them, smoke. Both women inhaled deeply.

"What do you say we have a celebratory cigarette?" Veronica asked Jane, hoping Jane's willpower was as pitiful as her own.

"Not me," Jane said. "Since I quit, I've been saving quite a bit of money. In fact, I calculated my savings over the next ten years, then went to Tiffany and invested in a rock. She held up her hand. Veronica had already noticed the diamond the size of a kumquat on Jane's middle finger. Several lichee-seed diamonds and pearls crowded round.

"Wow," Veronica said. "That's what I would call truly creative accounting."

"I'm quitting *Ordinary Matters* to write that novel," Jane said, her already blushing cheeks turning a deeper pink.

Veronica raised her glass. "I will happily drink to that. Congratulations, Jane."

"I was hoping I might serve as an example," she said, using her bejeweled hand to shape the dome of her freshly dyed strawberry-blond hair.

"I want to quit, too, but what if *Quid Pro Quo* is a big flop?"

"What if?" Jane repeated. "What if? Imagine if Christopher Columbus had said, 'What if I don't find the New World?'

Or if Elizabeth Taylor said, 'What if no one will marry me?' What do you do? You write another."

"Now I really do need a cigarette," Veronica said, glancing around the room in an effort to determine who might be the most likely donor of a bummed cigarette. An older man was the easiest target but the most potential trouble. A younger woman was less potential trouble but might cast a look of withering disdain, or, worse, say no.

"Besides," Jane said, "how can you stay at *Ordinary Matters* now that all the cool people have left — Ashley, Alex, me."

"Did Nigel and Laralee divorce?" Veronica drained the Veuve Clicquot from her glass and poured herself another.

"Still so naïve," Jane said, shaking her head. "They had a passionate and very public reconciliation. The whole thing, start to finish, was staged by the magazines, with Nigel and Laralee very professionally playing their offscreen parts. When soap-opera stars are offscreen, they're onstage. How is Alex's nose?"

Veronica focused on a guy about her age with tattoos on his arms. "Fine. A little crooked. That would explain why Nigel's lawyers have been calling offering gobs of money to settle out of court." She noticed the guy with the tattoos was smoking a filterless cigarette, dismissed him, and moved on.

"So what's next?" Jane asked.

"Next? What do you mean?" Veronica asked, spying a new prospective donor — a woman in her fifties with leatherlike skin who had no doubt tried to quit more than once and would be sympathetic.

"What's the next musical about?" Jane persisted.

"Oh, that." Veronica looked at the stage, hoping someone would spontaneously groove so that she didn't have to respond to Jane's question. "I don't know," she shrugged. Then, as if Bryan Byrd had heard her wish, he walked through the door wearing a linen suit the color of dark chocolate, his arm wrapped around his tuba as if around a girlfriend. He wore a white shirt, no ascot, and his bald head gleamed. She waved him over, perhaps a little too vigorously, introduced him to Jane, and asked him what music he and his group would be playing that evening. After he responded, in a desperate effort to keep the conversation going so that she wouldn't have to talk to Jane about her next opus, Veronica asked Bryan, entirely inappropriately, how the meeting had gone between Lillian and his mother.

Bryan laughed. "My worst nightmare come true. The first thing my mother does when she sees Lillian is point to her abdomen and say, 'I sincerely hope you are not going to try to pass that thing off as my son's.' For the rest of the evening, it was as if I didn't exist. We never even went to dinner."

"I'm sorry," Veronica said.

"Yes, it was terrible," he continued, although he seemed more pleased than disappointed. "They just couldn't get enough of each other. It's really the worst thing when a parent actually likes the person you're interested in. It almost feels like incest."

Jane chuckled, Veronica stared. In this world, do all roads have to lead to incest?

"Enough delaying, let's have it," Jane said, as soon as he left.

"Have what?" Veronica asked innocently. Then she stood up and — it was like jumping into a swimming pool on a brisk morning — approached the leather-skinned woman, who happened to be smoking Veronica's favorite brand. With all the charm she could rally, she explained that she was trying to quit but was dying for one last cigarette, and so on. The woman took a long drag, blew the smoke in Veronica's face, and said, "Sorry, can't handle the karma. Try someone else."

"Okay, I'll tell you my idea," Veronica said, returning defeated. "But then I buy a pack of cigarettes."

"It's your nickel," said Jane. "Go on."

"Well, it's about a guy who is put away in a mental institution by his wife after a car accident in which he suffers severe brain damage. The wife convinces everyone, including her two young daughters, that her husband, their father, is dead. Twenty-five years later, a neurologist at the institute reads a manuscript this patient has been writing for years. The manuscript is mostly unreadable, but certain sections are lucid. In those sections, the father writes everything he remembers about his daughters, his wife, and his life before he was put away — but due to his neurological disorder he writes these memories in strict lyric-song forms using classic rhyme schemes. The neurologist, who has Tourette's syndrome, decides to hire a private detective to find the daughters — who might or might not exist. In the meantime, the daughters, who never knew much about their father, hire another detective to search for information about him.

"It sounds like Oliver Sacks meets Raymond Chandler."

"Really?" Veronica asked, trying to hide her disappointment. "I kind of wanted it to be a screwball romantic comedy."

"Screwball maybe, but where's the romance?"

"Oh, I forgot. During the course of their search, the detectives fall in love."

"A gay screwball romantic comedy musical. I like it," Jane said, sounding genuinely positive.

"Oh, no, actually, one of the detectives is a woman. She's based on that redhead you met, remember, Sybil Noonan. I'll change her name, of course."

"How does it end?" Jane asked.

"I don't know." Veronica sighed. "I was thinking about the play-within-the-play solution, although this would be a musical within a musical staged by the patients at the mental institution."

"One more question," Jane said, "and then I'll leave you alone. Where is the mother?"

"Oh, right, the mother," Veronica said. "She shows up at the end."

"And what happens?" Jane asked.

"I don't know yet."

Veronica was about to flag the waiter down and order a pack of cigarettes when she noticed that a number of people in the club had turned their heads toward the front door. She followed their stares and saw Lillian, question mark shaped and wearing a tight black dress, heading for their table. Lillian sat down, ordered a glass of milk, and told the story of her encounter with Bryan Byrd's mother. Veronica's craving for a cigarette was soon entirely forgotten.

XXXIX

Rocco, three days old, born with ten fingers and ten toes and in all ways healthy, screamed bloody murder. Grandmother Agnes had him perched over her shoulder as she bounced around the hospital room patting his back, and saying, "There, there, it's just a little gas. Give us a big old burp. Make your family proud." Lillian, upright in the hospital bed and wearing a black negligee, was talking on the phone. Veronica noticed that her speech was slightly slurred from the Percocet, but otherwise she was doing very well, giving birth having in no way softened her edge. Kate

Cornell had made sure that Lillian was given a private, corner suite, with baby-blue decor. If Rocco had been a girl, Veronica wondered, would the room have been in pink?

Veronica was sitting in one of the two rocking-horse-and-teddy-bear-print upholstered armchairs watching *Ordinary Matters* on a television screwed into the ceiling at the far end of Lillian's bed. She was trying desperately not to worry that her mother would drop the baby or that Lillian had made a terrible decision by choosing not to breast-feed. She'd read innumerable studies in *The New York Times* proving that formula-fed babies had lower IQs, compromised immune systems, and a far greater chance of committing a federal crime. On the television, Eve White, Dr. Trent White's nymphomaniac wife, was angrily accusing her daughter, Lily White, of passive-aggressive vindictiveness epitomized by her recent decision to become a novice in an order of Carmelite nuns.

"A cesarean," Lillian was saying. "My water broke and he was breech. Kate offered to try to turn him around by hand, but I just wanted him out. I never even went into labor. It was over in twenty minutes, but it hurts like hell — as if I've been

420

ripped apart, eviscerated. Luckily, I'm on a lot of painkillers."

The baby continued to howl and Veronica was sure that her mother, who had arrived on the day of the birth, must be doing something wrong — the fact notwithstanding that her mother had worked for years as a nurse. And since Veronica now knew, after having been with Lillian during the birth, that she would never have a child herself, she wanted to be certain that they did everything right with this one.

"Veronica was there, but I'm sure she wishes she hadn't been," Lillian went on.

Three days earlier, Lillian, after awakening in a pool of warm water, had called Veronica in the middle of the night and said, "I'm sad to announce that the zygote won't be born on Halloween after all."

"Oh, my God, Lillian, should I call 911?" Veronica asked, sensing the onset of paralysis and wanting to act before it hit.

"Relax, Veronica. I'm not even in labor yet. We can take a taxi."

When Veronica arrived at Lillian's building minutes later, Lillian was waiting in the lobby with her overnight bag, which, Veronica later learned, contained a toothbrush, underwear, a black negligee, two outfits for Rocco, and a baby blanket. In the cab on the way to the hospital, Veronica sized up the driver, a certain Jean Baptiste, probably from Haiti, and decided, to her great comfort, that he would be able to deliver Lillian's baby if need be.

"I'm glad you're with me, Veronica," Lillian said. "But once we're at the hospital you don't have to actually watch this birth happen. In medical school, I had some experience with obstetrics, and no matter how well it goes, everything about the event, in my opinion, is traumatic. Human reproduction is a perfect example of evolutionary failure. The birds got it right. Lay an egg and sit on it. There is nothing natural or intelligent about pushing a watermelon through a straw. I also don't want to be responsible for your PTSD."

"PTSD?"

"Post-traumatic stress disorder."

Veronica told Lillian she was exaggerating, that many, herself included, believed that childbirth was the most beautiful experience in life. She wasn't, however, at all certain about the truth of this statement. When she had seen a documentary in high school about the birth of a calf, she had fainted. The taxi pulled up in front of the hospital. Veronica was relieved that it had not been necessary to ask Jean Baptiste to put on his other hat. She and Lillian rode the elevator to the fifth floor, where Kate Cornell, wearing a pinstriped suit and three-inch heels, was waiting — her lipstick and mascara fresh, her hair blown dry — as if it were perfectly normal to be so well put together at 4 a.m. Kate examined Lillian, pressing her hands over Lillian's belly for a few long minutes.

"He feels breech," she said. "Let's do a sonogram."

Wasn't breech something that happened to a ship or a contract? Veronica had heard the word before but wasn't exactly sure what it meant when referring to a baby in the womb. It wasn't a pretty word, rhyming, as it did, with *screech* and *leech*. She was about to ask Kate when a nurse hauled in a large machine with a monitor. Kate grabbed a bottle and squirted some gel onto Lillian's bared midsection, then rubbed her skin with a small device like a metal detector for what seemed an age.

"I can't find it," Kate finally said, sounding frustrated. "Do you think that might be it?" she asked Lillian, pointing to the side of the screen.

"Can't find what?" Veronica blurted out.

She could make out nothing on the screen but a cluster of circular gray shapes.

"The head," Lillian said.

Veronica leaned against the hospital bed in order to keep from falling. What did they mean they couldn't find the head? Was it possible to have a genetic birth defect and be born without a head? She didn't even want to know the answer. She looked at Kate and Lillian, neither of whom seemed particularly freaked out.

"Ah, there it is," Kate said, pointing to the top of the screen. "Hiding up by your heart." She ran the baby-body-part detector over Lillian a bit more, then said, "It looks to me like a complete breech, and, since your water broke, I wouldn't recommend an ECV. But you know I would do anything for you, so if you really want me to try, I will."

"No," Lillian said without hesitation. "If he wants to come out feet first, I'll give him that luxury. Just don't leave a sponge in me or anything," she said.

Kate left with a wink to Lillian, saying, "Okay, then, I'll see you very soon in the OR. Ideally, we want to get that guy out of there before labor starts." To Veronica, she said, "Glad to meet you. Lillian has told me so many wonderful things about you."

Veronica looked at Lillian for an interpretation.

"She's lying," Lillian said. "She's just like you, says whatever she thinks will make someone feel good."

While nurses came and went, taking Lillian's blood, putting in a catheter and an IV, Lillian explained to Veronica that the word *breech* with two *ee*s meant buttocks or rump, and a breech baby was one whose butt was where his head was supposed to be. A C-section was standard protocol, since the risk of complications to the mother and child in a vaginal delivery were far greater than the risks of a cesarean section. An ECV, or external cephalic version, which involved turning the baby by manually manipulating the fetus through the abdominal wall, was possible but painful and worked only half the time.

"Look, Veronica, there's truly nothing 'beautiful' about this operation, so if I were you, I would skip the OR and go to the waiting room until it's over. There is a reason for waiting rooms. Buy some cigars, pace, bond with the other fathers."

Veronica shook her head. "I want to be with you."

Lillian was wheeled off to the OR and was given an epidural. When Veronica tried to go with her, the nurse stopped her and said the procedure was now off limits to all but the patient. She explained that too many husbands had fainted at the sight of the huge needle going into the spine. Veronica was escorted to a bathroom by another nurse, who gave her socks, a mask, and a gown, and told her to put them on and scrub her hands thoroughly. She did this meticulously, then waited about ten minutes until the nurse returned and showed her to the operating room.

In an array of shiny chrome, blinking machinery, and bright light, a jolly young man with curly dark hair and a foreign accent was touching Lillian's feet, legs, and pelvis, asking, "Can you feel this? And this?" A couple of nurses were putting up a white sheet that stretched, like a curtain, across Lillian's chest. Someone brought a stool for Veronica to sit on.

The jolly young man introduced himself. "I'm Juan, the anesthesiologist." To Veronica he said, "You're brave." He looked over a chart and adjusted some knobs on a monitor. "Half the husbands, I mean partners" — he blushed — "decline to be here, and half of those who do assist, faint." Veronica had a vision of fathers falling down unconscious all over the hospital. Juan asked Lillian how she was feeling, then, as an afterthought, said to Veronica, "You're not queasy, are you?"

Veronica shook her head. In fact, she was feeling nauseated and light-headed, still not having completely recovered from the idea of a headless nephew. She wondered if she hadn't made a colossal mistake. If she bowed out right now, would Lillian, despite all she had said, feel abandoned? Would anyone notice if she kept her eyes shut the whole time?

"She's my sister, not my partner," Veronica said.

Juan looked at Lillian, then back at Veronica. "Sure thing," he said. "I usually advise the partners that the best thing is to hold the mother's hand and focus on her face. That's not to suggest," he faltered, "that you're not a mother too just because you're not giving birth." Veronica smiled and nodded, and wished he would just hurry up and say his piece. "The worst thing for you to do is to close your eyes or let your eyes wander elsewhere in the room."

Veronica decided to take Juan's advice and placed her hand in Lillian's. She was surprised by the force of Lillian's fingers around her own. Lillian's eyes were closed, but every muscle in her face, especially near her mouth and brow, appeared to be in high tension.

"I'm not hearing much from you, Lillian," Juan said. "Everything is fine. Are you panicking?"

Veronica was ready for some snide retort but her sister didn't answer. Could Lillian possibly be panicking? Even though Veronica was in a frenzy of fear herself, she couldn't fathom that Lillian, lying there on the table under bright lights and about to be cut open, could be anything but the picture of calm.

"I'm going to give you some Valium, Lillian," he said.

Veronica wanted to scream for him to stop, to tell him that her sister hardly needed any drug, when she realized that Juan probably knew what he was doing. She even considered asking him for a little Valium herself, when Kate and her team of doctors — scrubbed and dressed — walked into the room. They gathered on the far side of the white curtain. All Veronica could see was a bunch of masked, bobbing, and bodiless heads.

"Alright, everybody, let's do it," Kate's voice announced. "Lillian, everything is fine and this is going to be quick. Everyone in the room and many more beyond know that there is no one better, more precise, more elegant than I am at this procedure." The bouncing heads acceded, saying things like "the scarless wonder," "obstetrician to the stars," and "below-the-bikini-line Cornell."

The hint of a smile appeared on Lillian's lips. She was shivering, though her grip on Veronica's hand remained viselike.

"Lillian, I'm going to make the first incision. Once I start, I don't tend to talk much, because I'm concentrating on what I'm doing, but if you want to know anything at all, just ask. And you can always grill me afterward. You ready?"

Lillian nodded. Veronica then did exactly what she had been told not to do. She turned and looked toward the team of heads. Thick sprays of red splattered across the white sheet as if Jackson Pollock were on the other side. In horror, Veronica whipped her head back around, catching Juan's eye on the way, and was silently scolded with an "I told you so."

She looked down at Lillian, who was much paler than she ever was normally. Veronica felt dizzy. She was simply not up to this. She should have listened to Lillian. Veronica tried to indicate to Juan that she desperately needed help, but he was concentrating on his equipment.

"Veronica," Lillian whispered, "sing to me. Sing me one of the songs from *Quid Pro Quo.*"

"Sing to you?" Veronica said, thinking the only thing more terrifying than being in that room right then was singing one of her songs to Lillian. On the other hand, when would there ever again be a better circumstance than with Lillian under the knife and full of Valium?

"Okay," Veronica said, her eyes fixed on her sister. "The song is called 'My Girls.' Boss Tweed sings it after one of his two daughters has betrayed him and he has been arrested for grand larceny and fraud. Remember, it's a rough draft, really just an idea for a song. And the tune I use is dreadful."

Lillian said, "Veronica, stop quibbling and sing."

"Here goes," and Veronica sang.

> My girls are pearls
> One white, one black
> one shiny, one dull,
> one flawless, one cracked.
>
> My girls are dreams,
> one good, one bad

one delightful, one frightful
one pleasant, one best never had.

My girls are flowers
one fragrant, one sour
one bright, one blah
one glorious, one dour.

Theodora so adorable
Mary Amelia so deplorable,
but I'm their father
(what a bother)
And I love them both the same.

My girls are pets
one tame, one wild
one friendly, one nasty
one pure, one defiled.

My girls are cars
one sleek, one heap
one purrs, one coughs
one glides, one leaks.

My girls are books
one open, one shut,
one eloquent, one hack
one innocent, one smut.

Theodora so adorable

Mary Amelia so deplorable,
but I'm their father
(what a bother)
And I love them both the same.

As she was singing, Veronica watched
Lillian's face relax and her slight smile blossomed into a grin. Thank God for Valium,
Veronica thought. Veronica was feeling a lot
better, as if she just might make it through
this experience, when she heard the most
hideous noise, raspy and hellish, like the
snicker of a demon. The sound, she deduced, was the grotesquely distorted cry of a
newborn.

"Don't worry about the sound, Lillian,"
Kate said, "you haven't given birth to
Rosemary's other baby. We're just giving
him oxygen, which is routine, but makes
him sound peculiar. He's fine, beautiful,
everything's totally normal. We'll clean
him up and bring him to you in recovery
after I've finished closing you up."

At which point Veronica apparently
fainted, falling off of the stool and onto the
floor, luckily not harming herself. She remembered coming to in a hospital bed
next to Lillian's in the recovery room.
Lillian was holding Rocco, who was quietly
staring up at her.

"The whole OR team loved your song, Veronica," Lillian said. "They were truly sorry you weren't available to sing an encore."

In the same manner that Rocco had stared at his mother soon after birth, he now gazed at his grandmother in the hospital room three days later, absorbing her features, making a pattern of her face. Veronica was surprised by how little Agnes had changed in fourteen years. She was still beautiful, still curvy, still wore dark lipstick, and was still entirely unpredictable. Rocco had stopped his inconsolable racket. Was it possible, Veronica asked herself, that her mother would disappear back to New Zealand for another fourteen years? The way Agnes and Rocco were visually devouring each other, such a separation was, for the moment, hard to imagine.

Lillian hung up the phone.

"Who was that?" Veronica asked.

"Ben," Lillian responded. "He and Charlotte are stopping by later."

Veronica turned off the TV and looked at the baby. He was wearing a black cotton hat decorated with white stars and silver moons and was wrapped in the black fleece blanket Lillian had brought with her in her night bag. His face wasn't at all prunish and his head was perfectly round — common for a C-section baby, she had been told by a nurse, because he didn't have to squeeze through the birth canal. "C-babies tend to be smarter too," the same nurse had told Veronica, "because they don't get their brains squashed." Veronica figured that what he was losing in IQ through lack of breast milk might have been gained by avoiding the birth canal.

The baby's eyes closed. Agnes laid him down in his clear plastic hospital bassinet on wheels, then sat down in one of the armchairs and pulled out her knitting. She was making a red wool cardigan for Rocco. Veronica went over to the window and stared down Park Avenue. A small herd of brightly painted sculptures of cows grazed in the median while a fleet of taxis, limos, and SUVs raced by. Lucky cows, she thought, to have been crafted and not born.

There was a knock on the door and Alex walked in. "How's the little guy doing today? Does he still look just like me?"

Lillian sighed audibly. She said, "I was just thinking there wasn't enough family in the room."

Agnes aimed her needles at the bassinet. "See for yourself. He's the spitting image."

Veronica smiled at Alex as he walked over to the bassinet. She was surprised at how tolerant Lillian was being toward him. He had come every day since the baby was born, and he stayed for hours on end. Lillian had thrown him out only a few times.

"You've been here three days now," Lillian said to Agnes. "And once you go, who knows when we'll ever see you again. So I was thinking we might just clear up a few last little details."

"Of course, dear," Agnes said. "It was my intention to tell you girls and Alex the whole story as soon as you, Lillian, were feeling up to it. I gather you're feeling that way now?"

Lillian pulled a fallen negligee strap back up over her shoulder. She said, "Veronica and I went to see Charles at the Acme Neurological Institute a few weeks ago."

"I know. The director with Tourette's called me. He said he always knew I was lying to him when I told him Charles had no children. He told me he hired a detective to find you. It seems to be a good line of work these days." Agnes's needles were clicking as she spoke. "I have no reasonable explanation for what I did, no justification, and I have had plenty of time over

435

the past twenty-five years to come up with the one or the other, but I offer you none. I can only tell you what happened at the time of the accident." She put down her needles. "When the neurosurgeon had finished operating on your father, he told me that if he ever recovered he would be severely brain damaged and would almost certainly need around-the-clock care. I imagined all of our lives ruined. Once he was out of surgery, and it had become increasingly clear that his brain functioning was fully compromised, I made an entirely selfish decision to fake his death and institutionalize him. It was surprisingly easy to pull off. Charles was transferred by ambulance in the middle of the night to an institution in upstate New York. It was called, at the time, Mountain View Mental Home. I forged Charles's death certificate, and bribed the mortician on duty that night. An empty casket was cremated at the hospital morgue."

"Leave it to Agnes to be in the vanguard of bioethics," Lillian said. "You might find a second career at Princeton University's Center for Human Values. But that's not all you were the harbinger of, right, Agnes?" A nurse came into the room and took Lillian's temperature and her blood pressure. Agnes began knitting again. When the nurse had gone, Lillian said, "Brad Fitzgerald sent me Charles's medical history. Since I'm a neurologist, he thought I would be interested. It appears that Charles had Hodgkin's disease when he was a teenager, which left him sterile."

"Oh, yes, that," Agnes said. Her needles clicked furiously. "I imagine you would like to know who your biological fathers are?"

Veronica turned to Lillian. "Why didn't you tell me?" she asked.

Lillian said, "You may remember, I broached the subject with you, but I didn't pursue it because I don't think it matters," Lillian said. "And if there is one thing we might learn from Agnes it is that secrets — especially in families, no matter how ill or well meant — tend to have a way of becoming uncontrollably divisive."

There was another knock on the door. Bryan Byrd, his linen suit black as licorice, sauntered into the room carrying a huge bouquet of pink, yellow, and blue orchids.

"Agnes, Alex," Lillian said, "this is Bryan Byrd, the family private investigator." To Bryan she said, "Agnes is in the process of creating a proliferation of work for you. She was just about to tell us

437

who we really are."

Putting the orchids in the sink, he said, "I've retired from private investigating."

"What a shame. It seems to be such a thriving profession," Agnes said.

"How's your mother?" Lillian asked.

"Fine, thanks," Bryan said. "The orchids are from her."

Agnes put down her knitting, stood up, and walked out of the room. Veronica pushed aside the baby-blue gingham curtains and opened the window to get a little air. She wondered where her mother had gone and if she would ever return. Veronica also wondered if knowing who provided half her genes could make a difference in her life now. It would be interesting to know, she decided, but was not a pressing issue. After all, she'd lived with those same genes, day after day, year after year; it wasn't as if she was suddenly in for a radical change.

Agnes came back into the room carrying a large glass vase. As she arranged the orchids in the vase, she said, "I have no doubt that each of you has a very good idea who you are. It is true that the man you each think is your father is not. And in the case of Alex" — she stopped her orchid composition — "the woman he has recently been led to believe is his mother is not. Alex is not my son. He is in no way related to me or to Lillian or to Veronica."

Lillian said, "That tidbit will save Rocco a few years of therapy."

A thrill went through Veronica as she looked over at Alex, who had paled at the news. He sat in one of the teddy-bear chairs and put his head in his hands. Veronica wanted to go comfort him but was too confused to know exactly what she would be comforting him for. For not being her brother? Isn't that what they had wanted all along? She realized that she should actually be elated by the news. The man she once thought was the love of her life was now no longer her half brother and therefore freshly available. Yet, absurdly, all she could think of was whether or not Alex was going to be able to write songs she would be happy with for her musical. Would he be able to sing to her?

Agnes turned to Alex and continued. "I agreed to let your mother, who was fourteen years old, put my name on your birth certificate because she was terrorized. She thought that if her family ever found out she had a baby, they would kill her. She never would tell us who the father was. The father's name on the birth certificate is also false. It's the name of a colleague of mine. The hospital arranged for your adoption."

Before continuing, Agnes placed the vase of orchids, a paroxysm of color and intricate design, on the hospital tray table next to Lillian's bed. "I have given you enough information, Alex, so that you could hire someone like the now-retired Mr. Byrd here to find your birth parents, but I wouldn't recommend it. You would cause a lot of strife. And it seems to me you have found another family of sorts." Her gaze swept the room. "Naturally it's up to you. Sometimes we just need to know things whatever the cost."

Alex looked up, his radiant blue eyes so like Lillian's that Veronica had once been convinced the two of them had to be genetically related. He said, "My dental healer told me the other day that ninety-six percent of the universe is made up of some kind of mysterious dark matter and energy. He said that ordinary matter — the stuff of stars, planets, and people — makes up only four percent of the universe. He pointed out to me a skewed logic: If most of the universe is made up of something mysterious, why do we call ourselves and our physical world ordinary? Because we

440

simply don't *know* anything about the rest of the universe, we claim that it is exotic. The other ninety-six percent of the universe is probably looking at us and saying, 'That's some very weird shit.' No offense, Bryan, but I am done with detectives. You guys are too much like scientists and shrinks — always trying to explain the inexplicable. If I want to know something from now on, I'll be consulting my dental healer." He looked over at the still sleeping Rocco. "Besides, why pay to learn about an uncertain past when I can participate in making a future?"

"I work for an insurance company now," Bryan reminded him.

"Cruel, cruel destiny," Lillian said, shaking her head. Veronica wondered if she was referring to Bryan's new job or to Alex's putative collaboration in Rocco's future.

"As for you girls," Agnes continued, "there was an international exchange program at the hospital where I worked and many of the doctors participated in a sperm-donor project. The project was supposed to be anonymous, but I peeked. Lillian, your father was a Swedish cardiologist from Uppsala named Sven Rolfson. Veronica, your father was Lino Alegre, a Portuguese neuroscientist from Lisbon."

Lillian sat up. "Are you sure you have that right, Agnes?"

"I'm quite sure," Agnes said. "Why?"

Lillian said, "Lino Alegre is a world-renowned neuroscientist whose ground-breaking work on the neurobiology of happiness, and in particular on the neurophysiology of smiles, is likely to win him a Nobel Prize. If he's Veronica's father, as far as I'm concerned the nature-nurture question is settled."

Veronica was impervious to her purported father's accomplishments, but she smiled in spite of herself. It would be the way of fate, she thought, feeling an awful weight in her chest, if she and Lillian, no longer full sisters, were to now drift apart, especially since it was Veronica who had launched this ludicrous odyssey of lost and found fathers, brothers, mothers, and lovers all because she had been terrified that she would somehow lose her sister to a zygote.

Bryan said, "I recently read about an evolutionary theorist who claims that in primitive societies women conceived children with different fathers as a survival strategy for both themselves and their children. The fathers would look out for all the children because they didn't know exactly who was theirs and the mothers were dipping into a greater gene pool for their children. I think of it as the eggs-in-many-baskets theory."

"I had never quite thought about it that way, Mr. Byrd," Agnes said.

"And Charles was alright with this arrangement?" Veronica asked her mother.

"We made the decision together," she said, taking up her knitting again. "Your father said he didn't care if you weren't his children in blood, you were his children. And that never changed for him. Charles was anything but conventional, and I fell in love with him because of it. He wrote poetry. He got involved in political movements. He was a terrible flirt. He went back to school to get his master's in social work. He liked to be alone. He drank too much. To make money, he sold hairbrushes and vacuum cleaners. Then, when you girls were little, he got a job selling insurance. But Charles was never interested in having one steady job. He wanted it all, wanted to do and see and be everything. I loved this about him and then condemned him for it. He was just a man faced with the impossible task of being a man. Let's hope Rocco here has an easier time of it."

"You might stick around and see how he

does," Lillian said.

Agnes nodded and continued to knit. "Several months before the accident," she went on, "Charles changed. He began accusing me of deceiving him in all sorts of bizarre ways. He thought I was having affairs, that I was stealing money from him, and that I had convinced him he was sterile when he was not." Agnes looked up from her knitting. "I knew Lillian was aware that something was very wrong, and I was beginning to worry about the effect he was having on you girls. When he took you off in the car on the day of the accident, Veronica, I believed he might have been taking you to meet your biological father, who, we had heard, had been made a fellow at the Institute for Advanced Study in Princeton."

"Isn't that a soap-opera ploy?" Lillian asked Veronica. "When a character becomes too inconsistent or difficult or confusing, you just give him a brain tumor and all is explained?"

"Infallible trick of the trade," Veronica said. "I'm still curious about one thing, Agnes. Why did you take up knitting?"

Agnes responded, "I read not long ago in the journal *Brain* that knitting increases the activity in the left prefrontal cortex,

444

causing less susceptibility to stress and a more positive attitude toward life. The article said meditation and trampoline jumping had similar neurological benefits. I chose knitting because the outcome includes a scarf, a blanket, a sweater."

In hopes of further enlightenment, Veronica, Bryan, Alex, and Lillian were all staring at Agnes, whose needles continued to click away, when the nurse walked in and said cheerfully, "Percocet time."

"I bet she knits," Lillian said, indicating the nurse.

Bryan Byrd, standing by the bassinet examining the sleeping Rocco, said, "During the first few years of life, some thirty thousand new synapses are being created every second under each square centimeter of the brain's surface. And intelligence is in the connections between the neurons, not in the neurons themselves."

"True enough," Lillian said, before swallowing her pills, "but I think we should all keep in mind that inhibition is fundamental to a healthy brain. Too many connections gone amok, too much neuronal firing, and you'll have seizures."

A match made in heaven, Veronica thought. She looked back out the window and down Park Avenue at the cows. A man had placed a child on the back of one and a woman was photographing them. A few people had stopped on the sidewalk to watch the scene. One of them offered to photograph the three of them together among the cows. Veronica moved from the window and sat next to Lillian on the bed. Veronica wondered if the ending to her new musical was somewhere in here or not. It didn't really matter — everything always ends one way or another. She did hope, however, that her mother might be around to see *Quid Pro Quo* performed in the Fringe Festival next summer. Rocco began to howl. Veronica got off the bed and went to pick him up. She thought he might be hungry, so she grabbed the bottle and brought him to Lillian. Agnes, Alex, and Bryan gathered around to watch as Rocco made little snorting sounds while his tiny pink lips eagerly sucked on the brown plastic nipple, an ordinary infant doing the ordinary things he was supposed to do. And yet this child was already anything but ordinary, Veronica thought. Or perhaps he was very ordinary, since in this world the extraordinary was commonplace.

About the Author

Jenny McPhee is the author of *The Center of Things*, a novel, and the coauthor of *Girls: Ordinary Girls and Their Extraordinary Pursuits.* She is the translator of Paolo Maurensig's *Canone Inverso* and of *Crossing the Threshold of Hope* by Pope John Paul II. Her short fiction has appeared in numerous literary journals including *Glimmer Train*, *Zoetrope*, and *Brooklyn Review*, and her nonfiction has appeared in *The New York Times Magazine*, *The New York Times Book Review*, and *Bookforum*, among others. She is on the board of the Bronx Academy of Letters.

The employees of Thorndike Press hope you have enjoyed this Large Print book. All our Thorndike and Wheeler Large Print titles are designed for easy reading, and all our books are made to last. Other Thorndike Press Large Print books are available at your library, through selected bookstores, or directly from us.

For information about titles, please call:

(800) 223-1244

or visit our Web site at:

www.gale.com/thorndike
www.gale.com/wheeler

To share your comments, please write:

Publisher
Thorndike Press
295 Kennedy Memorial Drive
Waterville, ME   04901